PRAISE FOR
BARBARA NICKOLAE
and her masterwork of suspense
Finders Keepers

"_Finders Keepers_ is my kind of book . . . A neat, suspenseful plot about the kind of people you worry about, written with skill."
—Tony Hillerman

"This hooked my interest from the start and never let me go. A tantalizing puzzle with unexpected twists, engaging characters, and high suspense."
—Phyllis A. Whitney

"I've been reading mystery and suspense novels for more than a couple of decades, and I can't remember one that beats _Finders Keepers_ . . . Barbara Nickolae delivers."
—Dick Lochte, author of
Sleeping Dog and _Laughing Dog_

"An ever-twisting tale . . . The action moves quickly!"
—_Chicago Tribune_

"Fast-paced, well-drawn and believable . . . _Finders Keepers_ is a splendid find."
—_Baltimore Sun_

"Suspense . . . fleet pace . . . frequent surprises."
—_Booklist_

"A nifty thriller . . . energetic . . . no loose ends."
—_Kirkus Reviews_

Books by Barbara Nickolae from Berkley Books

FINDERS KEEPERS
TIES THAT BIND

TIES THAT BIND

BARBARA NICKOLAE

BERKLEY BOOKS, NEW YORK

TIES THAT BIND

A Berkley Book/published by arrangement with
the authors

PRINTING HISTORY
Berkley edition / January 1993

ISBN: 0-425-13573-X

A Berkley Book ® TM 757,375
Berkley Books are published by The Berkley Publishing Group,
200 Madison Avenue, New York, New York 10016.
The name "BERKLEY" and the "B" logo
are trademarks belonging to Berkley Publishing Corporation.

PRINTED IN THE UNITED STATES OF AMERICA

10 9 8 7 6 5 4 3 2 1

Dedicated to
Esther Keveson
and Nick Baker

With love and appreciation

TIES THAT
BIND

CHAPTER 1

Tara Nyborg focused her camera and snapped a long view of the Santa Inez Mission. A morning mist hovered, creating a mystique she might not capture, but the yellow and lavender flowers heralding California's early spring brightened the scene.

In her handbag was a letter postmarked in Solvang; angling her tripod to the north, she zoomed in on the rooftops of that quaint Danish community. She didn't take the picture. She sighed, no longer optimistic about locating the person who had mailed the letter almost twenty years ago.

Uncle Matt. Amazingly, she thought of him that way even though she had never met him—until three months ago, she hadn't known he existed. She had tried to phone him, but his name wasn't listed in the area directories, so she had written to him: *My name is Tara Nyborg. I'm your late brother's daughter. I found a letter you wrote to my maternal grandmother years ago asking about me, and I would like to know you.*

But her letter had been returned to her. Yesterday she had gone to the address, planning to question the neighbors, but she'd found a new condominium complex. No one she talked to had heard of Matthew Nyborg.

She heard the crunch of gravel, the hiss of hydraulic brakes,

1

as a turquoise bus pulled into the parking lot. The doors opened and a stream of gaily clad tourists flowed out. The cacophony of voices broke the meditative silence, but Tara didn't mind. She had shot enough film from this vantage and was ready to move on.

As she broke down her tripod, a woman in an orange straw hat hovered close. "All this equipment! You must be a real photographer—and you're so young! I just take pictures with my Instamatic." She thrust a small camera toward Tara. "I bet you know how to load this."

Tara laughed and reached for the camera. "Sure, let me have your film." She inserted the cartridge, then pointed out the camera angles that would make the best pictures.

"Flora! Where are you? The gift shop is open!"

The woman looked distracted. "My friends are waiting. Thank you!"

Tara watched the orange hat flutter off; then she hoisted the tripod into the trunk of her rented hatchback. Slinging her camera case over her arm, she followed a path to the back of the mission.

In the old days, a man on horseback traveling the Camino Real from Mexico to San Francisco would find the hospitality of a Franciscan mission at the end of each day's ride. Tara was trying to highlight the spirit and history of the old highway in a calendar layout. The Santa Inez was midway on the route, but it bordered Solvang, so she had arranged her week of shooting to make it her last stop.

In the old burial ground, graves were sheltered by a large stone grotto where a statue of St. Francis fed a gathering of forest creatures. Tara studied the names and dates on the humble markers. The earliest burials dated back more than two hundred years, and some of the life spans had been only a flicker in time: *Maria Teresa Calderon, May 18, 1837–July 7, 1837,* a tiny baby. Next to her was a child with the same last name who died at age three, and at their side rested *Señor* and *Señora Calderon,* who had not followed their children into the ground until decades later.

Señora Calderon. Querida Madre. "*Madre,*" Tara whispered. "Mother." It was a name she had never used.

Her mother had been tall and red-haired, like Tara herself, that much she knew. And her mother had been spirited enough to defy Grandmother and marry John Nyborg. But Grandmother had rarely been able to talk about her, and Tara knew nothing at all about her father's family.

Tracking the nostalgic whistle of a meadowlark, she caught sight of it perched on the rim of a stone fountain, its yellow breast and glossy black collar brilliant in the early sun. With a minimum of movement, she positioned her camera. A few flicks to adjust the f-stop, and she centered the bird. She stood patiently until it turned her way. At the sound of her shutter, the bird cocked its head quizzically, and Tara snapped several shots in succession, turning the camera to get a view that included the mission bell tower.

Tourists were beginning to mill through the cemetery. It would be impossible to get any more good shots, but Tara was satisfied with—

A scream, a piercing wail. Tara froze, her camera poised in her hand. Now a burst of screams came from inside the mission.

Someone bumped into her, running toward the sound, and instinctively Tara followed. A heavy, wooden door was open. The woman in the orange hat was staring into a large, carved chest, screaming, catching her breath, and screaming again.

Without thinking, Tara rushed to her. She looked into the chest, and a scream rose in her own throat. The body of a woman lay tangled in a splash of magenta.

Freeze frame. The shutter clicked once and then again— random, unfocused—almost without Tara knowing it. The magenta was a silk pantsuit, but the ruffled jabot of the blouse did not hide the ugly, purple bruises encircling the neck. Dark hair was splayed around the face; makeup looked stark against bloodless skin—and the eyes. Bulging, pale blue, they stared into endless space.

Someone crushed against Tara. Shrieks. The babble of voices. People crowding forward.

Backing up, Tara stumbled through a door that led to the inside entrance of the sanctuary. She was trembling and pressed her forehead against the cool adobe wall.

Holding one hand in front of her, she entered the church and grasped the back of a pew. The heavy oak was reassuring, and lifting the kneeler out of the way, she slid into the seat.

"Padre, venga!" someone yelled from behind her. *"A la ropa. La ropa! Pronto!"*

A bearded priest in brown robes hurried past her, his sandals slapping against the tile floor. She tried to block out the commotion—tried to focus on the altar in front of her, colorful with Indian drawings—but the image of the dead woman superimposed itself on the scene.

In nomine Patri et Fili et spiritu santi. She heard the resonant voice of the priest intone a blessing, then switch to rapid Spanish. Tara thought she recognized the word for police.

The mingled fragrance of incense and candle wax was soothing, and she took a deep breath. Soon her heart would stop hammering, her legs would regain their strength, and she could leave. When she was outside, she would be all right—walk to her car, get away.

The other voices quieted as the priest's voice rose in prayer, and Tara felt strengthened by foreign words she could not understand. Rising to her feet, she steadied herself, then tried to exit the way she had entered. The priest blocked her way. He stood near the open chest, sprinkling holy water.

Abruptly he stopped and faced the bystanders. "Please, step outside in respect for the deceased, but do not leave the mission.

The police have been notified. They'll be here soon and may want to talk to you."

Someone held the door open, and wordlessly, the group filed out. Tara moved, too, but despite herself, she looked back at the chest. It was deep. The body was not visible from where she stood, but she *knew* . . . She started to sway and reached to grasp the doorway.

A hand grabbed her arm. "Are you all right?" The priest did not release her until she nodded.

"There's a bench just outside. Sit down, but I don't think anyone should leave before the police arrive."

In the distance, sirens screamed. The sound got louder and louder, and several sheriff's cars careened onto the grounds. They braked to a stop, and officers leapt out and strode into the mission.

Tara overheard them talking to the priest about the body. She shuddered, wishing she could leave.

One officer came outside and surveyed the clusters of stunned tourists. The woman in the orange hat bustled toward him. "Officer! Officer, my name is Flora Ripley. I'm the one who found her. Just walked past the chest, opened it, and bang! There she was."

The officer was good-looking in the clean-cut manner Tara associated with policemen everywhere. He reached for a notebook and pen. "Why did you open the chest, Mrs. Ripley?"

The woman's eyebrows shot up. "Because it was there! I certainly never expected to find a body."

Tara moved closer. "Excuse me—Officer Ream," she interrupted, reading his name badge. "I wasn't in the vestibule when the . . . the discovery was made. I'd like permission to leave."

He glanced at her. "Are you with the tour group?"

"No. I'm here alone."

"You from this area?"

She shook her head. "I'm from Seattle. I'm here doing a

photographic study of the missions."

"What's your name?"

"Nyborg. Tara Nyborg."

Someone spoke behind her. "Nyborg? Did you say Nyborg?"

"Yes, I—" Turning, she faced a tall man with a full head of dark hair and a thick mustache that had the strange effect of making him seem boyish. His manner was official, but he wore a sports coat, and the top button of his shirt was undone.

"Nyborg," he repeated. "Any relation to—"

Officer Ream broke in. "Detective Castle, we didn't expect you this soon. We just called up to Major Crimes."

"I wasn't at Major Crimes. I was in the area and heard about it on the scanner." He turned back to Tara, and his smile revealed the suggestion of a dimple. "You wouldn't be related to Matt Nyborg?"

Tara was amazed. "He's my uncle. Do you know him?"

"Sure, he's my boss."

"Then he's with the sheriff's department!"

Detective Castle stood hands on hips, studying her. "He's the lieutenant in charge of the Major Crimes Unit in Santa Maria."

Tara had to resist clapping her hands. "I had no idea. I've never met him, but if you can tell me where—"

"He's your uncle, and you've never met him?"

"I want to meet him. I tried to find him, but the address I have is old."

"*I* found the body." Flora Ripley cleared her throat. "Like I said, I was just—"

Officer Ream interrupted. "Ma'am, Detective Castle will take charge of the investigation. Wait over there, and he'll get to you as soon as he can."

"If you want to meet Matt, I'll introduce you." Detective Castle nodded to Tara, then shouted, "Let's get the area cordoned off!" He walked away, toward the chest that served as a crypt.

CHAPTER 2

"Did you call that thing a *ropa,* Padre?"

"We refer to it that way, Officer. *Ropa* means clothes in Spanish. The chest goes back to eighteenth-century Spain. It was meant to carry clothes."

"Clothes?" Officer Ream looked up from his clipboard. "Pretty heavy for a suitcase."

Tara overheard and tried not to visualize what now lay in the bottom of that heavy, ornately carved chest. Her emotions were a strange mix. She was staggered by the grisly find and excited to know she would meet her uncle.

"I need your name, Padre."

"Riley. Father Dennis Riley."

"And do you know who *she* is?" Ream's question was accompanied by a gesture toward the mission. Then he signaled the uneasy tourists to clear the way for the arrival of another police car.

"I don't recognize her, so I don't think the poor woman is a parishioner. But Sofia Reyes—she works in our gift shop—said she thought she knew her."

A blond officer thrust a notepad at Ream. "Right. I just talked to Reyes. She said the victim and her husband were new in town. Asked Sofia about baby-sitting. Jessie Boo-shard, is the way Reyes pronounced it, but she didn't know how it was spelled."

"Do you have an address?"

"Reyes wasn't sure but thought it was a ranch near Ballard."

The priest broke in. "Leon Bouchard, that's spelled B-O-U-C-H-A-R-D, had a ranch in Ballard. He died recently, but maybe this is a relative."

Detective Castle reappeared. "I heard we have a possible ID."

Ream nodded. "We may have. A woman who works in the gift shop thinks she recognized her—that she might be Jessie Bouchard."

"Bouchard," Castle repeated. He cleared his throat. "Any idea where she lives?"

Ream nodded. "Possibly on a ranch in Ballard."

Detective Castle looked intense. "That gives us a place to start. Nail down the address. I'll go over."

Tara couldn't let him get away. "Detective Castle, don't forget my uncle!"

"I won't forget. Where can I reach you?"

"I'm staying at a motel right next to Anderson's Restaurant, in Buellton."

"Okay. I'll be tied up for a while, but I'll be briefing Matt on this. As soon as I talk to him, I'll get in touch. Meantime, you don't have to wait around."

Tara waved her thanks, then rushed to her car. She was still dazed, but at least she could distance herself from the staring eyes in the *ropa*. But suddenly she remembered. *She'd taken pictures of the dead woman.*

Her hands tightened on the wheel. Maybe she should go back and tell the police. She could print the whole roll and give them— No, that wasn't necessary. The police had their own photographer. Her pictures weren't important.

She concentrated on Solvang, a picturesque village with

cobblestone streets, delft blue windmills, and a myriad of gift and pastry shops, but she couldn't enjoy the fairy-tale atmosphere. She was drained, but not too drained to be glad about one thing.

Suddenly the scenery blurred, and she blinked hard. Perhaps it was the ordeal she'd just been through, but she couldn't fool herself anymore. The mission calendar was not her real reason for coming to California. It was just an excuse. She had come because she wanted to find her uncle. *Uncle Matt*. Detective Castle would introduce them.

Detective Peter Castle watched Matt Nyborg's niece walk to her car, appraising her almost by reflex. Tall, too thin maybe, but she carried herself with elegance, and she wasn't another Nyborg blonde. The thick hair haloing her face was a rich red and tightly curled, naturally curled if he didn't miss his guess, and she had the look of a model.

He turned back to the mission. The coroner would be here soon to take custody of the body, and he wanted to make one more careful check before the lab crew moved in. He was tired, but the adrenaline was flowing. This was his investigation, and he knew what to do.

He pulled off his sunglasses and walked back into the vestibule, which was already cordoned off. It was cool inside and reverently quiet. Even the officer standing guard didn't disturb the sanctity. But the body in the *ropa*—she did. He wasn't eager, but he took a final look around.

Outside, Ream was waiting with the Bouchard address. "Here. It's about three miles—"

"I'll find it." Castle pocketed the slip of paper and headed for his car.

Ream called to him. "Do you want us to roll a black and white behind you?"

Castle started to wave him away, then reconsidered. "Sure.

I don't look official in these clothes, and I may need help."

Minutes later Castle pulled up in front of the Bouchard residence. Surrounded by several acres of horse property, the large frame house wasn't dilapidated, but neither was it as fastidiously kept as most ranch houses in the area. Castle swung his long legs out of the patrol car and headed up the asphalt driveway.

A blond boy came running from the side yard. "Where's my mommy?"

Castle knelt in front of him. "Hi there, fella. Your mommy isn't here." He glanced over his shoulder at Ream, coming up behind him. "My name is Peter. What's your name?" As he spoke, he held out his hand.

The boy looked quizzical. "I'm Patrick."

The front door opened, and a middle-aged woman in a loose-fitting dress peered out at them. Her gaze fixed on Ream. "I was afraid of this," she said, stepping outside. "Something's happened. I knew it when—" She hesitated, glancing toward the boy. "I knew I should have called you."

"I'm Detective Castle, ma'am. County Sheriff's investigator. This is Officer Ream. May we come in?"

"Patrick, you stay outside and play. I'll make you lunch in a little while." She opened the door, and Castle and Ream followed her into a wood-paneled living room. "Mrs. Bouchard has been late before, but she's never been gone all night. And her husband's not here, either. Didn't know what to do. Couldn't leave Patrick alone . . ."

"Ma'am," Castle held up a hand, "are you related to Mrs. Bouchard?"

She shook her head. "I'm Lottie Nielson. I baby-sit. What has happened to Mrs. Bouchard, Officer?" she asked, her voice unsteady.

"Mrs. Nielson, first maybe you'll tell me when you saw her last."

The woman peered at him. "Yesterday. Yesterday afternoon. Mr. and Mrs. Bouchard both. She was taking him to the airport."

"What time was that, ma'am?" Castle reached to get a notebook and pen from Ream.

Mrs. Nielson looked at her watch. "I got here at a quarter to three. They left ten, maybe fifteen minutes later. Mr. Bouchard had a plane to catch. They were going to the Santa Barbara Airport."

Castle wrote quickly. "Do you know where he was going?"

"Phoenix—he's due back the day after tomorrow."

Castle looked up. "Thursday?"

"That's right. Mrs. Bouchard said she'd call me if she needed a sitter when she picked him up."

"Are there any relatives who could take care of the boy until his father gets home?"

"No one that I know of. But . . . maybe I can take him home with me." Her voice dropped to a whisper. "Detective Castle, you *have* to tell me. What happened to Mrs. Bouchard?"

Castle took stock and decided the woman wouldn't fall apart. "A body was found this morning over at the Santa Inez Mission. We think it may be Mrs. Bouchard."

Mrs. Nielson clapped a hand over her mouth. "My God, how horrible! The poor woman. And poor little Patrick—he's only three. And his daddy. A nice man, Mr. Bouchard. He'll take it hard."

"Where's Mommy? And where's Daddy? I want my daddy!" Peter Castle hadn't heard him come in, but Patrick Bouchard was standing just inside the open doorway.

Mrs. Nielson dropped to her knees and put her arms around him. "Patrick dear, we thought you were outside. But don't worry. Your daddy . . . your daddy will come—" Her voice broke.

Castle felt an unexpected sympathy for the slightly built

child and couldn't respond, but Ream held out his hand. "Come on, Patrick. Let's you and me go outside and have a look at that fire engine I saw."

The boy whimpered. "Daddy, I want my daddy."

When Ream took the boy outside, Detective Castle continued. "I'm sorry, Mrs. Nielson, but I do have to ask a few more questions. Do you know Mr. Bouchard's first name?"

She thought a minute. "Derek."

"Derek," Castle repeated. "Derek Bouchard." He paused. "What time did you say he left for Phoenix?"

CHAPTER 3

The church sparkled white in the sunlight, and the graceful steeple reached deep into an azure sky. The door to the church opened, friendly voices welcomed her, and Tara rushed inside. But it wasn't a church at all. She was in a dark cemetery, and from misty shadows, tall gravestones glided toward her. Horrified, she tried to escape, but the door was gone. She heard the voices again, but now they repeated her name in a sinister chant. *Tara. Tara.*

She was running, struggling, but slimy vines grasped at her like tentacles. She couldn't break free. Then a soothing voice called and, in desperation, she held out her hand. A shadowy figure grasped it and led her toward a distant light. The light grew brighter. The figure who guided her was draped in a magenta cloak. Tara tried to pull her hand free. The figure turned. She saw a face. A dead face. A smiling face. A face that stared at her with unblinking eyes.

A sound rose in the distance. It grew louder, demanding. Tara groped for the phone. It was a dream. She was safe, and a vibrant, masculine voice brought her awake. "Miss Nyborg, this is Peter Castle. Do you have plans for dinner?"

"Peter Castle." Tara shook off the horror of the nightmare. "Of course," she murmured, "the detective at the mission." Again she saw the dead woman's face—the real woman. She squinted, forcing the image out of focus.

"That's right. I just talked to your uncle, and he's expecting us for dinner. You still want to meet him, don't you?"

Tara swung her legs over the side of the bed and felt for her shoes. "Of course! I'm dying to meet him."

"Good. I'll pick you up in an hour, hour and a half."

Tara checked her watch. It was after five. When she'd arrived at the motel, she had concentrated on making notes for her photo captions. Later she had lain down, but when her eyes closed, she'd envisioned the chalk-white face floating in a sea of magenta. No wonder she'd had a nightmare, and she struggled against the lingering effect. She was unnerved and had to tell herself that the terrible death scene was no threat to her.

A sliding glass door opened onto a tiny patio, and Tara stepped outside. She was getting used to California weather—warm, sunny days that rapidly turned cold at sundown—and now the brisk air helped to clear her head. Her room was the last one in the row and the farthest from the road. It was quiet, and closing her eyes, she welcomed the breeze that played across her face. It had been a traumatic day, but she would be calm and poised when she met her uncle.

After a quick shower, she decided against a sporty pants outfit and put on a jade blouse, brown woolen suit, and muted gold earrings. Her usual style was more flamboyant, but she would look very respectable when introduced.

When the phone rang again, she was eager. "Yes," she bubbled, "I'll be right there."

It was dark, and Tara didn't recognize the man in a blue jacket waiting for her outside the motel office until he stepped toward her. "Miss Nyborg—"

"It's Tara." She shook his outstretched hand. He was taller than she remembered, and his strong, regular features made him marvelously photogenic.

"And I'm Peter. It's nice to see you under more pleasant circumstances."

Something was familiar, as if she had seen him before. Of course she had this morning, but still . . .

"My car is just outside." He led her to a black sports car with a matching rag top. He opened the door, holding it as she eased into the depths of the leather seat; then he slid in beside her. "Matt and Sylvia live in Santa Maria, about forty miles from here."

"Santa Maria," she repeated. "I checked every telephone book in the county. They must not be listed."

"Of course not. Cops don't publish their addresses and phone numbers." He winked at her. "We make too many enemies."

He turned onto the freeway. "You said you were from Seattle. Is that why you've never met Matt?"

Tara shifted in her seat. She always felt uneasy when questioned about her family. Grandmother was the only relative she'd ever known, and she'd grown up feeling, not abandoned exactly, but isolated. Maybe that was why meeting her uncle meant so much to her.

She looked out the window, seeing the city lights grow farther apart as they traveled north. "My mother died shortly after I was born. I was raised by my maternal grandmother, and I never knew until after her death that my father had a brother."

"So old Matt has a brother, too," Peter said softly. "Apparently they don't get along."

"My father died a few months after my mother. But years ago Uncle Matt wrote to my grandmother asking about me. I found the letter among my grandmother's papers."

Tara was still amazed that the letter had been saved, perhaps the single oversight of a woman usually in command of every detail. She stared into the darkness, remembering how she had read the single page over and over.

Dear Mrs. Ainsley,

    I am writing again to ask about my niece, dear little
Tara. It would sure mean a lot to me to know my
brother's daughter or to at least know how she is . . .

His niece, Tara. She had an uncle, but yesterday when she
couldn't trace him through his old address, finding him had
seemed hopeless—and then she'd met Peter Castle.

"I doubt my grandmother ever replied, but in the letter my
uncle asked if I could visit him and his wife in California. He
cared about me then, but it was so long ago . . ." Suddenly she
felt uneasy. "I'm not a child anymore. I don't know if he's still
interested in me."

"Matt will be interested," Peter said, pulling up for a stop
sign at the off ramp. "Family. It's all important to some people.
They can't get away from it—the ties that bind."

Tara felt encouraged and at just the right moment. Peter
turned into a driveway, then drove up a short hill to a two-
story Victorian-style house. The bright porch light seemed
welcoming.

Opening her door, Peter winked. "Don't be nervous. When
Matt finds out who you are—"

"He doesn't know? You didn't tell him?"

He walked ahead of her toward the house. "I thought it
would be a great surprise." He glanced back. "Come on."

A man bounded across the porch. He was not much taller
than Tara, but he was lean and wiry, and every movement
suggested strength. His white hair was tightly curled, like her
own, and he was smiling. "Just in time," he called, waving.
"Sylvia's putting dinner on the table."

"And I brought you something better than wine." Taking
Tara's arm, Peter ushered her up the steps to the porch.

Matthew Nyborg held out his hand. "Pete, your friend
is . . . ?"

Peter put one hand on her shoulder and the other on her uncle's. "Matt Nyborg," he said, his voice deep and steady, "it is my pleasure to introduce you to Tara . . . Tara Nyborg."

Matt Nyborg stared at her. His lips moved, but at first no sound came. "Nyborg?" he said finally. "Tara Nyborg? Johnny's daughter?"

Tara nodded, hearing the crickets, the creak of the floor-boards under her feet. His expression was inscrutable, and she tensed. Maybe coming here was a mistake . . .

But then Matt reached for her and crushed her in a bear hug. "Tara, my God. . . . Sylvia! Sylvia! Come out here! Sylvia, it's Johnny's daughter!"

Tara was trying to catch her breath when a small, trim woman joined them—a rush of words, a tangling of arms—and she was led into the house.

They sat her between them on a sofa. Their questions over-lapped. "Here, let me look at you—"

"How long have you been here—?"

"Where on earth did you meet Peter?"

Peter had been standing to one side, but now he came closer. "We met this morning. She's a photographer and was taking pictures at the mission. I heard her name and found out she was your niece."

"My niece." Matt savored the word. "My brother Johnny's girl. I can hardly believe it after all these years. Twenty-five, you must be about twenty-five now."

"Exactly."

Matt hit his forehead with the palm of his hand. "Hard to believe. I can't stop staring. Don't see too much of Johnny in you, but you sure look like Olivia. Doesn't she, Sylvia?"

"Tara dear, I only met your mother once—a lovely girl—and you do resemble her." Sylvia smiled. "That magnificent red hair, just like hers. But perhaps we're being unkind, talking about your parents when—"

"Oh no! I want to hear. I know so little. I mean, my grand-mother—it was difficult for her to talk about them. All my life I've wondered . . ." Tara's voice was pitched higher than usual, and she stopped, annoyed at herself for sounding childish.

Sylvia took Tara's hand. "Dinner will be ruined if we don't get to the table. Peter, there's a bottle of chardonnay in the refrigerator. Do you mind?"

"Happy to." Peter headed toward the kitchen while Tara, flanked by Matt and Sylvia, entered the dining room. It was more formal than Tara had expected—crystal and silver, heavy mahogany, richly textured wallpaper. She had just met them, but already Tara knew the gracious room reflected Sylvia. Her uncle would have been just as content over a Formica table.

"Sit here, between us," Sylvia said, pointing, "and Peter, you take your usual place."

Peter poured the wine. "A good California label, Tara. I hope you like it."

"So far, I've been fascinated by everything in California." She smiled. "I'm thrilled to be here."

Sylvia raised her wineglass. "Thank you, Peter, for bringing us together. It was a wonderful accident, you two meeting this morning—even under such awful circumstances."

Smiling, Tara lifted her glass. "To Aunt Sylvia and Uncle Matt. I hope I can call you that. I'm leaving California on Thursday, and I'd almost given up hope of finding you."

"Thursday?" Uncle Matt echoed. "You're leaving that soon?"

She nodded. "But now that we know each other, we can keep in touch."

When they passed a cut-glass salad bowl, Tara realized she was hungry. The food was good, and as they ate, she told them her grandmother had died recently. "That's when I found out I had an uncle."

The phone rang and Peter jumped up. "I'll get that. I left word at the station that I'd be here."

Matt waved his fork as he talked. "So you take pictures for a living. Pretty as you are, I would have expected you to be on the other side of the camera."

Tara laughed. "I did a little modeling after college, but it's more exciting to take pictures than to pose for them."

"Speaking of pictures, Tara, don't you think Peter looks a lot like his brother?"

Tara looked at her aunt. "His brother? I don't think I know—"

Matt's voice boomed. "Ryan Castle! The actor. You've heard of him. The women around here fall all over themselves to see his show on Friday night."

"Of course! That's why Peter looks familiar. And he did say something about a brother—"

Peter slid back onto his chair. "I hate to bring this up at a family celebration, but I have to update you on that murder, Matt. We've got the official ID now. The dead woman is definitely Jessie Bouchard."

"Pete, I can't think about anything now except Tara. I'm totally sidetracked, and I'm glad I've got you on the job."

Sylvia shook her head. "Peter, I think you need some rest. You look exhausted."

Tara decided Peter did look tired, but he grinned. "Sylvia, didn't your husband ever tell you—no rest for a good cop."

"Not until they retire," Sylvia said smugly. "But, Peter, I mean it, you shouldn't run yourself into the ground."

Peter pushed his plate aside. "I want to get a line on the husband before he gets back from Phoenix. Maybe it's early, but I've got a hunch . . ." His voice faded.

"I don't have to tell you that later the case will get my full attention—but right now you have to hack it alone. While she's here, I can't concentrate on anything but Tara."

Peter leaned toward her. "Do you hear that? You can't scoot back up to Seattle so quick. Your uncle can't let you out of his sight."

Peter was right. Her uncle's gaze hardly left her face, and she stared at him, too. "I wish I could stay longer, but I have clients who depend on me and work to get out."

The front door rattled. "Walker," Sylvia said, rising from her chair.

"Stay put, Sylvia. He's got a key."

Aunt Sylvia sat down again, and in a moment a slender, blond man appeared who could have been no more than a few years older than Tara. Peter stood up and extended his hand. "Walker, haven't seen you for a while."

Walker looked startled, but before he could answer, Sylvia broke in. "Walker, we have the most wonderful surprise. This is your cousin Tara. Dear, this is our son, Walker. Did you know you had a cousin?"

Tara rose from her seat. "No! It's wonderful to meet you."

Sylvia set a place for Walker. "Tara is your uncle Johnny's daughter. Peter brought her to us. She's a photographer and was shooting pictures at the mission. They just ran into each other."

"At the mission?" Walker directed his attention to Peter. "Then you know about—"

"Of course, I know. I'm in charge of the investigation."

Walker slumped into a chair.

"Walker, aren't you going to say hello to your cousin?"

"Matthew, give him a chance! He's stunned. We were stunned, too. Tara's taken us all by surprise."

Walker thrust out his hand. "Mom's right. I'm surprised. A cousin. A red-haired cousin."

Peter broke in. "So, Walker, how did you hear about the murder?"

Walker stared at him. "It's all over Solvang. They say the victim's been identified."

Peter drained the last of his wine. "Her name was Jessie Bouchard."

Walker gave Peter a long look. "Yes, I heard. Jessie Bouchard."

CHAPTER 4

Tara was roused by a sharp knock. "Compliments!"

Pulling on her robe, she opened the door. She didn't see anyone, but hooked over the doorknob was a dainty pink plastic bag. She checked the contents: two luscious sweet rolls were wrapped in a large white napkin; one was dotted with cherries, the other with pineapple.

She yawned. It was too early to sample them, but they looked much better than the sweet rolls the motel had provided yesterday. But yesterday she had made her own selection from an assortment on tables in the gazebo near the pool. Apparently when the complimentary breakfast consisted of a special treat, the management made sure it wasn't overlooked.

It was almost seven o'clock, no point in going back to bed. She stretched, feeling vastly contented. Last night she had met her relatives, and they had accepted her as family. She had felt welcome, cherished, and was still basking in a glow.

The water in the tiny electric kettle was boiling by the time she was dressed, and she mixed a paper cup of instant coffee. Outdoors the air was chilly, but it mingled ocean smells with the fragrances of spring, and she took her rolls and coffee out on the patio. She put the rolls on the little metal table and was deciding which one to try when the phone rang.

"Tara, it's Aunt Sylvia. I know it's early, but I have to see you this morning—just to make sure you're real! Can I take you out for breakfast?"

Tara heard the affection in her aunt's voice, the catch in her own when she responded. "That will be lovely. Where shall I meet you?"

"I can be at the motel in less than an hour. Your uncle had to be at the station early, so he won't be with me. But, Tara, I should warn you. I have something in mind, and I won't let you say no."

When Tara stepped back out on the patio, a bird fluttered off the table. Apparently it had wanted a bite of her breakfast, and it might as well have it all. She broke both rolls into fragments and scattered them on the patio. Birds swooped down in minutes, apparently accustomed to handouts.

When her aunt arrived, they went to the restaurant next to the motel, a place famous for pea soup. "It's not usual breakfast fare," her aunt told her, "but I'm going to order it. It's delicious."

Tara joined her, so instead of sweet rolls, she had pea soup for breakfast and it was tasty. But even before the soup was served, her aunt was insisting she extend her stay in California. "Your uncle hardly slept a wink last night, he was so thrilled. You just can't leave tomorrow. We have to have more time to get to know you."

Tara broke off a piece of crusty bread, trying to control a rush of emotion. "My return flight is scheduled for tomorrow morning. I don't know if I can change it so late."

"No matter! If you can't change your ticket, your uncle and I will see that you get home—but not until after a nice, long visit."

"But I should go. I have work—" She broke off. Her aunt's smile was mischievous, and for once in her life Tara was willing to give in. "You win—and so do I! I'll stay a few days longer."

After breakfast, they went for a drive through Solvang. Most of the shops were still closed, but Aunt Sylvia wanted to show Tara something. "See that shop right there with the red-and-white-striped awning?"

Tara read the sign aloud. "Sylvia's Gift and Import Shop."

"It used to be Cara's Gift and Import Shop. I worked for Cara, and when she moved, I took over. Walker was little then, and we lived in Solvang."

Even in an area crammed with stores and boutiques, the shop stood out, as fresh and inviting as a stick of peppermint candy. Tara was impressed. "Do you still run it?"

Aunt Sylvia shook her head. "It's still mine, but Walker manages it for me. When he moved back to Santa Maria, he needed something to do, and I'd been at it long enough. When your uncle retires, it'll be nice having so much free time." Her sigh sounded like regret.

"Aunt Sylvia, I just thought of something! I should get back to the motel and try to get my flight rescheduled."

It was a quick drive back to Buellton, but maid service had already cleaned her room. Tara was glad, remembering the robe and shoes she'd left scattered. Aunt Sylvia was dainty and had an aura of tidiness that Tara didn't want to jar.

"Take the chair and I'll sit on the bed while I make the call. It shouldn't take long." As she spoke, Tara drew the drapes and slid open the door to the patio.

A sparrow was on the table and didn't fly away. A dove lay on its side under the chair. Its eyes were open and sightless. A third mass of feathers was humped almost at Tara's feet. The head rested on a piece of sweet roll with a glazed bit of cherry still visible. A fourth bird was in the far corner.

Someone knocked. "Maintenance. Housekeeping reported some dead birds."

"Dead birds! My goodness, they're all over the patio. Tara, where did they come from?"

Tara tightened her grasp on the door frame. "I . . . I don't know." But of course she knew. Birds had eaten the rolls she put out for them, and they had died.

A dozen people straggled off the America West commuter flight on Thursday, and Detective Peter Castle had no trouble deciding which one was Derek Bouchard. He noted every detail of the sandy-haired man's appearance, from his tailored slacks and sheepskin-lined jacket to his dazed expression.

"Derek Bouchard?"

The man nodded.

"I'm Detective Peter Castle. My condolences, sir."

Bouchard's voice was stiff. "You're sure—you're absolutely certain—it's Jessie?"

"You can see her if you want to, but at this point there's no doubt—"

Bouchard cut him off. "I want to see my son. Mrs. Nielson has him at her house."

"I know. I can take you to him, but it would help if you could answer questions first. I'll keep it short."

Bouchard looked around as if trying to get his bearings. "Okay," he murmured, "if you think I can help."

On the ride to a nearby substation Peter was silent, waiting to see what Bouchard would volunteer, but the man didn't speak until they were inside. "I still can't believe . . . God, who did this? Detective Castle, do you know who killed my wife?"

"That's what we're hoping you can help us with." Opening the door to a small interview room, he motioned Bouchard inside. "Can we get you coffee or maybe some water?"

"No. Let's get this over with."

They sat, and Peter rested his hands on the table between them. "To your knowledge," he said slowly, "did your wife know anyone who might have had reason to harm her?"

Bouchard looked taut. "I don't think so. She didn't know many people—not that she was unfriendly, but—well, she was selective."

"A business associate, a family member, someone who could have benefited from her death?"

"No, of course not. At least—no one that I know of."

Peter leaned across the table, tensing at the significance of his next question. "I know this is tough, but I have to ask. Do you know if she had another man in her life?"

Bouchard grimaced and looked away, giving Peter his answer.

Peter took a moment to collect himself. When he spoke, his voice was soft. "Do you know who he is?"

"No—yes." Bouchard sighed. "It was finished. She had broken it off."

She had broken it off. Peter leaned back. "How long ago? Who was he?"

Bouchard shifted. "It was over. I'm sure it was, so there's no point in going into it."

"Maybe, but we can't afford to overlook anything."

Bouchard sighed. "Well, I don't know exactly when it started, but it was after she got to L.A. Jessie and I had been living in Dallas. I'm a piping engineer and was there on a project. Anyway, we'd been married just over three years when things changed . . ."

"What happened?"

"I got a new assignment in Aurora—"

"Aurora?"

"Colorado, just outside of Denver. Jessie didn't want to go. She wanted to go to L.A.—take a stab at modeling or the theater." His voice broke. "God knows, she was beautiful enough."

Peter studied him, trying to decide if Bouchard's show of emotion was convincing. "So she went to L.A. alone?"

"She took Patrick. I went to Colorado. But it wasn't that we actually separated—only that circumstances kept us from being together."

Peter nodded. "So she was in L.A. And that's where she met this . . . other man?"

"Lauer . . ." Bouchard's voice hardened. "His name was Helmut Lauer."

"Lauer," Peter echoed. He took a file folder from his brief-case and made a notation. "What do you know about Helmut Lauer?"

Bouchard shrugged. "About all I know is his name. Their relationship ended when Jessie and I came up here."

"When was that?"

"A little over a month ago—when I inherited the ranch."

"So now you're trying ranching?"

"I am. The ranch belonged to an uncle. Growing up, I spent most of my summers there, working for him. I loved the place. I still do, and I thought I could make a go of it—and put my family back together."

Peter looked down at the file. "How did Jessie feel about it?"

"She was happy. She took a real interest in the ranch. Even insisted on spending her own money to put in new fencing."

"Hmmm." Peter stared down at the folder, deciding how to continue. "In other words, you're telling me that your marriage was back on track?"

Bouchard passed a hand over his face. "Better than what I'd hoped for when we moved up here."

"You were willing to overlook her affair?"

Conflicting emotions played over Bouchard's face. "I had my son back. That was more important to me than anything else—and Jessie was trying hard."

"To save your marriage?"

"Yes, I think so."

If Peter was holding a bomb, it was time to drop it. "Then why was she filing for divorce?"

Bouchard stared at him. "Filing for divorce?" He shook his head. "She wasn't. Maybe *before* she might have thought about it, but not . . . not now."

If Bouchard had known about his wife's divorce plans, he was putting on a good act. But Peter wouldn't give up. He went through the folder and drew out a document. "Two weeks ago, your wife met with Robert Komac in Santa Barbara. He's a divorce attorney, Mr. Bouchard. According to him, she wanted to determine what her percentage of the community property would be *when* she divorced you. Not *if* she divorced you. Komac said she made her intentions clear."

Bouchard looked baffled. "I don't believe . . . No, there must be some mistake. I told you, she had just insisted on buying new fencing, and—"

Peter cut him off, guessing that it was time to take a harder line. "New fencing? That fits, because according to Komac, she wanted advice about whether the ranch you had just inherited could be considered part of her settlement." He read the paper in front of him, then thrust it at Bouchard. "Komac told her that if she helped you maintain the property or if it was maintained with commingled funds, then it would be considered community property in California."

Bouchard slumped forward. He put his head in his hands. "Then all of it—her questions, her enthusiasm about the ranch—it was just a trick, a scheme . . ."

"If you *had* known what she was planning, would it have made you angry?"

"No—yes. I . . . I don't know."

It was time to move in. "How angry, Mr. Bouchard? Angry enough to kill her?"

"Kill her?" Derek Bouchard jerked to his feet, knocking his chair over. "You can't think . . . You can't believe . . ." He sputtered, but Peter had heard people sputter before.

"I think, before we go any further, Mr. Bouchard, that it's my duty to read you your rights."

Bouchard's eyes widened. He looked incredulous, then angry. "You can't be serious."

Peter Castle held up his hand. "I'm serious, Mr. Bouchard, but understand that it's just a technicality for your protection." Opening the door, he signaled the desk officer, who came into the room and, at Peter's nod, recited the Miranda from memory.

Bouchard remained standing, hands on hips, and said he understood his rights.

"And are you willing to proceed without an attorney?" The desk officer didn't sound threatening. He could have been asking if Bouchard wanted a beer.

Bouchard shrugged. "What difference does it make? I didn't kill my wife."

Peter cleared his throat. "Then you won't mind if we catch this on videotape?" He flipped a switch. "Mr. Bouchard, you've been read your rights and have agreed to continue, correct?"

Bouchard nodded.

"Please speak up, Mr. Bouchard."

"Yes, yes, I did."

"When was the last time you saw your wife?"

"On Monday. She drove me to the airport."

"What time was that?"

Bouchard seemed to calculate. "We left about three-thirty, so it would have been about four-fifteen when she dropped me off."

"Three-thirty? Are you sure that's when you left home?"

"Yes, that's about right. Three-thirty."

Peter looked at his notes. Mrs. Nielson reported that the Bouchards had left the ranch at three o'clock. A thirty-minute discrepancy.

"Did you make any stops on the way to the airport?"

"None. We drove straight there, and she dropped me at the terminal. It was early. My plane didn't leave until five but I told her she didn't need to wait." He met Peter's stare. "That was . . . that was the last time I ever saw her, ever talked to her."

Peter reviewed quickly. *The mission closed at five. If Bouchard had left home at three, he would have had time to kill Jessie, dump her body in the* ropa, *and still get to the airport in time to pick up a five o'clock flight.*

The next question was critical. "Mr. Bouchard, did you talk to anyone or see anyone you knew at the airport? Someone who could substantiate that you were at the airport at four-fifteen?"

"I *was* at the airport at four-fifteen!" Storm clouds darkened Derek Bouchard's eyes, but then he slumped down. "But I didn't see anyone. Not that I remember."

Peter leaned across the table. "Mr. Bouchard, think. This could be important. Is there anyone who can place you in the Santa Barbara Airport between four-fifteen and the time you boarded?"

Bouchard clenched his fist. "I don't think so. But you could ask. The airport's not that big, and I waited at the gate, reading a newspaper. Someone must have seen me."

"What time did you check in?"

He grimaced. "I didn't. I already had my seat assignment."

Peter thought it through, just to be sure the scenario worked. *Bouchard inherits a ranch. His wife is cheating and wants a divorce. If she leaves, she'll take half his property with her,*

and he can't let that happen. They leave for the airport at
three. If he's quick, he has just enough time to strangle her,
dump her body, and still make his flight.

So far, so good, but there was one jagged edge. Could he
explain why Bouchard dumped her at the mission?

It took Peter a moment, but then it came to him. *The road-*
block. He remembered the roadblock. A diesel had overturned
just outside Solvang that day, spilling a load of chemicals.
The road between Ballard and the major highways had been
snarled for hours, with only one car at a time snaking through.
Bouchard could have killed his wife, then panicked when he
approached the roadblock and saw all the black and whites.
He could have pulled onto the mission grounds just to get off
the road. But then, desperate, he spots the *ropa* and decides
to take his chances.

The evidence wasn't strong enough to book him, but thinking
it over, Peter was convinced. The scenario played.

CHAPTER 5

Tara realized that the Nyborg home reflected Aunt Sylvia's taste, but on Friday when she stepped into Uncle Matt's office at the Major Crimes Unit in Santa Maria, she felt his personality. The ten-by-ten room was crammed but tidy—truly his domain—but it wouldn't be for long. He'd said he was getting ready to hang it up for the last time, and Aunt Sylvia was already planning their retirement.

After dinner that first evening Uncle Matt had insisted that Peter was too tired, and he'd driven Tara back to Buellton himself. On the way he had mentioned his retirement. "I'll find things to do to keep busy. That doesn't worry me too much," he had said, "but I've been in police work for thirty years and it'll take me another thirty to get my office cleaned out."

Laughing, she had told him she'd love to help, but wouldn't be in California long enough. Then Aunt Sylvia talked her into staying, and Tara had insisted on living up to her word. She was family, volunteering to pitch in, and Uncle Matt seemed eager to keep her busy. So here she was taking pictures off the wall and packing them into a carton. She was standing on a chair, her back to the door, when it opened. "Uncle Matt?" She turned around.

In the doorway stood a woman with waist-length hair and

outlandish attire. Of indeterminate age, though probably younger than fifty, she wore a wide-brimmed felt hat and draping garments that covered the tops of her boots. When the scraggly boa around her neck moved, Tara flinched, almost losing her footing on the chair. Keeping her eyes on the animated fur piece, she stepped down.

The woman peered at her from under the wide-brimmed hat. "Don't be afraid of Prince. Possums are affectionate. I'm here to see Lieutenant Nyborg. Is this his office?"

Tara was as captivated by the owner as she was repelled by the marsupial. "Yes," she managed, "but Lieutenant Nyborg isn't in now. Did the desk sergeant send you back here to—"

"Do you mean that nice-looking fellow? He was busy so I just ducked back here on my own." The woman rummaged in an outsized straw bag and brought out a folded newspaper. "I've come to see the lieutenant about this case he's in charge of— Jessie Bouchard. Do you know about it? Her body was found at the mission."

Tara blinked hard, blocking the image of the magenta shroud. "Yes," she said. "I do."

"I have something very important to tell the lieutenant."

Tara eased around the desk, her gaze still focused on the possum, which was asleep and hanging head-down around the woman's shoulder. "He's not here right now, but you can wait—"

"Can't wait too long. Had to take a bus to get here, and I want to catch the early bus back."

"Lieutenant Nyborg could phone you, or perhaps you'd like to talk to someone else, Miss . . ."

"My name is Pudget Vandermeer. Actually it's Margaret Vandermeer. I still sign myself that way, but no one's called me Margaret since I was in school." She stroked the possum. "I should talk to the lieutenant, but I guess I can leave him a message."

Tara picked up a pen and notepad, curious about what this bizarre woman had to say.

"This newspaper story says Jessie was put into the *ropa* on Monday before the mission closed at five o'clock. That can't be right. I saw Jessie Bouchard in the Ballard cemetery on Monday, and it was after six. The mission would have been locked up by then. You tell the lieutenant. And I know it was after six, because I was hurrying home to see Jordan Jourdain."

"Jordan Jourdain?"

"Don't you know him? He's the star of *Yesterday's Tomorrows*. He's the dearest thing, and they were going to interview him on *Celebrity Watch* at six-thirty."

Tara wrote quickly, trying to keep up.

"Anyway, Jessie was wearing my earrings. I recognized them right away. They were a bright blue abalone-shell seahorse in a gold-and-magenta setting."

"She was wearing *your* earrings?"

"I made them. I make earrings from shells I find along the beach, and I sell them to gift shops in Solvang."

"Are you sure the woman you saw was Jessie Bouchard?"

"She was Jessie all right. I know her because I talk to Patrick—he's her little boy. A cute little thing. She scolded him for coming near me, but Patrick likes me anyway. Once I let him hold Prince, but when Jessie saw—well, she set to hollering."

Tara ripped the message off the pad and placed it in the middle of her uncle's desk.

"Be sure your uncle sees that," Pudget said. "The newspaper story is wrong." She snapped her fingers. "Wait a minute! I saw a man near the entrance of the cemetery. He was walking in her direction and had to have seen her."

Suddenly Tara felt very professional. "Did you recognize him?"

"Not by name, but he looked familiar. He must live around there." She nodded to herself. "I remember now—I said good evening and he sort of waved."

Tara added the information to the note. "How can my uncle reach you?"

Pudget Vandermeer recited her phone number and address. "It's off the main road through Ballard, not too far from the cemetery. It's a frame house with a cactus garden in front and an eight-foot-high totem pole you can't miss. I carved it out of a tree trunk."

Tara grinned. "I'd like to see that and maybe take a picture. I take scenic photos—and portraits, too," she added, thinking Pudget Vandermeer was a once-in-a-lifetime subject. "Can I drive up sometime and look around?"

"Of course! Come anytime. Come this afternoon."

Tara pondered. "I could stop on my way back to Buellton. And I want to get some shots of you."

"Pictures of me? Whatever for?"

"I think you would be an interesting study—with or without Prince."

Pudget looked pleased. "That's because I'm an artist. My earrings aren't my best work even though that's how I make a living. I'm really a sculptor, and I have several pieces I'd love to show you." She looked at her watch. "I'm on my way home now to watch *Yesterday's*. But I'll count on seeing you."

When the woman left, Tara went back to wrapping pictures, and a few minutes later she heard Uncle Matt. "Tara, how's it going?"

She wiped the dust from her hands. "Hi! You just missed someone. Her name is Vandermeer. Pudget—no, Margaret Vandermeer. She wants to talk to you about the Bouchard case. Claims the newspaper story is wrong—that she saw Jessie Bouchard after the time she was allegedly put in the crypt."

Handing him the note, she repeated everything Pudget Vandermeer had said. "She was adamant about it. Said she even recognized the earrings Mrs. Bouchard was wearing as a pair she'd made herself."

Uncle Matt's expression changed. He was Lieutenant Nyborg and at attention. "Did she have any way of fixing the time?"

"Yes, she did. She was on her way home to watch a television show. She was very aware of the time and said it was definitely after five."

He nodded his head just perceptibly. "That would alter Pete's theory."

Tara felt a glow. She was doing more than packing her uncle's belongings; she was taking part in his life. "She was an adorable woman," she blurted. "I was startled by the possum, but—"

"The possum?"

"Prince, she called him. Wore him around her neck like a fur piece. And the clothes she had on—"

"Now wait a minute." Uncle Matt's eyes narrowed. "The woman was *wearing* a possum?"

"At first I thought it was strange, but after a few minutes it didn't seem that odd and—"

He interrupted again. "We'll definitely check it out. But she sounds like a loony. In murder cases they pop up like mushrooms. They all have vital information."

Tara wouldn't argue with her uncle, and yet—well, he hadn't seen the woman. "Uncle Matt, she wasn't a loony. Offbeat maybe, but convincing. I thought she knew what she was talking about."

He glanced down at the piece of paper. "Well, you don't have to worry. We'll give it a thorough check. But it's nearly noon, and Sylvia will have my head if I don't get you out of here in time for lunch."

Tara hesitated, wondering if she should kiss him good-bye,

but he took the decision out of her hands. Gathering her in a quick hug, he planted a kiss firmly on her cheek. "Now get going," he said gruffly.

In the parking lot, the door of the car next to hers was wide open, and a man was leaning inside. He undid the straps of a car seat and picked up a little boy. "Stand still," he said, "while I tie your shoe."

The man was adjusting the child's clothes when he noticed Tara. "Excuse me. We'll be out of your way in a minute."

Tara studied the boy. "You've got a cute little guy there."

The man rested his hand on the boy's head, an almost solemn gesture. "Thank you." He smoothed the boy's hair. "And the two of us are going to stick together."

It was a strange thing to say, and Tara took a good look at the man. He was well-built, with sandy hair and good features—and then she noticed his eyes. They were brown, ringed with dark circles, and hauntingly sad.

CHAPTER 6

Raymond Andrews hated watching his dumb sister. She was only seven. Stupid for a guy eleven—twelve in August—to be stuck playing with a baby. But he would fix her. He doubled his left hand into a fist to hold the sleeve of his jacket closed. He had something up that sleeve, and when he was done with Vanny, she would never follow him around again. He'd bet on that.

"Raymond, if you're just going to look around, take Vanessa with you. She wants to go. But watch her, d'you hear? Don't run off and leave her alone." Mom stood balanced on the step of the trailer, one hand grasping the door frame, but the other on her hip, her no-nonsense look.

He smiled at her. "Don't worry, Mom. I'll take *good* care of her." He sure would. He'd take good care to scare her half to death. She'd wet her pants. Ha! That would be great. Show the world what a baby she was. Maybe then Mom would realize it wasn't fair to make him watch her. He started hiking with Vanny running behind him.

"And don't go too far," Mom called after them. She said something else, too, but Raymond couldn't hear. The dog at the trailer next to theirs was barking. Barking loud. It wasn't happy.

When they were clear of the trailer camp, Raymond thrust a little garden shovel toward Vanny. "Here, you carry this."

She took the shovel and studied it like she was going to find a treasure map engraved on it. "What's it for?"

"It's for digging, Stupid. What'd ya think?"

"Digging what?"

Raymond tightened his hold on his sleeve. "You'll find out."

He walked faster toward a dry bed that had once been part of Lake Cachuma. Or so Dad had told him. At least two or three times a year they pulled their trailer up here from Los Angeles, and every time Dad complained that the lake and the fishing weren't what they used to be. Not that Raymond could remember the lake as ever being much different. It was five miles long now and a mile wide, but according to Dad, it used to be eight miles long and at least twice as wide. The drought was responsible. The unending drought. Ever since Raymond had been a little kid, he'd heard people talking. "If we don't get rain soon . . ."

Looking out over the wide expanse of cracked earth and brush, it was hard to believe the water had ever come up this far. Hard to believe the lake would ever reach this far again. But the dry bed was exactly right for what he had in mind.

"Did you know," he said sweetly, "that this used to be an Indian cemetery?"

"It was not. It used to be part of the lake. Daddy said."

Raymond grimaced, but wasn't stuck long. "Sure it was part of the lake. The Indians buried people underwater so that enemy tribes couldn't dig them up. Read all about it in social studies class."

"Underwater," she repeated. "How did they do it? I mean . . ." She stopped, a puzzled look on her face.

"They did it with totem poles. They sunk a pole deep under the water, then pulled it out quick and pushed the body into the hole before it closed up again."

"They did?" Vanny's eyes were getting wider. She was staring at him. Jiminy Christmas, she'd believe anything.

"Sure they did. So let's dig up a few old, dead Indians, 'cause maybe they were buried with fancy beads or something." He had stopped walking and was looking for a likely place to dig. Vanny stood still. Very still. Her arms were crossed like she was hugging herself. Wow, it was working.

It took a while, but he found a lonely spot totally sheltered by brush. She wouldn't be able to see what he was doing, not until he was ready. "Okay, give me the shovel. And stay put. Don't go getting lost to get me in trouble."

"I'll stay right here. But I don't want to dig up old Indians. And I don't think they're buried here anyway."

"They're buried here. Just wait and see." The tangle of brush around him was high enough to hide a man, but Raymond crouched low. It was more exciting that way. He jabbed the shovel into the ground and turned over a handful of earth. The ground was firm but gave way easily. Excited, he dug quickly. This was going to be fun.

About six or seven inches down, the earth turned to jelly— a damp, oozing stuff. He kept digging, and when the hole was large enough, he released his sleeve and slid out a long bone. A beef bone most likely. The dog had been reluctant to give it up, but Raymond had distracted him with half a sandwich. In a second the sandwich had been gulped away, but by then the bone had been up Raymond's sleeve. The dog had barked, complaining, but fortunately no one but Raymond had understood.

He called to his sister. "Vanny, come here. I want you to see something. It's nice." First she had to see the bone in its grave. And then . . .

She came toward him cautiously. So maybe this wasn't the first trick he had played on her, but it was the best one yet. "Look here. Down in the hole." He grasped one end of the bone.

When she peered down, he screeched. "Dead Indian bones. Dead Indian bones." He pushed the bone toward her. "Ugh," he groaned. "Dead Indian bones. Now the dead Indian will haunt you for sure."

She shrunk back, her eyes wide with fear. "Haunt," she gasped. "What's haunt?"

He waved the bone at her. "When somebody's alive and comes after you, that's hunt. When somebody's dead and comes after you—that's haunt."

She shriveled. Any second now, she'd go running back to the trailer, wet and crying. He was sure of it—but she was staring at the bone. Suddenly she put her hands on her hips, just like Mom. "That's no dead Indian bone. It's a dog bone. And you took it away from that dog in the trailer by ours. I'm going to tell."

"It's an Indian bone, honest, and I—"

"Humph. It is not. There's nothing in that old hole. You just dug it to scare me."

"No, look. I'll dig some more. Bet I find more bones." She *would* tell, the tattletale, if he couldn't talk her out of it. Quickly, he shoveled more dirt. "Hey, look, here's something else." It was just a button, but it was coated with mud and maybe he could fool her. "See, a bead—an Indian bead."

She glanced into his outstretched hand. "A button. Humph."

"Well, wait. Let's see what else I can find." He dug deeper. The mud was oozing, and something smelled bad. Real bad. He came to a firm lump. He slipped the shovel under it and pulled, but it wouldn't come free. It was anchored, like the branch of a tree. He grasped it and wiped away the ooze to see what it was. Another hand was holding his.

A cold, prickly feeling ran through him. A roar burst in his ears. Something pounded in his chest, and his insides somersaulted, threatening to give back everything he had ever eaten. He heard a sick moan, then a terrified voice: *Jiminy. Jiminy Christmas!*

Vanessa knelt at his side, squealing. "That's a real hand. This *was* an Indian cemetery! Let's look for the pretty beads. But oh, it smells yucky."

Jerking wildly, Raymond let go of the thing. It fell back in the grave. He rubbed his hand against his pants leg. That didn't help. He had touched it—touched a dead body. The prickly feeling engulfed him and held tight. He was too scared to move, but he had to move. Had to get away from there. Run. Get back to the trailer.

"Hey, Raymond! Wait for me!"

He ran the whole way. He'd tell Mom. She would know what to do. But first, he had to change his clothes.

CHAPTER 7

Sitting across from her in the dining room, Tara decided that Aunt Sylvia possessed the same inherent graciousness, the unerring sense of what was proper, that she had admired in her grandmother. Even the taste of their Hollandaise was similar—just the right tartness. The difference between them, Tara realized with a burst of affection, was that Sylvia made her feel so . . . *welcome*.

"You have the oddest little smile on your face, Tara," Sylvia said. "It's almost as if you want to tell a secret."

"Not a secret really. It's a hard thing to say, but—Aunt Sylvia, I feel at home here. More at home than I ever did with Grandmother."

Aunt Sylvia put her hand over Tara's. "Remember, we've known you far longer than you've known us. We always wished you could be part of our lives."

Tara let her hand nestle in her aunt's. "I wish it could have been that way, but my grandmother was—" She shrugged. To this day, she didn't know how her grandmother's mind had worked.

Aunt Sylvia responded as if she had said the words aloud. "I only met your grandmother once. She was very reserved, but she loved your mother very much. Adored her."

Tara shook her head. "Then why didn't she have pictures of her? I've seen pictures of her when she was young, but none after she was grown-up and married. And never any of my father."

Aunt Sylvia pushed back from the table. "Come with me."

Tara followed to a large, white-walled room with a gleaming hardwood floor and a bed decked with a quilt of colorful spring flowers. Aunt Sylvia opened the window, and the lace curtain fluttered on a breeze.

"It's been a while, but I'm sure those albums . . ." As she spoke, Aunt Sylvia opened the bottom drawer of a 1920s dresser, polished until the dark mahogany shone like glass. "Yes, here they are!" She took out two large boxes.

They sat side by side on the bed, sorting through albums and dozens of loose photographs. Most were snapshots taken with no photographic flair, but they fascinated Tara in a way few pictures ever had.

"Here it is!" Sylvia cried. "This is the one I was looking for. Your father sent it to us right after they were married. It was taken just before an auto race."

For the first time Tara stared at the face of her own father. He was in racing attire and smiling, his face ruggedly attractive, his expression almost brash. One arm was raised in a triumphant salute; the other encircled a woman—her mother, red-haired, proud, and adoring.

Aunt Sylvia's sigh was audible. "Johnny loved racing. That's what put him in wrong with your grandmother. That—and of course the accident."

The accident. Her mother had fallen, that much she knew. But now she heard the details. *Her mother, pregnant, falling down stairs at a raceway, hitting her head. Tara's premature birth, and her mother's death. Her father distraught and driving fearlessly, recklessly, to relieve his grief. Grandmother's unyielding resentment, even after her father careened into a wall and out of their lives forever.*

The couple in the photos adored each other—it was obvious—and they would have loved their daughter. "I . . . wish I had known them."

"They would have been very proud of you. Your uncle is right. You're a daughter that anyone would cherish." Tara sat quietly, not moving, and her aunt continued. "Tara, I know you have to return to Seattle next week. But come back soon and stay with us awhile. This room will be yours for as long as you like."

The room was charming, and she felt at home. With a rush of feeling, Tara knew she wanted to return.

They heard the front door open, and Aunt Sylvia looked startled. "Walker, is that you?"

"Who are you expecting—one of your boyfriends?" Grinning, Walker appeared. He wore a pink dress shirt and dark slacks, and although his blond hair was windblown, his appearance had style. But his face! Startled, Tara stared again at the photo in her hand. *Her father.* Walker was about the same age now as her father had been in the photo, and he looked just like him.

Walker planted a kiss on his mother's cheek. "I thought I'd stop off and— Whoa! My pretty new cuz! So that's your car outside."

Tara extended her hand, but he kissed her, too. "Glad you're still in California."

"And we're going to keep her. Aren't we, Tara?"

"You're making it very tempting." Tara laughed, but couldn't stop staring at her cousin. "Walker," she blurted, "you look just like this picture." She looked back and forth, from the still to real life.

"Yes, he looks very much like your father," Aunt Sylvia said gently. "And we gave him your father's first name."

Tara was puzzled. "Walker?"

"I'm John Walker Nyborg—but to the family, your father was Johnny, so I've always answered to Walker. And speaking of names, Tara suits you. With that red hair you look more like an Irish colleen than a Dane."

This was only the second time she had ever met him, but suddenly they were bantering as if they'd known each other all their lives. Riffling through the pictures scattered on the bed, Walker picked one up and handed it to her. "Did you see this one of Grandpa Nyborg? He was even fiercer than he looked."

Their Grandpa Nyborg. She was an adult, but she felt like a child who had found a dollhouse under the Christmas tree, complete with a family and a special room for her.

Later Walker accompanied her to her car. "If you're going to be around awhile, maybe we can do something." He took her key and opened the car door. "I could borrow a friend's boat and take you for a ride on Lake Cachuma, but the lake's down so low, it's not much fun." He brightened. "But we can think of something."

As she slid onto the driver's seat, he said, "Going back to the motel now?"

She shook her head. "I met the strangest woman today. Pudget, she calls herself. Pudget Vandermeer. Wears a possum like a scarf. I'm going to stop at her place and get some shots of her and her totem pole."

"Where did you meet her?"

"She came into your father's office while I was there. Claims she saw Jessie Bouchard on the day of her death, *after* the mission would have been locked up for the night and after the time the husband is supposed to have left for Phoenix. She was strange, but I was impressed."

Suddenly Walker seemed distracted. He stared into space, and time passed before he responded. "This Pudget person could blast Pete's theory about Bouchard's husband bumping her off." Before she could answer, he seemed to catch himself. "See you, Cuz." He slammed the car door.

Turning out of the driveway, she waved to him. She felt lighthearted and ridiculously pleased with herself. She had friends in Seattle—people she cared about—but here in California, she had found a family.

Walker stared after his cousin, reviewing what she had said: *Pudget Vandermeer had claimed she saw Jessie Bouchard on the day of her death, after the mission would have been locked up for the night.*

If Pudget knew what she was talking about, she could give Bouchard an alibi by proving he was already out of the area when Jessie's body was put in the crypt. Then Pete's contentions would be shot to hell, and the investigation would have to be broadened. *And the old man would be in charge*. Walker shook his head. The whole thing was crazy.

He drove to Solvang, but was in no mood to work. He would stay just long enough to relieve Inge at the counter—let her take a break—then he would take off. Inge could stay until closing and tally the day's receipts.

He was behind the counter when several women stomped in, all carrying identical satchels that identified a tour. Walker heard the usual comments and sighs of appreciation: "This shop is different, such lovely things—and look, music boxes! Aren't they darling?"

"I need a couple more gifts. Maybe those earrings. Aren't they fascinating?"

"They are! Sir, how much is that pair there, in the front of the case?"

Just his luck to get stuck with a crowd as soon as Inge walked out. Walker removed several pairs of earrings, placed them on top of the showcase, then answered questions for another customer. "No, the needlework is imported from Denmark, but most of the music boxes are Swiss— Yes, I'll be right with you."

He rang up a sale, then assisted the woman looking at earrings. "They're forty dollars a pair, and each pair is unique. Absolutely one of a kind."

Absolutely.

"No, not that pair. These green ones. Sir. Sir!"

Struggling, Walker roused himself. "What . . . what was that? The gold ones? No, you said the green. Fine. I'll get a box."

When they trooped out, Walker fingered a pair of earrings, bright blue abalone shells in a gold setting. It was true. He hadn't been giving a sales pitch, and he stared transfixed. *Every pair was unique.*

Inge returned, but before he left the shop, he dialed a San Francisco number. "Nance, it's me. How's it going?"

"Walker." When she said his name, she sounded soft, vulnerable, not like the efficient nurse. He visualized her, felt her presence right beside him. But he couldn't let her know how much he missed her.

"I just phoned to see . . . well, to make sure you're okay. Are you working tonight?"

"Yes, I'm still on swing—three long shifts a week."

He cradled the phone. "Take care of yourself."

"Walker, how are you?"

"The same. Nothing's changed." It was a lie. His whole world was turned inside out.

"Walker, is there something you want to talk about?"

"No, Nance, nothing important . . ." Now that their divorce was almost final and his life was a mess, how could he tell her he had realized too late that he loved her?

CHAPTER 8

Matt Nyborg put his feet on the desk and folded his hands behind his head. It wasn't a familiar pose. Relaxing was definitely not one of the things he did best, as Sylvia made a practice of telling him. He did his best thinking on his feet, walking or, better yet, running. He'd been a devoted jogger long before the word worked itself into the language, but now it felt good to lay back.

Johnny's daughter. She was beautiful, just like her mother, but he could see Johnny in her, too. She had his flair, his self-assurance. Matt had always wanted to look after her for Johnny's sake, but Olivia's mother had been adamant. Her granddaughter could have nothing to do with the family of the race-car driver who had caused her daughter's death. But Tara had grown up to be a gem, and Johnny would have been proud.

Matt shifted in his chair. He sure wished he could be proud of his child. Walker had been a good kid—exceptional, if he said so himself—but Sylvia had babied him too long. Matt shifted again. Well, he had to admit he'd had his hand in it, too. An only son, an only child—it had been easy to spoil him, but the damage hadn't shown up until he was grown.

Together he and Sylvia had raised a son who lacked ambition and, worse yet, self-respect. Selling lace and souvenirs—it had been fun for Sylvia, but it was no work for a man. But that wasn't the worst of it. What really galled Matt about his son was that he was seeing Louise again.

Matt felt a rush of adrenaline and sat up. Damn, a man had to be weak in the gut to crawl back to a woman who'd pulled the kind of stunt she had. Nance was one nice lady—too crazy about Walker for her own good—but apparently Walker was still off his rocker about Louise, so no wonder that marriage had failed.

His thoughts had shifted, so it was time to get to work. But he had to find a way to get Tara to move to California. Be great for Sylvia—the daughter they never had—and for him, too. Matt nodded to himself. He had a pretty damn good idea.

"Matt?" Knocking, Pete opened the door. "I need to brief you on something."

Think of the devil. For a moment Matt felt like rubbing his hands together, the spider welcoming the fly. But the web he had in mind for Pete would be a great place for a man to get caught. Tara was a wonderful young woman. She would make a terrific wife, and it was time Pete settled down. Hell, Matt had lost track of Pete's girlfriends. Never dared call one by name just in case it wasn't the right name. But Pete was like him—had to find the right woman, the perfect woman. Well, he had won Sylvia, and maybe Pete would win Tara.

"Matt." Pete repeated his name.

"Sure, Pete," he answered, aware he was smiling more warmly than usual. "Come on in. Let's hear what's up."

"It's the Bouchard case. New evidence."

"Meant to talk to you about that case. Mike Franklin was in here yesterday, griping as usual and claiming that, by rotation, Bouchard should be *his* case. For once he's right. He was due to handle the next homicide. If you want to turn it over to him—"

"No point—with the new evidence, we're ready to go to the D.A." Pete dropped into a chair and extended his legs in front of him. "It's a shame! The husband's as guilty as hell—but that poor little kid!"

"Yeah?"

Pete peered out the little window. "Bouchard's grief could pass for the real thing, and I tried to buy into his story. But it was too hinky. And there's the car he reported missing when he came in here this morning with his little boy. Said he couldn't locate it. Claims the last time he saw it was when she dropped him off at the airport."

"And you found it?"

"At the airport, in long-term parking."

"But he said he watched her drive away."

"Yep. We've got that on videotape."

"How was the car located?"

"Well, Matt, I had a hunch. Initiated an inspection of the entire airport lot. And now everything falls into place. Bouchard strangled his wife, dumped her at the mission, and drove to the airport in her car. He reported the car missing and was waiting until he thought our backs were turned to move it to a place where it would be found, substantiating his story."

Matt nodded. As usual, Pete was thorough and efficient. "Look, you're right. There's no reason to gift Franklin with this. You've been on the case from the go, and you've done a hell of a job—and quick. Your case, your credit."

Matt leaned back in his chair. Years in police work had made him adept at reading people, but to most people, he himself was an enigma. Generally speaking. Suddenly he felt as if Pete could read him as easily as a banner headline on a tabloid, but what the hell, his motives didn't disgrace him. "Look, you know I may be out of here in a few months. Haven't done anything official yet, but Sylvia doesn't know that. Guess I'd prefer to hang around for another five or ten years, but I've promised her— Well, that's another story. What I'm getting at is—I'm recommending you to replace me."

Pete shook his head. "Franklin is next in line and—"

"The hell with that," Matt barked, slapping his hand on the desk. "You're the man for the job." *Both jobs. Peter Castle, replacement at this desk and husband for Johnny's girl.*

"Matt, Franklin will raise one hell of a—" The phone rang.

"Lieutenant Nyborg." Matt listened, then scribbled notes on a pad in front of him. When he hung up, he looked at Pete. "Well, well. Franklin won't have to bellyache about your taking his case. I've got one to hand over to him. Seems a couple of kids dug up a man's body at Lake Cachuma."

Pete coughed. "Lake Cachuma?"

"In the dry bed area, just down from the 245." He picked up the phone. "Got to get the coroner over there, then locate Franklin."

Pete stood up. "How did the kids happen to find him?"

Matt shrugged. "The park patrol said it was a brother and sister. The boy was digging a hole to bury a bone and found a hand. Must have scared him shitless."

Pete headed toward the door. "Some kind of luck."

Matt put his hand over the mouthpiece. "See if Franklin's out there, will you?"

"Sure, but Matt—if he wants the Bouchard case, fine with me. It's wrapped up. I can take over this one. I'll head down to Lake Cachuma—"

"Nothing doing. You're going to take a bow whether you want to or not. So keep working on Bouchard—and check this out." He tossed Tara's note across the desk. "My niece was helping me this morning and took a message from a woman who wore a possum."

Pete glanced at the note. "There's something else I haven't briefed you on."

Matt held up his hand. "Hold on a second." He gave orders over the phone, then looked up. "More evidence? What is it?"

"Jessie Bouchard's purse. It was in her car. That blows Bouchard's whole story to hell. He killed her, probably in the car. The lab men are analyzing bloodstains now. When they get through, we'll have enough to get a conviction."

The totem pole was a true landmark, colorful and more intricately carved than anything Tara had imagined. She saw the top of it from the main road, and it served as a beacon to lead her to the home of Pudget Vandermeer.

The house was painted blue, not a pale shade, but azure. White wooden stars stood out in bas relief against the window frames, and over the front door, the white globe of a light fixture simulated the moon.

Awestruck, Tara had her camera clicking as soon as she stepped out of her car, her telephoto lens picking up every detail of the higher reaches of the totem. In the last couple of frames she caught Pudget, coming out of the house. "Welcome to the sky," Pudget called.

"I love the place," Tara answered, focusing tight on Pudget's face. She snapped the shutter one more time.

"You're unusual. Most people can't tolerate creativity. In town, neighbors would raise Cain, but out here, I'm so secluded I can do as I please."

A shaggy, cream-colored dog charged toward Tara. "It's all right, Zephyr, settle down. This is Tara. She's an artist, too, an artist with a camera."

The dog quieted, and Tara bent to ruffle its coat. "Hello, Zephyr."

After a tentative wag of its tail, the dog nuzzled against Tara's legs until Pudget shooed it away. "Come in, come in." Pudget opened a screen door to let Tara inside. "Did you give

Lieutenant Nyborg my message? Let him know I saw Jessie
Bouchard—" She broke off and looked back over her shoulder.
"Look there," she said, pointing. "This road turns and goes
straight through Ballard. Probably the way you came up. The
cemetery is off to the left, and that's where I saw her."

"I told my uncle exactly what you said. I'm sure he'll be
in touch with you."

It startled Tara to see that the interior of Pudget's house was
as conventional as the exterior was unusual. The living room
was small and dominated by an upright piano. The couch was
upholstered in a floral print; several bookcases were jammed
full, and an overstuffed chair faced a large-screen TV. Stepping
around the chair, Pudget said, "I'll just turn the volume down
so we can talk."

"Don't miss your show on my account. Maybe tomorrow—"

"No, no. This is nothing special. I just keep the TV on for
company."

"I took pictures of the totem pole. It really is a piece
of art."

"I worked on it for two years. That's a long time, but I wanted
it to be perfect." Her pride indicated she had accomplished
her goal.

"It's marvelous, and I'd love to see more of your work."

"Well, I don't have anything else that big, but come in here.
I'll show you some of my sculptures."

Her work area was crammed with a strange array of materials—blocks of styrofoam, panes of stained glass, wooden
dowels, mosaic tiles, the remains of clocks, and broken
discards from furniture. To Tara it looked like a roomful
of junk until she noticed two fascinating—she didn't know
what to call them—*things* against the far wall. "Those," she
said pointing. "What are they?"

Pudget took a deep breath. "Come here. I'll introduce you."

Tara changed the f-stop on her lens and circled both pieces, snapping from all angles.

The first piece was a mountain of inverted plastic champagne glasses, each housing a tiny light bulb and a treasure—scapular medals, gemstones, glass animals—suspended from the interior of the glass by a fine silver thread. The sculpture rested on a blue mirror sea, and when Pudget flicked a switch, the bulbs began blinking on and off, creating a kaleidoscope of reflected light and design.

Enchanted, Tara was still studying it when Pudget whispered, "And this is my masterpiece."

At first the piece looked less interesting—a pedestal supporting a drum of alternating wood and stained-glass strips. But the drum was rotated by a handle on its side, and when tiny lights blinked, reflecting on inlays of silver, the effect was truly hypnotic. Watching the drum turn and the lights flash, Tara felt as if she were being pulled into a different reality.

Flicking off the lights, Pudget said, "I call it *Meditation*."

Tara blinked, refocusing on the room and looking at Pudget with stark admiration. "I can see why. It's spellbinding—consuming." She blinked again. "I don't know what to make of it."

Pudget chuckled. "Nobody does. But people are willing to pay well for my work whenever I can bring myself to part with something. But most of the time I just sell those." She indicated a collection of earrings on a black velvet display board. "Had to hurry to finish this batch. They're being picked up tonight."

Next to the earrings were several carved figures, and Pudget handed one to Tara. It was a sturdy little rocking horse of dark wood, about eight inches high, and the wild mane and tail were made of yellow yarn. "I made this for Patrick Bouchard. They're not far from here, and it's on your way. Maybe you'll drop it off."

"Stop at the Bouchards!" Tara caught her breath. "Of course, Pudget. It's very sweet of you."

Pudget gave her directions, then offered to put on a pot of coffee. "Don't have visitors often. I expect you have something better to do, but if you have time . . ." Pudget looked diffident, but Tara wasn't eager to get away.

She had already been convinced of Pudget's genius, but after sitting over coffee with her, Tara felt something more. Pudget Vandermeer was compassionate, vital, and unmistakably one of a kind. When Tara left, she threw her arms around the woman and gave her an affectionate hug.

Beaming, Pudget returned the embrace, squeezing hard. "A new friend—that makes this a special day." She walked with Tara to her car. "Remember, turn left at the main road. The Bouchard place is about the third one down."

Tara thought of something. "Prince—where is he?"

"Sleeping. Possums like to sleep. I don't. My head's always full of ideas, so I'm up all hours. So come back any time. Maybe tomorrow." She gave Tara a final wave.

CHAPTER 9

Tara rapped softly on the door of the Bouchard house. If no one answered, she would leave the horse, scribble a note to let them know who had sent it, and be on her way. She was digging in her handbag for a pen when the door opened.

It was getting dark, and a man stood in half-light. She couldn't see his face. "I'm Tara Nyborg. I have a present from Pudget Vandermeer for Patrick Bouchard. He lives here, doesn't he?"

"Yes, I'm his father."

Tara caught her breath. *His father. Derek Bouchard.* "Sir, I . . . I'm sorry to bother you. And I'm very sorry about your wife." Her hand shook when she held up the horse. "Pudget made this for Patrick."

He opened the door. "Give it to him if you want. He's in the kitchen."

Tara swallowed. If she went inside, she might see pictures of Jessie Bouchard alive. She didn't want to see them and be reminded of Jessie Bouchard dead. She could hand the horse to the father, repeat her condolences and leave, but Derek Bouchard opened the door wider, expecting her to enter.

He pointed. "That way."

In the huge country kitchen a towheaded boy knelt on his

57

chair to reach the table. He lowered his cup as she entered. Recognizing him, Tara spun around and looked at his father. Derek Bouchard was the man she'd seen in the parking lot.

"Mr. Bouchard." Tara wanted to speak, but she faltered until she remembered why she had come. "Patrick, I'm a friend of a lady you know, Pudget Vandermeer. She made this and asked me to bring it to you." She held out the horse. When he didn't reach for it, she set it on the table.

She could leave, but something held her back. She knew Derek Bouchard was a murder suspect, but they both seemed so desolate. "Mr. Bouchard, is there anything I can do? Maybe play with Patrick for a while . . ."

"I'm sorry. Your name, I didn't—"

"Tara Nyborg. If you need me, I'm not busy."

For the first time he actually looked at her. "Nyborg," he repeated. "I've heard the name—and I think I've seen you."

"You did see me, in the parking lot of the police station. Lieutenant Nyborg is my uncle."

"Your uncle." He yawned. "I'm sorry, but I'm just so, so . . ."

"Tired," she finished for him.

"That's true. I just can't . . . can't put things together."

"Is this my pony?" Patrick was down from his chair and standing beside Tara, clutching the horse with both hands and holding it up for her approval.

She knelt beside him. "Yes, Patrick. It's your pony. A lady who likes you very much made it for you."

Solemn-faced, the child patted it. "Can it go night-night with me?"

"Of course it can. It's yours." She looked up. "That is—if it's all right with your daddy."

"Sure, Patrick. And I think it's bedtime now. It's early, but we've had a long day." He sighed. "I . . . I'll help you with your bath."

As if in response, the boy yawned and rested his head against Tara's shoulder. Instinctively, she folded her arms around him. "May I give Patrick his bath and get him to bed?" Tara knew she was being forward, but Derek Bouchard was exhausted. They both needed help, and she was there.

His father seemed too weary to protest, and Patrick directed her to his pajamas and towels, insisting she put "bubble bears" in the water. He was soft and slippery, and kneeling beside the tub, Tara felt uneasy. She had never bathed a child before, and he looked so small and vulnerable. But almost at once she began to relax.

"A lady who likes me gave me the pony?" he asked, a peak of bubbles on his nose.

"Yes, her name is Pudget. My name is Tara, and I like you, too."

When she tucked him into bed, he wanted his horse beside him, ignoring several stuffed toys. "Nice pony," he said. "I'll show it to Mommy when she comes home."

When Mommy comes home. Tara's heart ached for him and she stroked his hair. "Patrick, can I kiss you good night?" He didn't answer, and she pressed her lips against his forehead.

When she tiptoed downstairs, the house was quiet. Derek was probably asleep, and she crept toward the door.

"Miss Nyborg." He was standing just inside the kitchen.

"Patrick is tucked in. I'm sure he'll go right to sleep."

"Thank you. You're very kind, and I'm just not myself."

She nodded. "I understand. It must be terrible for you."

He shrugged. "It's a nightmare, but the alarm never rings."

Tara couldn't think of anything to say.

"It was nice of you to bring the horse—to help us—and I shouldn't keep you . . ." His voice faded. He didn't want her to leave.

"I'm not in a hurry."

"Would you like a cup of coffee or maybe some tea? I'm

new in the area. I don't really know anyone, but—forgive me—
I guess I'm imposing."

Twice this evening she had been offered coffee. She hadn't
refused the first time. She couldn't refuse now. "I'll have coffee
with you, Mr. Bouchard. And talk, if that's what you want."

He carried two mugs of coffee into the living room. He
never touched his, but he did talk. Words—emotion—seemed
to flow out of him. "We hadn't been getting along, Jessie and
I. She . . . wanted a world, a life-style, that turns me off. She
was beautiful and wanted to show the world she was beautiful,
but I thought—I hoped—that up here on the ranch we had a
shot at making a go of it . . ."

Rambling, he seemed unaware of Tara. He was talking to
himself, sorting things out. "I wasn't in love with her, not the
way I had been in the beginning, but I could have learned to
care again. At least it was worth the try—for Patrick."

He paused, but she remained quiet. He didn't need her to
speak; he needed her to listen.

"But now they tell me—I don't want to believe it—but the
detective told me that Jessie had hired a divorce attorney.
She wanted to arrange things so she'd get half of the ranch.
That means she was just pretending. She never had any real
intention . . ."

He set his mug down hard, slopping coffee onto the table. "I
can't believe I'm doing this! Unloading on a stranger. I don't
even know your—" He stopped. "Nyborg. You said your name
was Nyborg."

"Tara Nyborg. And I don't mind. You need someone to talk
to and, well, when I saw you this morning, you looked—" She
broke off. She couldn't tell him how sad he had looked, so she
tried again. "You looked like someone who needed to talk."

He sighed. "I guess I do, but I'm not usually like this. But
first I find out my wife is dead and then I'm told she planned
to divorce me. And now . . . now . . ."

He threw his hands in the air. "The police—it's impossible to believe—but they suspect me. They think I might have killed Jessie. They read me my rights. Apparently they think I might have killed her before I left for Phoenix. I don't know exactly what time she was found at the mission, but—"

"It was just past nine in the morning," Tara whispered.

"I was in Phoenix then—a horse auction. I left home the evening before. Jessie dropped me at the airport."

Tara could hardly get the words out. "What time did you leave for Phoenix?"

Derek Bouchard looked up. "My flight left at five o'clock."

Tara stood up. "Five o'clock! But then the police can't suspect you, because—" There was a loud knock.

Derek went to answer. Tara couldn't see, but she heard voices. First a man, then a woman. He had other company, and it was time for her to leave. She picked up her handbag and headed toward the door.

Derek's voice raged. "My son's sleeping. You can't—"

"There's no other family member here, so we have to take him into protective custody."

Several police officers surrounded him, and moments later a woman in civilian clothes carried Patrick down the stairs. He was crying. "Mommy! Daddy!"

Derek moved toward his son. "Patrick, it's okay. Daddy is just going with these men for a little while." He rumpled the boy's hair, then patted the shoulder of the woman who carried him, indicating she was a friend. But Patrick's cries for Daddy continued, and crooning, the woman carried him into the night.

"We have to cuff you. Put your hands behind you."

Tara was so shocked that at first she didn't realize the second officer was talking to her. "Excuse me, ma'am. I asked your name."

"I— It's Tara, Tara Nyborg."

"Nyborg?" When he peered at her, she recognized the officer who had been with Peter at the mission. "Hey, you're Lieutenant Nyborg's niece. Does he know you're here?"

She couldn't answer. Her attention was on Derek Bouchard, who was being led down the driveway flanked by two officers. He stared back at her, the anger and accusation clear in his eyes. She was the niece of the lieutenant in charge of the investigation, and her being there right before the police arrived was no accident.

CHAPTER 10

Tara sat in her car and watched the police vehicles until they disappeared down the dark country road. She had entered the Bouchard house hoping she wouldn't see pictures of the woman whose corpse had lain twisted in the *ropa*. She hadn't, but she had seen something harder to deal with—the look on Patrick's face when he was separated from his father.

She'd been at the mission when Jessie was found, and now she'd been on the scene when Derek was arrested and taken away. Maybe it was irrational, but she was frightened and remembered her terrible nightmare.

She turned the key in the ignition. Poor Patrick. His nightmare was real and just beginning. She ached for him, understanding the pain of a child without parents. But even though she'd never known her own father, he hadn't been wrested away before her eyes.

Her motel room was stuffy, but she wouldn't open the door to the patio. The memory of the dead birds lingered, making her uneasy, and she didn't want to be reminded. She switched on the TV. It might not be company for her the way it was for Pudget, but any distraction would help.

Flipping channels, she was startled to see Peter's face. Only it wasn't Peter, and then she remembered. Ryan Castle. They really did look alike.

She pulled a chair close and watched, her face hardly a foot from the screen. The name of the series was *Darn,* taken from the nickname of Ryan Castle's character, Tony Darnell. It was a long-running, highly rated show, but Tara had seen only a few episodes. It wasn't a format that appealed to her, but now—watching Peter's brother—she was fascinated. It was almost like watching Peter. Ryan had the same strong jawline, the same well-defined profile. His features were similar, and even his movements and voice were reminiscent of his brother. But Tara decided Peter was better looking.

After watching a few minutes, she had the feeling she'd seen this episode before, but they all followed the same pattern: Darn was a detective, like his brother in real life, but the time frame was the 1930s. Detectives were supposed to be tough, handsome, and outrageous, and Tony Darnell was all three. He was as quick with one-liners as he was to pull a gun, and adoring women littered themselves in his path. He had a soft side, but when he was on a case, anyone who got in his way was greeted with fists. Tara shook her head, realizing Ryan couldn't have modeled his TV character on his brother. If he had, Darn would have been more realistic.

As the show ended, the phone rang. "Tara? It's Peter. I planned to call you earlier, but I was assisting with a homicide."

Tara flinched. "I know. Derek Bouchard was arrested."

"Not Bouchard. This is another case—a body buried at Lake Cachuma—hasn't been identified yet."

"Another body, I—"

"Hold on! I shouldn't have mentioned it. I don't want to scare you out of Santa Barbara County. Anything but. Fact is, I want to take you out tomorrow night. Something special—my brother is giving a party."

"Your brother," she repeated. She had just seen the man on television. An invitation to his party hardly seemed real.

"Yes—Ryan. It's at his place in Santa Barbara." There was a pause. "I hope you can make it, so we can get to know each other better."

Tara warmed. An evening with Peter sounded ideal, and it would be nice to meet his brother, but nice because he was Ryan Castle, not because he was Tony Darnell. "I'd love to go," she murmured. She started to say she had just seen Ryan's show, but checked herself. People would always be telling him they watched his brother's show. He had to be bored with it. "Peter, I'll meet you at my uncle's. He and Aunt Sylvia are insisting I stay with them."

Getting ready for bed, Tara decided to shop for a new outfit because nothing in her travel wardrobe was suitable for a celebrity party. Perhaps in the morning she would phone her aunt and ask where to shop. Perhaps—if she tried hard enough—she could press Derek and Patrick Bouchard out of mind.

She spent a restless night, and it was early when she made a final check of the motel room and loaded her suitcases into the car. The door to her room was painted turquoise, the last in a row of identical doors, and Tara inspected them all. No dainty pink bags were attached to any of the knobs.

She inquired when she settled her bill. "The other morning sweet rolls were delivered to my door. Does the management do that often?"

The desk clerk looked up from the computer. "We never deliver breakfast. Complimentary breakfast is always served in the gazebo back by the pool."

"But on Wednesday, someone hung a sack of rolls on the doorknob. Called out either 'complimentary' or 'complimentary breakfast.' It was about seven o'clock."

The clerk shook his head. "It must have been an outside delivery, but don't worry. There are no charges for it on your bill."

Tara was baffled. "But I didn't order any rolls! And they killed the birds."

"*What*?" The clerk stared at her.

"Listen to me," she demanded. "I fed the rolls to the birds and then the birds died. I want to know where those rolls came from."

"Maybe you should talk to the manager when she gets here." The clerk sounded helpful, a recorded message, but his expression told her she wasn't making sense.

Tara signed the bill, but before she left the motel grounds, she circled back toward the room she had occupied. It was the farthest from the road and hidden from easy view by a stand of trees at that end of the property. Tara thought hard. When she had opened the door and found the rolls, she hadn't seen a car or heard anyone knocking on other doors.

It was baffling, but perhaps the rolls had been ordered by someone else and simply delivered to the wrong room. Certainly the thought that teased was foolish. The rolls couldn't have been poisoned. The birds had died, but surely they had ingested something else that was on the patio—scouring powder perhaps, or insecticide. It was insane to think someone might have been trying to harm her. Seeing a murder victim had left her wary, that's all.

It was a quick drive to Solvang, and she decided to stop for breakfast before heading north to Santa Maria. She selected a restaurant with an orange-and-blue windmill facade and ordered a feast of Danish pancakes with eggs.

Across the front of the dining room was a display case filled with an attractive array of Solvang's specialties—breads, rolls, and decorated pastries. It was early, but Pudget kept odd hours, and Tara decided to take her an assortment.

She put her cup down, thinking it would be nice to have coffee with Pudget. And she could tell her about Patrick— what had happened to him and how he had been clutching his little horse when the social worker took him away.

Suddenly she clapped her hand over her mouth. Witnessing Derek Bouchard's arrest had been so shattering Tara had all but forgotten Pudget's story. Now she racked her brain for details: Pudget claimed to have seen Jessie Bouchard walking in the Ballard cemetery *after* the mission would have been closed. Derek had left for Phoenix at five o'clock— he'd told her that himself—in which case, he couldn't have . . .

Jerking up from her chair, she ran outside and bought a newspaper from a vending machine at the door. The story headlined the front page: *Mission Victim's Husband Charged With Murder*.

A Ballard man, Derek Bouchard, has been charged with the murder of his wife, Jessie, whose body was found at the Santa Inez Mission on Tuesday morning, hidden in an antique chest. The mission is locked to visitors at 5 P.M., indicating the body had been placed in the chest before 5 P.M. on Monday. This is consistent with the coroner's report that when discovered, the victim had been dead from 12 to 24 hours.

Bouchard claims to have last seen his wife when she left the Santa Barbara Airport Monday, after dropping him off to make a 5 P.M. flight to Phoenix, Ariz. Airline officials confirm that Bouchard did make the flight, but inside sources speculate that he had hidden his wife's body in the chest earlier.

According to Sergeant Elaine Nicoles, information officer for the Santa Barbara County Sheriff's Department, Bouchard voluntarily reported to police that his wife's car was missing. Police later located the car in the parking lot at the Santa Barbara Airport. Jessie Bouchard's purse containing money, her wallet, driver's license, and car keys was

found in the car, shedding doubt on her husband's claim
that he watched her drive away . . .

No! If Pudget was right—if she had really seen Jessie
Bouchard in the Ballard cemetery after five o'clock—then
Derek couldn't have killed her!

Tara closed her eyes. Her impulse had been to like Derek
Bouchard, and her heart had gone out to Patrick. The murderer's
identity didn't really concern her—as long as it wasn't Derek.
Pudget has to be right. She has to be right.

She was so eager she almost forgot the pastries, but at
the last moment, she picked out an assortment—no cherry
or pineapple; they had lost their appeal. Then she headed
down the road toward Ballard, eager to hear Pudget repeat
her story.

The totem pole, then the blue house, white stars and moon.
Tara hurried to the front door, balancing the box of pastries
in front of her.

Zephyr was whining and scratching to get in. He ignored
Tara. "Zephyr, is Pudget off creating something and not paying
any attention to you?"

She knocked on the door. "Pudget, it's me, Tara." When
Pudget didn't answer, Tara knocked again, shifting the pastry
box to her left arm. She knocked a third time, louder, but heard
nothing from within.

Pudget, where are you? Tara had never wanted to see anyone
so badly, but finally she gave up. Pudget had to be out, but she
would leave the pastries and a note. The door opened when she
turned the knob, but before she could enter, the dog yipped and
pushed past her. Tara set the pastries on a stand inside the door.
"Zephyr. Zephyr, you come here!" she commanded, but she
heard the dog whimpering.

She stepped inside. "Pudget?"

Except for Zephyr's whimpering, the house was silent.

Heading for the kitchen to get the dog, Tara noticed clutter—odd items and materials—strewn over the living room floor. Suddenly she felt apprehensive. Her muscles tightened. "Pudget," she whispered, then tried again, louder. "Pudget, are you here? Are you all right?"

She moved toward the kitchen. From the doorway she saw that a cupboard door was open. A can of coffee lay on its side on the counter. Ground coffee was splashed everywhere—she noticed that first—then she saw Pudget, lying facedown at an odd angle on the floor.

And blood. A river of blood. Crying out, Tara dropped to her knees beside Zephyr who bayed at Pudget's side. She touched her friend's cheek. It was cold.

Horror was even more paralyzing than grief. Dead birds, dead bodies. She really was caught in a nightmare.

CHAPTER 11

Uncle Matt held Tara close, soothing her as if she were a child. "Poor Tara. Another body and this time someone you knew."

They were in Pudget's yard, standing in the shadow of the totem pole. His arm was around her, strong and protective. He wasn't someone she had met only a few days ago. Uncle Matt was her father's brother. He had known about her, cared about her, all her life. It felt natural to put her head on his shoulder, to accept his handkerchief to dry her eyes.

When Tara had called the police, she had hardly been able to speak. Struggling with tears, she'd gasped a report of Pudget's body to the dispatcher. Then she had asked that Lieutenant Nyborg be told she had made the call. "He's my uncle," she had said.

He had arrived in his own car, immediately behind the first county sheriff's unit that screamed to a stop at the blue house. She was distraught, and he comforted her a long time. Then he said, "I know it's hard, but we need you to answer some questions. And first of all, Tara, what were you doing here?"

Tara steadied herself. "Yesterday I came to take pictures of the totem pole. When I left, Pudget asked me to drop off a little horse she'd carved for Patrick Bouchard. Uncle Matt, I was with Derek Bouchard when he was arrested."

Tara glanced at the front door of Pudget's house. The entrance was already cordoned off with official yellow streamers. "I came back today to bring Pudget some pastries. The dog ran in when I opened the door. I went to get him and . . . found her on the floor." Trembling, she closed her eyes tight. "There was so much blood!"

"We're still waiting for the coroner, but it doesn't look like an accident."

Tara couldn't speak. She already knew—had known from the first moment—that it wasn't an accident.

"Tara, what time did you get here?" As he spoke, Uncle Matt guided her to her car, nodding to an officer to join them.

Officer Ream. Tara recognized him from the mission. Suddenly she remembered she was a Nyborg in an area where the Nyborgs had a reputation to uphold. She pulled herself together. "I arrived between nine and ten-after."

Uncle Matt signaled to Ream to take the report. "Did you touch anything in the house?"

She shook her head. "Only the phone." She answered Uncle Matt's barrage of questions, then persisted. "Remember what I told you yesterday? Pudget came to your office because she saw Jessie Bouchard the day she was killed. She was certain it was past five o'clock, and Uncle Matt, that would have been *after* Derek Bouchard left for Arizona."

He mulled it over. "I hear what you're saying—and it might be important. Tara, do you know if Pudget Vandermeer told anyone else that she saw Jessie Bouchard that day? If word had gotten around—" He broke off in midsentence.

"I don't know whether she told anyone else. But she was aware of the time because she was hurrying home to watch a particular program on television." Tara stressed the words. "She was *positive* it was after five."

"She was certain of the day?"

"Positive."

Uncle Matt was concentrating. "Sorry there wasn't time to question her, but we have your statement. And now, I'm sending you to your aunt." He called out, "Ream, will you take Miss Nyborg to my house? Drive her car. Fernandez will follow in a patrol unit."

Tara hopped in her car. "Uncle Matt, I can drive myself." Despite his protests, she drove away, keeping her attention riveted on the road. The vision of Jessie Bouchard's corpse had finally begun to fade, but now a heart-wrenching picture replaced it. *Pudget. Dear Pudget.*

In her fifty-five years, Mildred Tatum had never seen a morgue before, except on TV shows, and the little building didn't match her expectations. Located in a residential area bordering a cemetery, it was freshly painted with an open beam roof. If she hadn't known, she would have guessed it to be a recreation center or rangers' station. She parked her old Buick and walked slowly to the entrance, reluctant to face what was waiting.

Going in, she caught her breath, holding it as long as she could. But when she breathed, no odors assailed her. No formaldehyde. No disinfectant. It was just a building. "Mrs. Tatum?" A young woman rose from behind a desk to greet her. "Are you alone?"

"Yes, the detective who called wanted to pick me up, but I told him I would be all right. Drive myself at the end of my shift."

"Then come with me. Deputy Gilbert is expecting you."

They entered a short corridor, and when the receptionist opened a door, Mildred closed her eyes tight. This was it.

"Mrs. Tatum." It was a man's voice—brisk. She forced her eyes open and, steeling herself, glanced around. *No gurney with the shape of a body clearly defined under a drape of white sheets. No pathetic foot exposed with an identification tag laced to the toe.* The room was just a small office with two desks and a television, and a uniformed man was holding out his hand. "Mrs. Tatum," he repeated, "I'm Deputy Gilbert." They shook hands; then he pulled a captain's chair away from the wall. "Please—have a seat."

She sat down, holding her purse in her lap and grasping it with both hands.

"Would you like a glass of water?"

When Mildred shook her head, the deputy sat down behind a desk. Looking at him, she decided he was too pleasant-looking to be perpetually furious like the coroner on an old TV series she had followed. And he didn't look like a ghoul out of a Frankenstein movie either. His nameplate read *Deputy Larry Gilbert*. She stared at that nameplate. At the moment anything would do as a distraction. But he was talking, and she had to listen. He was explaining that the body found at Lake Cachuma matched the description of the man she had reported missing.

"My nephew, Handy—Andrew Arthur Mason, my late sister's son," she told him. "But I want to see the body—make absolutely sure."

"Yes, ma'am. But you don't want to see him." Gilbert sounded gentle. "I know this isn't easy for you, but I have to explain. The body was buried for at least a week. Decomposition is advanced, and the facial features are not recognizable."

Mildred felt the flutter of hope. "Then how can we be sure?"

Gilbert leaned forward, extending his arms across the desk. "We don't have a hit on his fingerprints yet. We're still working on that—but there's something else."

Mildred looked at him.

"The victim's tattoo—an American flag on his left arm—looks like what you described." He spoke slowly, patiently. "When the epidermis—that's the top layer of skin—first wears away, the dermis is still visible. Tattoos are permanent because they are in the dermis. We've taken photographs, but we can do a positive ID right now if you're willing." He glanced toward the TV. "It's closed-circuit, and you won't have to see the body. All we'll show you is a close-up of the tattoo."

Mildred consented, dreading it, yet wanting to be sure. Maybe, maybe there was a chance—

Deputy Gilbert called down the hall, then turned on the TV. He adjusted the dials, suggesting she look away until he was ready.

She stared in her lap, waiting.

"Mrs. Tatum."

Blinking, she looked up. Hope was over. It was Handy. "That's his tattoo," she said, emotion thickening her voice. "I told him it was wrong. The bottom stripe is supposed to be red, not white." She wiped her eyes. She wasn't going to break down, but still—poor Handy.

Someone rapped on the door just as Gilbert turned off the TV. Sniffling, Mildred glanced up, then, startled, she took a long look at the man who entered. "Why," she exclaimed, still sniffling, "you're Tony Darnell!"

"Excuse me, I'm Detective Castle. I'd like to ask you some questions if you're—"

"Detective Castle—Ryan Castle! You're one of my favorite shows. But, my goodness, what are you doing here? You're not a real detective, are you?"

"I'm not Ryan Castle. I'm Detective Peter Castle with the Santa Barbara County Sheriff's Department, and I need—"

Mildred blinked. "But you look just like him. And the same name. You must be related."

He looked down at his open notebook. "He's my brother. Now, if you don't mind—"

"Yes, of course, but it's amazing, isn't it? He's such a *famous* detective."

"Amazing. When was the last time you saw your nephew?"

"Nine, no, ten days ago." She explained to Detective Castle that Handy had lived with her whenever he was in the area. "When he wasn't following the rodeo, you know. He used to be a roper."

"Yes, ma'am—"

"He still followed the circuit, but it was too dangerous for him to ride anymore. Not after his accident and that head injury."

Detective Castle looked up. "Head injury?"

"Took a fall from a horse and cracked his skull a good one. The concussion healed, but he walked funny and the doctors said he'd never be the same. They said any trauma to the head could kill him."

"Any trauma to the head could kill him," the detective repeated. He had been standing near her chair, and now he sat down on a low file cabinet.

"That's why I reported him missing. I knew something was wrong. If he'd left for the rodeo, he would have taken his saddle. He always takes it with him, even though he can't ride, so I was afraid maybe he'd got his head hurt. Maybe landed in a hospital . . . or in jail." She felt her lower lip quiver. "I didn't expect this."

Deputy Gilbert spoke up. "According to the preliminary autopsy report, the probable cause of death was a cranial hemorrhage of unknown etiology. In other words, Mrs. Tatum, there was bleeding in his head and, as yet, we don't know why. But it's a homicide based on the fact the body was buried."

"Poor Handy." Mildred shook her head. "I can't imagine anyone wanting to kill him. But maybe he got in a fight. Before the accident, he used to be a scrapper. But, big as he was, he still never hurt anybody. It was just fun, but maybe someone hit him in the head, not knowing what could happen—"

Ryan Castle's look-alike brother cleared his throat. "Do you know if he had any enemies? Anyone he might have fought with?"

Mildred looked at the detective. *My goodness, he's handsomer than his brother, if you get right down to it.* It took her a moment to collect herself. "No, he didn't have any enemies. Nobody I knew about, anyway."

"But he had been in trouble with the law. We have his rap sheet—I mean, a printout of his arrests, and—"

Mildred cut in quickly. "I know. He was arrested for disorderly conduct a couple of times and once for being drunk in public. Had to pay fines—I know 'cause I loaned him the money. And he paid it back. Every cent. He was like that. Honest. Good-natured too, unless he was drinking, and he didn't start drinking until after the accident. Guess he never got over not being able to ride anymore." She sighed. "Maybe . . . maybe it's just as well now."

Detective Castle explained that they had a search warrant they hoped she would sign, giving them permission to examine all of Handy's possessions on her property. "It might give us a lead. Help us find out what we're looking for."

"Of course," she told him, reaching for a pen. She signed the warrant and handed it back to him.

Detective Castle stood up. "Is there anything we can do for you? Perhaps get an officer to drive you home?"

Mildred hesitated, taking a moment to dab at her eyes. "You don't suppose—" She paused again. "Well, would it be too much trouble to get me an autographed picture of your brother?"

CHAPTER 12

Tara woke up flooded with memories of a nightmare, but this time the nightmare was real—Pudget Vandermeer lying in a pool of blood. Pushing the horror out of her mind, she opened her eyes wide and saw a large mahogany dresser; she caught the movement of a lace curtain fluttering at a window. Startled, she wondered where she was, and it took a moment before she recognized the guest room of the Nyborg house.

Aunt Sylvia was in the doorway. "Are you awake, dear? Peter is on the phone. He's concerned about you. I told him I'd persuaded you to lie down, but that I'd see—"

"Peter." Tara sat up and looked at her watch. *Two o'clock.* "We had a date for tonight, but I don't think I want—"

"He knows what happened and suspected you would want to cancel. But he asked me to use my influence and I will. Tara, it will be good for you to get out. And tonight is special—his brother's party."

Tara dropped back against the pillows and put a hand over her face. Memories of this nightmare would never fade, but Aunt Sylvia was right. Dwelling on what had happened wouldn't help. "Tell Peter I'll be ready."

When Aunt Sylvia returned, she insisted on taking Tara shopping. "It will do you good, and you need something special to wear tonight."

79

At a boutique Aunt Sylvia coaxed Tara into trying on a designer dress in turquoise silk. Despite herself, Tara was pleased. The silk felt delicious against her skin, and the color highlighted her red hair. "It's a gift from your Uncle Matt and me," Aunt Sylvia said before Tara could take out her checkbook. "It's already on my charge."

Peter arrived promptly at seven, and Aunt Sylvia and Uncle Matt walked out on the front porch to see them off. Aunt Sylvia kissed her. "Tara, have a good time. I insist."

Uncle Matt kissed her, too, then patted Peter's shoulder. "You'd better take good care of my beautiful niece."

With that send-off, Tara felt like a teenager heading for the prom, but she wasn't annoyed. It was pleasant—comfortable— to be part of a family. And earlier, when Uncle Matt had praised Peter to her, she'd known he wasn't being offhand. He had something in mind, and she'd felt her cheeks warm, wondering if poor Peter had endured a litany of how wonderful *she* was. Driving away, she laughed, a good start for the evening.

Peter asked what was so funny, and she felt brazen enough to tell the truth. "Uncle Matt is trying to promote something between us. I have a hunch you're hearing whatever good things he can think of to say about me."

Peter didn't laugh. "He never told me anything I hadn't already decided on my own. And as for his promoting something between us—sounds good to me."

She studied his silhouette. It was too dark to make out his features, but he had a high forehead, a well-defined chin—a strong face. As she nestled in her seat for the long drive to Santa Barbara, the idea occurred to her: *It might be nice . . .*

But even appealing thoughts couldn't hold her attention. They were traveling south on the 101 freeway, and the early darkness of winter was settling in. She stared out at the rolling hills, at the trees looming as eerie shapes in the dimness. In the car with Peter she was safe, protected, yet somewhere in that night were murderers—one who had stuffed a body into a chest at the mission, another who had crushed the spark of genius that had been Pudget.

A shiver iced through her. *The two murderers were really one. Pudget had been killed because her witness could protect Derek and send the police searching elsewhere for Jessie Bouchard's killer.*

That morning she had rushed to the sky-blue house, eager to hear Pudget repeat her account of seeing Jessie Bouchard in the Ballard cemetery. Tara had wanted proof that Derek was innocent—but maybe someone else had wanted him guilty.

"Tara, I know what's bothering you."

"I'm sorry," she said, startled by the sound of Peter's voice. "I guess my mind was wandering. It won't happen again."

"I think we should talk about it. It will make you feel better."

She was touched by his understanding, but it took time to put the words together. "I know this is your business, not mine," she began, "but I think Pudget Vandermeer was killed because she saw Jessie Bouchard alive *after* Derek Bouchard left for Phoenix. I mean, if the person who killed Jessie knew—"

"At this point, nothing points in that direction. Vandermeer was murdered while a robbery was going down. He got in through the back door, hit her in the head, and ransacked the place. We don't know what was taken, because there's no telling what she had."

"Could someone have deliberately made it look like a burglary?"

Even in the darkness, she saw the shake of his head. "Did a mighty convincing job if it was faked. Hit exactly the spots a burglar goes for. No, Tara. We're not overlooking anything, but as of now, we don't see a tie-in to the Bouchard case."

"If it's just a horrible coincidence, what about Pudget's claim to have seen Jessie Bouchard? She was positive about it, but now she's dead, too. Could her evidence still be used to help Derek Bouchard?"

Peter reached for her hand and his grip was firm. "Tara, I doubt that what she had to say would make any difference even if she were still alive. The case against Bouchard is nailed shut."

Gesturing, Tara pulled her hand away. "But Pudget saw Jessie! It's just not possible—"

"If Vandermeer really saw her, it wasn't when she thought it was—or *said* it was. With most major crimes—and especially murders—we get a parade of witnesses who claim to have vital information. It goes with the territory. We check everything out, but most of it is crackpot garbage."

"But Pudget wasn't a crackpot. She was a gifted artist, and very intelligent. Uncle Matt can't ignore what she had to say. She was rational, and she—"

"Wore a possum around her neck," Peter finished for her. He cleared his throat. "Tara, your uncle will make sure nothing is overlooked. Unless the murderer is a transient—someone we have almost no chance of bringing in—we'll catch him. Matt has one of the best reputations in the state, and you don't have to be afraid he won't do his job."

"I wasn't questioning his competence!"

Peter laughed. "You're *his* niece, and you're like him. You both feel responsible for everything that happens. But I think you should let him worry about the Vandermeer investigation."

Peter was right. Murder was beyond her scope. Uncle Matt, Peter, and the other detectives would know how to evaluate Pudget's claims. It was their responsibility, not hers, and she had told them everything she knew.

They had reached Santa Barbara, and the lights of the city shone through the trees and dense hedges that bordered the freeway. Toward the ocean, giant palm trees swayed, bewitching dark shapes on the horizon. The view from the freeway was limited but inviting, and Tara became aware of a throbbing need to be with people. The horror of the morning was still with her. She needed gaiety, life, distraction. She couldn't forget Pudget, but perhaps for a little while she could ignore the ache.

"Peter, I'm in the mood for a party—more than I thought I'd be—and I'm looking forward to meeting your brother."

He laughed. "Of course you want to meet Ryan. Everyone does." As he spoke, he cut onto an off ramp, then circled down toward the water, into an area of palatial homes set on sprawling estates. Most of the homes were illumined, either by dramatic spotlights or by rows of lights encircling driveways and adorning entries.

It was a new scene to Tara, and she decided it would be a great place to return to with a camera. With her photographer's discernment, she caught glimpses of a variety of architectural styles—sometimes combined in a single structure. No two houses resembled each other; few houses reflected a unified design: Tudor turrets on a Victorian-style home; columns worked into the facade of a postmodern; and over there a house that belonged in the Black Forest to serve as an oversized abode for Hansel and Gretel.

It was an elegant hodgepodge and, at the end of a lane, Peter turned the car through gates that led up a long, circular driveway to a magnificent, white Mediterranean palace. It was a blaze of light, and sheer drapes in pale gold made the windows look like glowing feline eyes. Peter pulled to a stop, and parking attendants rushed to open the doors and assist them out.

As they approached the entry, Tara took Peter's arm. "This is your brother's house?"

"He leases it. Comes up here on weekends. But he's shooting a feature film in the area, so he's been up here quite a bit lately."

A man in a tuxedo greeted them at the door. Friendlier and less formal than a butler, he was obviously weeding out party crashers, and he recognized Peter immediately. "Mr. Castle," he said, beaming, "your brother will be delighted. I'll let him know you're here."

They entered the main salon, where a pianist wearing a floor-length red dress was rendering a Joplin rag on a concert grand. She was accomplished, and her music gave the scene the perfect touch of vitality. The throng was good-sized, but the room wasn't overcrowded, and Tara recognized several faces from movies and television. Then she saw Ryan moving toward them, shaking hands and greeting people on the route.

"Pete, you actually showed up!"

"You invited me, didn't you?"

Ryan laughed. "Yeah, I invited you. I've invited you before, but this is the first time you ever dusted off your suit and came."

"Well, I didn't have anything to read and there's never anything good on television. Here, I want you to meet someone."

Before Peter could make the introduction, a bejeweled woman snuggled close to Ryan. "How can he say that, darling? That there's never anything good on television? Your show is wonderful! My favorite, and I want to do a guest appearance—just for you." A fixture on television game shows, the snuggler was known for flamboyance and seasonal husbands, and even if her face—so much older and cosmetic-laden in person—had been turned away from her, Tara would have recognized the drawling foreign accent.

Ryan hardly glanced toward her. "Great, Suzette," he murmured, extending his hand and attention to Tara. "Hello. I'm Pete's big brother."

Suzette squealed. "Your brother! This big, splendid man is

your brother?" She touched Peter's cheek. "Of course he is!
I see the gorgeous resemblance."

Tara felt as if she were watching television and had somehow
got caught inside the picture. She wasn't at a loss for lines, but
didn't get a chance to say them.

"And what do *you* do?" Suzette asked, shifting her snuggle
from one brother to the other.

"I'm a detective with the Santa Barbara County Sheriff's
Department."

Suzette looked puzzled. "What show is that? I'll have to
watch—or maybe we could watch it together." She drawled
the words even more than usual, working on seduction.

Tara glanced at Peter. He wasn't moved. If anything, he
looked annoyed. "You don't understand, Miss Cordeau. I'm
a detective, not an actor. I don't have a scriptwriter to do my
thinking."

Ryan roared. "Not a bad line. If you can come up with more
of them, you can *be* a scriptwriter. It's a better-paying job."

Tara couldn't resist staring at Ryan. In contrast to Suzette,
he looked better in person than he did on the tube. His face was
gentler somehow. And already—hidden in the quick barbs that
passed so easily between him and Peter—she sensed a family
affection. In the past, displays of family regard had always
made her feel left out, but she relished this one. Now she had
a family of her own.

Ryan eased closer to take Peter's place beside her. "Pete
told me you were beautiful, and I have to admit—for once
he's right."

Tara felt herself blush, not from Ryan's compliment, but
from the implication: *Peter was already mentioning her to his
family.*

Suzette had Peter monopolized, holding him fast with one
arm and using the other to signal a waiter offering drinks on
a silver tray. "A drink, darling. Let's you and I touch each

other's glass—and whatever else we can think of."

"Would you like a drink, Miss . . ."

"Nyborg. Tara Nyborg. And I'll have a glass of wine."

"Come with me. I have quite a wine collection—more interesting than the labels we're serving. Let's pick out something." Taking her arm, Ryan guided her through the crowd. She glanced back at Peter, but Suzette devoured his attention.

"Peter!" She doubted he heard her over the piano and chatter, and she went with his brother.

"There you are, Ryan!"

People called and reached to shake hands with him as they passed. His responses were warm but quick, and he took Tara to what was more of an alcove than a traditional wine cellar. It was chilly, and she realized the area was specially cooled to protect the wines that lined the walls.

He whisked out a bottle to show her. "This is a California wine, and our wines are the best. But if you prefer a foreign vintage, let me know." He smiled at her, and suddenly it didn't seem real. *A famous actor coaxing her to select a wine.*

"Please—I'm not a connoisseur. You pick out something."

"Okay, then. I'll have this iced. It'll only be a few minutes." They walked back to the salon, and handing the bottle to a waiter, Ryan murmured instructions. "Now, down to business," he said, turning back to Tara. "Pete asked me if I could do anything about getting you a job. He never asked for a favor before—believe me, he almost choked getting the words out—and I told him I'd do my best. What experience have you had?"

Tara was so startled, it took a moment before she could answer. "I— Well, I'm mostly free-lance, but I have a clientele. Department stores, calendar work. Now I'm working on a calendar study of the California missions."

"What?" Ryan looked puzzled. "I mean—what acting have you done?"

She shook her head. "I've never done any acting. I'm a photographer. If Peter talked to you about a job for me, that had to be what he had in mind. But really—I'm not looking . . ."

Suddenly her voice broke as she realized: *Peter wants to keep me in California.*

"A photographer! I could have sworn Pete said—" Breaking off, Ryan chuckled. "I was so surprised when he called, I must have misunderstood. Anyway, I'll talk to the studio. Arrange an appointment for you. Do you have a portfolio?"

"Of course, back home in Seattle. I came to California to do the calendar, and then I met my uncle and his family and stayed on for a few days."

"Do you want to stay in California?"

Before she could answer, the waiter returned and flourished a tray in front of her. Centered was a single crystal glass of wine. She raised it to her lips and, sipping, caught Ryan's eye. He was waiting, but she took a moment to compose her answer. "Your wine is delicious, and yes—maybe I would like to stay in California. Your offer is greatly appreciated."

"What offer?" Peter had managed to untangle himself from Suzette Cordeau and had come up behind her.

Tara stared into her wineglass. "Your brother has offered to help me get a job in California."

Peter took a firm grip on Tara's shoulder. "The lady is doing very well without your help. She doesn't need the services of Tony Darnell."

Tara looked up. "But I thought you *asked* him . . ." Her voice trailed into embarrassment.

Peter looked surprised, then leaned to brush his lips against her cheek. "That was before. Fact is, I don't think this is your kind of crowd." Despite the kiss, he sounded brusque.

"Hey, Pete, these are my friends, so don't polish your badge and ride off on your high horse! I offered to arrange a job interview for her and I will—if she wants me to."

Tara saw a cloud pass over Peter's face, and it was almost impossible not to understand: Ryan was being so attentive, Peter was concerned she might fall for the wrong brother . . .

The wine was warming, the company heady, and winking at Peter, she held her glass to his lips. "Ryan, let's find out what a real detective thinks of your wine."

Peter's face softened. He tasted the wine, then stared directly at Tara. "Wonderful," he murmured. "Absolutely wonderful."

CHAPTER 13

A stinging wind slapped her legs, and Tara struggled to hold her coat down and attend to her luggage. It was late Tuesday afternoon, the beginning of rush hour, and she was hailing a cab outside Sea-Tac Airport.

The more Tara thought about moving to California, the more irresistible it seemed. She had been brought up to do the expected at the expected time. Grandmother had been devoted to maintaining order, and change could only follow long-term planning. As a teenager, Tara had battled her grandmother's tyranny and broken free. Now she relished quick decisions and wasn't afraid to take a risk. An exciting new life beckoned in California. She was determined to give it her best, but she needed her portfolio for the job interview, and she had to contact her regular clients. She had flown home, but it was temporary. California was in sharp focus.

The damp chill was jarring after the clement weather in California, but the heat in the cab was stifling. After a slow drive through heavy traffic, Tara was relieved when they pulled up to her red brick condo complex on Magnolia Hill. She'd been thrilled when escrow closed on the place and she owned her first bit of real estate. Now the place belonged to her past. The future was in California.

As she unpacked, she listened to the messages on her answering machine. Several were from clients and would be acknowledged later, but hearing the vibrant voice of Michelle Michaels, Tara picked up the phone and dialed.

"You're back!" Michelle trilled. "Welcome home!"

Michelle's voice returned her to a world that somehow seemed distant. It was hard to believe she had been gone only a couple of weeks. "I'm home, but not for long. I'm going back to California."

"You didn't finish the shoot for the mission calendar?"

"Yes, but . . . Michelle, I'm going back to California for a job interview. I have relatives in Santa Maria." She hesitated. "And I met someone—"

Michelle broke in. "A guy? Tell me about him."

Tara smiled. "His name is Peter Castle. He's a police detective and—well, I like him."

"A detective? So maybe that's not the highest-paid job in the world, but what does he look like?"

"He's good-looking. Handsome, actually. He resembles his brother Ryan, and—"

"Ryan! Ryan Castle? You're kidding! This guy is Ryan Castle's brother?"

"Yes, he is. He works for my uncle Matt." Tara felt a surge of pride. "I'd never met my uncle Matt before. He's a lieutenant with—"

"You met Ryan Castle's brother? How exciting. Do you think you'll ever get a chance to meet Ryan?"

"I met him. And I have to tell you about my aunt. She's the most—"

"You *met* him? You met Ryan Castle? Where? What's he like?"

Tara sighed. "It was at a party, and—"

"You went to California to shoot the missions, and you end up at a Hollywood party!"

"Not exactly. The party was in Santa Barbara, at Ryan's house. Peter took me. He—"

"Wait a minute. You were in Ryan Castle's house? What was it like? Who was there? Tell me everything!"

Suddenly Tara realized what Peter had to put up with, and she made a mental note: never mention Ryan's name to anyone if she wanted to get in a word about Peter. The screen cop would always seem more exciting than his flesh-and-blood brother. "Listen, Michelle," she said, trying not to sound exasperated, "I have to finish unpacking, and then I'm going to soup some negs of the missions. I have to update my portfolio and—"

"Oops, Tara. I'd better come over. I'm afraid I left your darkroom a mess. I shot a wedding and had to develop the prints in a hurry, but I'll get it cleaned up."

Tara glanced at her watch. "I'll forgive you if you come soon and stop for a pizza."

"Mushroom and olives with extra cheese—within an hour."

Tara continued unpacking, but a glance into the darkroom confirmed what Michelle had said. In a small bedroom, Tara had hung lightproof drapes, installed Formica tabletops to hold chemicals and equipment, and created a streamlined workplace. But now the trays were full of stale chemicals and unprinted negs hung from the drying racks.

Michelle. She wasn't exceptionally neat—Tara had known that when she offered her the use of the darkroom—but she was an excellent photographer and had been an invaluable help when Tara had been battling to establish herself as a professional. Although almost a decade older than Tara, Michelle retained a pixie-like quality, and Tara admired her gregariousness and dependability—if not her fascination with Ryan Castle.

Michelle was quizzing her about Ryan even before the pizza box was on the table. "So you met Ryan Castle and you're going back to California because of his brother?"

"No, Michelle. I told you I met my aunt and uncle, and I have a cousin, too. His name is Walker, and—"

"How long will you be gone? And is there any chance you'll see Ryan Castle again?"

Tara put slices of pizza on plates and mixed two tumblers of instant ice tea. "I don't know how long I'll be gone, Michelle, and I guess that's a problem. I told you I have a job interview that—" She caught herself. She couldn't mention that Ryan had arranged the interview, because that would set Michelle off again. "Well, if I get the job, I'll stay in California. That means I'll have to rent my condo." She paused to take a bite of pizza. "I won't be taking my darkroom equipment with me, so if you have a place where you can use it while I'm gone, then—"

"I have a perfect place to use it while you're gone. Rent the condo to me!"

"But you have an apartment."

"Month to month rental. I can move anytime."

"But if I decide to stay in California—really stay—then I'd have to sell."

Michelle popped out of her chair and looked around as if seeing her surroundings for the first time. "Hmmm, I've got an idea. Someone will have to handle your accounts while you're gone. It might as well be me. That'll boost my income enough so that if you stay in California, and we can agree on a price—well, I've always liked this place and the location is great."

Tara put the dishes in the sink. "And you're sure you want to move?"

Michelle opened cupboard doors and examined the electric range. "I've been looking, but haven't found anything—not like this."

Tara felt a rush of enthusiasm. Everything would work out better than she'd dared hope. "Come on, Michelle. Let's get to work. The job I'm interviewing for is a publicity photographer, but I've got some great mission shots, and I'll add a few to my portfolio."

In the darkroom Michelle stood beside her and hung up the first set of negatives that came out of the soup. "Who's this?" she asked, squinting.

Tara leaned toward her. "That's my uncle Matt. There, in the next shot, is Aunt Sylvia. And the next one is . . . is . . ." Tara stopped. The next one showed Pudget, beaming unmistakably even in the negative.

"Hey, that looks like a totem pole."

"It is," she faltered, "but these are personal shots—the last ones I took. Let's get to the next batch."

Tara quickly turned her attention to the shots she had taken at the Santa Inez Mission. She'd doubted she could catch the morning mystique that had hovered over the valley, but several of the negs were promising. It took a moment to remember the meadowlark, but then she was pleased with the close-up that caught its cocked head and quizzical expression against the background of the mission bell tower.

Michelle was studying the next frame. "What the devil is that?"

Tara glanced at the frame, then peered closer. She couldn't identify the subject. It was a woman, standing—no, lying down. And chartreuse green. Chartreuse—that would print magenta. My God! She staggered backward. Jessie . . . Jessie in the *ropa!*

Tara slumped against the door, breathing with her mouth open, almost as stunned as she had been at the actual scene. The moan she heard must have been her own, and Michelle grasped her arm. "Kid, what's wrong?"

Tara shook her head, not in response to Michelle, but trying to break free of the image swimming before her eyes. But Jessie wouldn't go away. She was right there in the darkroom, and the odor of stale chemicals mimicked the foul odor that had risen from the *ropa*. The eyes that stared into endless space stared at Tara, finding her even a thousand miles away.

Michelle snipped several negatives from the roll and put them in the viewer. "These are still damp, but—" She tipped the viewer toward her, angling it. "So this is what got to you! It's a corpse in some kind of chest."

Tara roused herself. "It's at the Santa Inez Mission. A body was found when I was there."

"Why did you take pictures?"

Tara shrugged. "A reflex action. A woman was screaming. I ran over. I had my camera and started shooting."

"You must have set your f-stops. These are good photos. The detail is excellent. Here, do you want to see?"

Tara grimaced. "No! I know exactly how she looked, and I wish I didn't." She opened the door and lunged into the light.

Michelle assailed her with questions. By comparison, the inquiries about Ryan Castle had been entertaining, but it was a relief to talk. "Like I told you," she gasped, "this woman had found the body and was screaming." The memory was jumbled, everything running together. "That's when I met Peter. He took charge of the investigation, and that night he introduced me to my uncle."

"Have the police solved the murder?"

"I don't know. They've arrested someone—her husband— but I met him and somehow I just don't think—"

"You met the woman's husband? How? I mean, that's weird."

"I took their little boy a pony that a lovely woman named Pudget Vandermeer carved for him. I talked to the man. He seemed stricken and devoted to his son. I can't believe he murdered his wife." Until she heard the words from her own mouth, Tara had never realized how sincerely she believed they were true. Derek Bouchard wasn't a murderer.

"Do the police have a good case against him?"

Tara dropped down on the couch, pulled her long legs close to her body, and wrapped her arms around them. "The police think they have a good case against him, but Pudget *did* see Jessie after five o'clock. That woman knew what she was talking about."

"Who's Jessie?"

Tara swallowed. "The woman in the chest. Her name was Jessie Bouchard. Her husband is Derek Bouchard." Quickly Tara explained about the mission's closing time. "So you see, if Pudget was right, it's proof Derek didn't murder his wife, because he was already on his way to Phoenix."

Michelle shrugged. "If Bouchard goes to trial, Pudget can testify and—"

Tara unwound and stood up. "Pudget can't testify. She's dead, too. Murdered."

Michelle gasped, but Tara continued. "And as far as I know, I'm the only person Pudget told. The only person who actually heard her say she had seen Jessie Bouchard." Suddenly Tara felt a chill worse than what she'd experienced standing in the wind. She shivered. "I'm the only person who knows she was telling the truth."

CHAPTER 14

"Sylvia, you won't want to hear this, but it can't stay secret for long. Walker is involved with Louise."

"Louise?" Sylvia blanched.

Much as Matt hated to, he'd thought he should tell her, and now there was no turning back. "Yeah. You'd think that after what happened, he'd keep her set loose for good, but he's seeing her again. That's what's wrong with him."

Sunday-morning breakfasts were Matt's favorite meals, and he usually whipped them up himself. Sylvia's cooking was the world's best, but once a week it was fun to take over the kitchen and fry a mountain of hash browns or flip pancakes. This morning he had served up a mushroom omelette—something he'd been sure Sylvia would enjoy—but she'd just toyed with it. Her expression was so forlorn it stabbed his heart—and galled him. She was worried about Walker, so he'd told her the truth.

"Maybe I should have kept it to myself, but eventually you'll hear about it. I hoped it would be easier on you if it came from me."

Sylvia shook her head. "You have to be mistaken. It's just not possible. Not after what she did."

Her slender hand rested on the table, and he took it in a protective grasp. "Walker was boating with Louise on Lake

Cachuma. Someone in the department spotted them."

"*Who* saw them? How can we be sure it was actually Walker and Louise?"

"It was her father's boat," he said softly.

"Matthew, I think Walker takes the Medford boat out occasionally. It could have been another woman, perhaps a friend of the Medfords who—"

He shook his head. "Sylvia, I checked it out. It had to have been Louise." His sigh could have doubled as a groan. "The woman was a brunette, somewhere in her late twenties, and a looker. Maybe that's not a fingerprint make, but on the Medford boat, it's enough to convince me."

He still held her hand, and she returned the pressure, squeezing tight. She clung to him, and he was torn between loving her gentleness and wanting to give her his strength. She was delicate and, with her dark hair hanging loose against her blue silk robe, as beautiful as a girl. He adored her still, and they were a great team. Walker came from good stock, and what made Matt so mad was that he didn't behave like it.

Sylvia stared at her cold omelette. "When he married Nance, I thought—I hoped—that he had finally gotten over Louise. But now he's separated . . ." Her voice quivered. "But even so, what about Louise? She's married."

"Her marriage is in the courts, the same as Walker's. In fact"—Matt sounded weary—"I think the one caused the other."

Sylvia looked struck. "What do you mean?"

Blasting himself for hurting her, Matt chose his words carefully. "I can't be sure, but the timing is suspicious. Brian and Louise separated last fall, and, if I've got the dates right, Walker left Nance about a month later. Louise lives in Santa Barbara, and with him putting up here, it's convenient for them."

Sylvia pulled her hand free. "I'm not ready to accept—no, I *won't* believe it. He can't be seeing her. It's something else—

maybe separating from Nance—and he's depressed."

Matt was at his wits' end. He didn't want to hurt Sylvia by coming down hard on Walker, but maybe that would help. If she held off on the sympathy, the whole situation might be less painful for her. "Look, maybe Walker is depressed but that's to his credit. What can he think of himself, chasing her again after . . ." His voice snagged. "After what happened?"

After what happened. Walker and Louise had been engaged, a stunning pair according to everyone's description. Walker was blond and Louise was a vibrant brunette who behaved like a queen and expected everyone to pay her court. Walker had obliged, groveling at her feet to his father's annoyance. A wedding date was set; invitations were out. The Medfords had a lavish wedding and reception planned and then—

Matt closed his eyes. Two weeks before the wedding, Walker, at the age of twenty-three, was stricken with an apparent heart attack. Sylvia and Matt camped at the hospital, and Louise visited frequently, usually in the company of Brian Holmes, Walker's lifelong pal and scheduled best man. After almost a week of tortured waiting, a diagnosis was made: Walker's heart was perfect. His symptoms had been brought on by a hernia resulting from an overly strenuous exercise regime. Sylvia had sobbed, and Matt had held back his own tears when they heard the prognosis—complete, uncomplicated recovery and his doctors promised to throw rice at the wedding. But no wedding took place, at least no wedding for Walker.

In a phone call to her parents, Louise announced that she and Brian had "found each other" and run away to marry amid the genuine tinsel of Las Vegas. Walker was utterly demolished— a ruin. Everyone else was staggered, and Matt felt tortured watching Sylvia's fresh anguish on Walker's behalf. Deep in his own heart, he harbored an "all's well that ends well" feeling. Walker was in good health and, his father was certain, better off without Louise Medford.

Matt had forced himself to like the girl as a prospective daughter-in-law, but the cop in him had sized her up. Her selfishness ran too deep, and her thinking was warped, reminding him of the crooks he dealt with. She wasn't apt to ever have a run-in with the law, but he didn't think much of her potential as a wife or a mother.

Sylvia's thoughts must have paralleled his. She pushed her plate away—his fancy omelette was a complete waste—and sounded wistful. "Louise's little girl must be five now. She was born the winter after . . . after Walker got sick, and Matt, you know, if things had gone differently, she'd be our granddaughter."

He had cooked the damn omelette, and at least some of it would get eaten. He forked a big bite into his mouth and washed it down with coffee. He didn't relish it, but eating gave him time to think, and he had to console Sylvia. "We're lucky it's not our grandkid. With Louise for a mother, we'd worry about it night and day. This way, it's the Medfords' problem."

Sylvia nodded. "I'm sure they do what they can. They're nice people, and so fond of Walker."

That tugged his heart. Anyone fond of Walker would be a nice person in her book, and the Medfords certainly qualified. They'd always thought the world of Walker and were probably in favor of the reconciliation.

Well, maybe it was a good thing he'd told Sylvia. Get her ready for the big blow. When their respective divorces were final, it wouldn't surprise him if Louise and their son finally strolled to the altar.

Matt hadn't heard Walker, but he entered the kitchen and leaned down to kiss his mother.

Matt took a plate out of the cupboard. "D'you want some omelette?"

Walker shook his head. "No, just a cup of coffee." He was dressed, but his clothes looked as if he'd slept in them, which, come to think of it, he probably had. Matt had no idea when he'd come in, but suspected it had been only a couple of hours ago.

"Walker, dear, you *should* eat something."

"I'll eat later, Mom."

"You look worried, dear. Is everything—"

"Fine, Mom. Everything's fine. I've just—well, I've got a lot on my mind." He sat down, not moving toward the coffeepot, and Sylvia was getting to her feet.

"Stay there," Matt told her. He poured Walker's coffee and set it in front of him.

"Anyone going to let me in!"

It was Pete, and Matt opened the door. "We're out in the kitchen, finishing breakfast. There's plenty for you, if you're hungry."

"Starved. After jogging a couple of hours, my body's ready for refueling."

"Good!" Matt started slicing the rest of the mushrooms.

Peter sat on a tall stool at the far end of the kitchen. "Sylvia, I'm going to keep my distance. I probably don't smell as good as I look."

Sylvia laughed. "Peter, make yourself comfortable wherever you like."

Grinning, Peter braced his back against the wall and hooked the heel of a running shoe on a rung of the stool. "Well, Walker, what have you been up to lately?"

Matt thought Walker hadn't heard, but finally he answered, sounding choked, as if a slug of coffee had gone down the wrong way. "Nothing interesting—but how's the Bouchard case coming?"

"Bouchard?" Peter echoed. "Matt, didn't you tell him? We've got that one sewed up. But I do have more information that I want to talk to you about."

"Sewed up," Walker repeated. "Derek Bouchard—her husband?"

Pete laughed. "That's what I read in the papers."

Matt broke in. "The papers aren't giving you half the credit you deserve. It was your case from the beginning. I've said it before, but I'll say it again—I'm impressed with how quickly you pulled it together."

"Hey, Sylvia, tell your old man I'm good at my job because I have one hell of an example." Pete sounded playful, but Matt got the message. They had more than a working relationship, the two of them. They had a bond, and it was a hell of a shame he couldn't get to first base with Walker.

Pete took a banana off the counter. "I feel sorry for the little Bouchard boy. He's only three and, from the looks of things—"

Suddenly Walker bolted. "I-I better take a shower, get to the shop—"

Matt handed Peter a plate, and it was gratifying to have someone enjoy his efforts. Peter plowed into his food and nodded to Matt's offer of orange juice.

"I've got to tell you, Matt," he said when he came up for breath. "I checked out the man Jessie Bouchard was involved with. His name is Helmut Lauer. It was hard to get a tag on him, but he's an actor-type, bodybuilder with his own gym in North Hollywood. According to him, he and Jessie—the Bouchard woman—had something hot going up to the time of her death, but he's got a good alibi for the evening she bought it. He was a contestant in a bodybuilding show—and he won. He's got witnesses, to say nothing of a couple of dozen photos he's eager to show." Peter grunted. "Would you believe he wanted to know if we would use one of his photos in a newspaper story?"

"And he'll testify?"

"Gladly. And he'll probably come to court wearing stage makeup. He's got telephone bills, letters she wrote to him . . ." Peter sounded harsh. "There's no question—the Bouchard woman was crazy about him."

"So her reconciliation with her husband was a hoax?"

Peter grimaced. "Complete. She wasn't interested in anyone but Lauer." He took a deep breath. "Unfortunately for her, her husband must have found her out."

Sylvia stood up. "You two! I may as well get dressed, because once you start talking cases . . ."

"Aw, come on, Sylvia. Matt and I'll be good."

Sylvia shook her head, but in the doorway, she hesitated, her expression coy. "Matt," she said softly, "have you told him?"

"I haven't," he said, winking at her, "but now is as good a time as any. Pete, we've got news that just might interest you." Matt relished the moment. "Tara pulled everything together in Seattle and is on her way back."

"That's great." Peter looked confused, and by God, he blushed. Pete, the ladies' man. Finally the right lady had come along. Well, it was a hell of a shame about Walker, but now they had Tara, and Peter Castle would make one hell of a nephew.

Sylvia started up the stairs and Matt called after her. "When Tara gets here, don't let me forget. A letter arrived at the station for her in care of me."

Sylvia eased back down a couple of steps. "Why would anyone write to Tara at the station?"

Matt rubbed his chin. "Can't say I haven't wondered, but I have no idea. There's no return address."

CHAPTER 15

Tara, I mean it. Be careful.

Tara crammed a final box into her car. Except for the driver's seat, not enough space remained to squeeze in an extra postage stamp. She would land the job in California, then arrange for a place of her own and send for the rest of her belongings.

Meantime, Michelle was already moving in. No, diving in was more like it. Her packing boxes were already stacked in the garage, and a pile of her clothes, on hangers and ready to be hung in the freshly vacated closets, lay across the back of the couch.

But despite her eagerness to take possession of the condo, Michelle had discouraged Tara from returning to California. Her usually animated face was solemn as she followed Tara to the car. "Look, you were down there for two weeks and met up with two dead bodies. That scares me. Just think—if that Pudget woman really saw the woman in the chest when she said she did, you may be in danger."

Tara slammed down the lid of the trunk, then pushed a damp wisp of hair off her forehead. "What do you mean?"

Michelle's voice was husky. "Maybe Pudget saw the murderer, too. Maybe that's why she was killed. And if the murderer knows that Pudget talked to you and thinks she might have described . . ." Her voice faded.

Tara steeled herself. "I told you—I don't want to think about seeing those poor dead women. It happened, but it's over—at least for me. My uncle is in charge of both murder investigations. He's very competent."

"But if the murderer is afraid you could testify, then—"

"Testify! I don't know anything! And Peter didn't think the two murders were related. But even if they *are* related, I couldn't be a threat to anyone."

"But what if the murderer doesn't know that? What if he thinks Pudget told you—"

"Stop it! You're dramatizing all of this, and you're silly. Silly, that's all. No one knows I talked to Pudget." She shrugged. "And how could anyone know who I am?"

"I don't know. But everything you told me is really scary. I'm worried about you, and—"

"Michelle!" Tara felt a rising uneasiness. Her friend's fears roamed in her own mind, but she refused to let her imagination run wild. "I don't want to talk about it. And I'd better get going if I want to reach the California border before I stop for the night."

Michelle caught her in a hug. "Okay, kiddo. Be happy. And let me know how the romance goes."

Tara returned Michelle's embrace, then hopped into the car. "Good-bye, Michelle. I'll keep in touch."

Driving away, she heard Michelle again. "Tara, be careful."

A bank of heavy clouds held the morning sun at bay. The pedestrians she passed on the drive to the freeway were dressed for rain, but through the grayness she could make out the Space Needle that identified Seattle as surely as the Eiffel Tower announced Paris. She paid it a silent farewell. Seattle was her childhood home; it was people and places she cared about, but she was heading toward a new life. Excitement washed over her. It was absolutely no time to feel afraid.

• • •

Patrick held tight to the handle of the teeter-totter. The big, smiley girl on the other side was making it go fast. She was laughing, but he didn't like it at all. He popped up and down, and his feet hardly touched the ground.

If he jumped off, she would go plop. That would be nice. But he couldn't jump off. He always flew right back up again as soon as he knew he was down. He blinked a lot of times. Everything looked all fuzzy, but that was all right. If he cried, Auntie Rose would come.

"Patrick is crying again." That Jenny girl was shouting. Good! Auntie Rose was hurrying toward him.

"Diane, stop, so I can see what's wrong with Patrick."

"Oh, he's always crying, and I'm having fun."

"Ask Jenny to teeter with you. And here, Patrick, don't you like to play? You come with me and tell me what's wrong."

She took his hand and led him toward the house. He was off the teeter-totter, but now that he was crying, it was hard to stop.

On the porch Auntie Rose sat on the big swing and pulled him up on her lap. She was soft all over, a people pillow. He leaned his head against her. She felt good and she smelled like nice soap, but tears were still spilling out of his eyes. He wiped them hard with his fists—both fists, one for each eye—but that didn't do any good. More tears were coming, and he didn't know how to stop them. He didn't know how to do anything.

"Shhh, Patrick, don't cry. Everything is all right."

"They took my mommy to heaven, Daddy said, and then they took my daddy. Is Daddy in that heaven place, too?"

"No, Patrick. I've told you—your daddy is fine, and you mustn't worry about him."

"Where *is* my daddy?"

She patted his head. Her fingers were soft when she pushed his hair back. It felt nice, but he wanted to know where his daddy was. And Mommy, too. But he didn't even know where *he* was. One of those big kids said it was a foster place. Maybe foster places were okay, but why didn't he go home at night? He wanted to sleep in his own bed.

"Is my daddy coming today?"

"I don't think so, Patrick. But we're going to have meatballs and spaghetti for supper. I bet you'll like that."

"Will my daddy come and eat with us?"

"No, dear, I don't think so, but—"

"Is he still on that bail place? Why doesn't he get off of it and come and get me?" Timmy had told him that the TV said his daddy was out on a bail. Timmy was big; he was learning to ride one of those bikes that won't stand up alone. He *had* to know what he was talking about, but Patrick couldn't understand.

Timmy was awarded the cat. Patrick didn't know what cat. Timmy said the cat could decide what would happen to him. Timmy said maybe he would leave the foster place and get a new mommy and daddy. He said maybe Patrick would get a new mommy and daddy, too. But Patrick didn't want a new mommy and daddy. He had a mommy and daddy, but he never knew where they were. He tried again. "Auntie Rose, where is my daddy? Why doesn't he come?"

"Maybe he will, one of these days. Now, you stop crying, and we'll go find something that you like. I guess you never played on a teeter-totter before, but you know we have lots of toys. Let's get you something to play with until nap time."

He followed her, kicking the little white stones that covered the path. Auntie Rose was wrong. He *had* played on a teeter-totter before. He remembered. It was down by great big water where boats were riding. There was a place for kids to play, too. He was there with Mommy, but she went away. He played all alone until a girl came. She was big, but not too big, and her daddy was there. The daddy helped them play on the teeter-totter. And he pushed them in the swings.

The daddy was nice. He didn't yell, but daddies don't yell. Mommies do. But Mommy didn't yell that day. She was all smiley. And the man was smiley, too. Not the daddy. The other man. Patrick saw him sometimes. Patrick remembered real good, but the man didn't remember him.

Patrick played with the little girl a long time. It was getting dark. The daddy said he wouldn't leave Patrick alone, and he waited until Mommy came back. When Mommy came, she had pretty ring things in her ears. When they got in the car, Mommy looked at the ring things in the little mirror that sees the cars in back. She told Patrick everything was a secret and not to tell Daddy. And she told him she would buy him an ice cream bar, but she forgot.

He didn't tell Daddy. He didn't tell anybody. But he knew about teeter-totters. What he didn't know was where his daddy was. It had been such a long time. Maybe Daddy forgot about him.

"Patrick, please don't cry again. Here, do you want to play on the tricycle? You liked it yesterday. No? Well, you must be tired. Let's go in the house. You're ready for a nap."

Auntie Rose took him back to the house and tucked him in a little bed. She always said it was his bed, but he knew it wasn't. His bed was at home. He picked up the little horse the lady had given him. That nice lady with the hair that sort of looked like fire. The little horse liked to sleep with him, and he held it close. Maybe, when he woke up, Daddy would come.

CHAPTER 16

Late Tuesday night, after a two-day, thousand-mile drive, Tara pulled up in front of the Nyborg home in Santa Maria. She flexed her stiff hands and, with a sigh of relief, let her weary eyes blink shut.

"It's Tara! She's here." The front door banged, and Uncle Matt ran down the front stairs.

Tara was caught in a bear hug. "You should have let me fly up to Seattle and drive back with you," he scolded. "Too far for you to drive alone—but I'm sure glad you're here."

Aunt Sylvia waited on the porch, her arms extended. "Tara, it's wonderful to have you."

For a heartbeat, Tara remembered how apprehensive she had been the first time she entered this house, but now she was coming home.

Uncle Matt insisted on unloading her car; Aunt Sylvia mothered her. No doubts lingered. This was where she belonged, so, she had to land that job tomorrow. No, not tomorrow—today. By the time she was settled in, it was past midnight.

In the morning, driving to Hollywood, she felt confident and eager. Her portfolio proved she was talented, and though she couldn't boast of years of experience, people were relaxed with her. She caught their essence, and her scenes and portraits were as interesting psychologically as they were creative.

And if she got the job, then what? Uncle Matt had told her how happy Peter had been when he knew she was returning to stay. Actually, Uncle Matt had told her that twice, and she would probably hear it again this evening. Smiling to herself, she puzzled over whether she shared her uncle's eagerness for Peter and her to get together.

Traffic slowed as she approached the Los Angeles area, and she kept busy studying the different neighborhoods. She would rent an apartment, but keep close ties to Santa Maria.

The movie studio was a complex of stark buildings, and she parked in the visitors' section of the lot. "Next time," she told herself, "I'll park in the employees' section."

The interior of Building E belied the bleak box exterior. Glass-block windows transmitted filtered light onto red tile floors and art-deco wall hangings; oversized plants grew out of shiny black containers. People hurrying through the lobby seemed deliberately groomed to look utterly casual, and they emitted a vitality, a locked-in enthusiasm. On the noiseless ascent to the fifth floor, Tara's spirits rose faster than the wood-paneled elevator. *This place was exciting.* She was caught up in it already.

"Tara Nyborg to see Mr. Brett Adam."

"I'm sorry. Mr. Adam does not see anyone without an appointment."

"I have an appointment. It was made over a week ago, but I'm early. If it's all right, I'll just put my portfolio over there and wait."

The woman at the immaculate reception desk looked like a cool cross between an army drill sergeant and a department store mannequin. Her attire was chic; not a strand of her graying brown hair wandered out of place, and she radiated the knowledge that she allowed *nothing* to be out of place. She stared at Tara. "Mr. Adam has no appointments scheduled for the next several hours. He's in a meeting. You have made a mistake." It had to be Tara's mistake. The woman did not allow mistakes to be the property of her domain.

Tara was baffled. "Please," she began, "will you check again? My appointment was for one o'clock. I've driven all the way from Santa Maria—" Her voice snagged. Actually, she had driven all the way from Seattle, but Santa Maria was sufficiently distant to make her point.

The mannequin's eyelids narrowed. "I'll go check, Miss—"

"Nyborg. Tara Nyborg."

"Miss Nyborg. However, I hardly think so."

While she was gone, Tara reviewed: At his party Ryan Castle had given her Brett Adam's name and telephone number, and on Monday she'd made the call. She was well-received— Ryan had already recommended her—and a half hour later Mr. Adam's secretary called back to confirm an appointment. She remembered it very clearly. She'd been having lunch with Aunt Sylvia and Walker.

"Next week Wednesday at one o'clock," she had mused. "I'll go for the interview with Mr. Adam and if I'm offered a job—"

"They'll offer you a job. I'm sure of it." Aunt Sylvia had been confident, and Walker had encouraged her, too.

"I have no doubts, Cuz. And you won't be able to resist. The glamour of Hollywood—plus us! You'll leave the Evergreen state and become a Californian." His voice had been mocking, but she'd already realized that was Walker's way.

"Miss Nyborg?" A young man, who would have been a handsome photographic study even without makeup highlighting his salon tan, appeared through a doorway. "I'm Mike Clark— Brett's secretary. We talked on the phone—last Monday I think."

Tara sighed with relief. "Yes, Mr. Clark. We certainly did, but I was getting worried. Your receptionist didn't know I had an appointment."

Mike Clark studied entries in a red leather appointment

book. "We certainly *had* an appointment with you, but it was canceled."

"*What?* Why didn't someone let me know?"

"But you called us. It's right here. 'Nyborg returned to Seattle and canceled.' The clerk who made the notation said a man made the call for you."

Tara tried to make sense out of what she was hearing. "But I never asked anyone—"

"And you didn't go to Seattle?"

"Well, yes, I was in Seattle for a week. But I always intended to return for my interview with Mr. Adam." She caught her breath. "There's a mistake somewhere, but that's all right. I understand that Mr. Adam is in a meeting, but I'll be happy to wait—"

Mike Clark coughed. "Miss Nyborg, I can't reschedule your appointment without taking it up with Brett. Not after you— Well, maybe there *has* been a mix-up. But he certainly won't have time to see you today. I have your number—it's this 805 one, right?" He smiled brightly. "I'll call you."

The mannequin-at-arms looked serene. She had been affirmed.

The rush of anger Tara felt did justice to her red hair. "Look, Mr. Clark, I counted on this interview and certainly didn't cancel it."

"Of course. Nice to meet you."

Tara was accustomed to combining her talent and self-assurance to unlock professional doors. It was infuriating to be denied a chance to present herself, but picking up her portfolio, she forced a dignified smile. "Please reschedule an interview for me as soon as Mr. Adam is available."

The elevator ride to the lobby was deflating—and baffling. Someone had canceled her appointment—someone who knew she had gone to Seattle. What could she possibly have said to make someone think that's what she wanted? And who had the information to cancel on her behalf?

Her portfolio seemed heavy now, and she was glad to deposit it on the backseat. She sat down behind the wheel, but with the door open and her feet on the ground. Her disappointment was understandable, and there was an uneasiness she couldn't ignore. *Whoever had canceled the appointment knew all about her.*

It didn't make sense, unless . . . unless . . . She swung her feet inside the car and locked the door, but she couldn't lock out the thought. *Someone didn't want her around.* Despite herself, she thought about the mysterious rolls that had been left for her. Birds ate them and died. What would have happened to her if she had eaten them? Tara's heart pounded, and suddenly Michelle's voice echoed. "Tara, be careful. You might be in danger."

No! She refused to let her disappointment and Michelle's dramatics distort her thinking. She couldn't explain the rolls, but as for her appointment with Brett Adam, a mistake had occurred—that was all. She turned the key in the ignition.

Breakfast had been hours ago, and in Santa Barbara she pulled off the freeway and found a diner. She ordered a sandwich and coffee, but wasn't really interested in food. Grandmother's legacy was tied up in trusts to be doled out in handfuls, but even more than she needed money, Tara had to be active and pursuing her career.

Starting out with nothing but courage and ability, she had forged a career for herself in Seattle. Now she had an outstanding portfolio backed up by excellent references. She could start over in California, but darn it, the atmosphere at the studio had fascinated her.

The sandwich was tasteless. Holding a coffee mug in both hands, she gazed out a window. Dramatic palm trees were sketched on the horizon, and she remembered the scene from another time. She had driven the freeway to Santa Barbara with Peter to attend his brother Ryan's party.

Ryan. She had an idea. It was brazen, but what did she have to lose?

Taking a notepad out of her purse, Tara wrote a brief message, then hurried to her car. She drove north for several miles and headed down a road that led toward the water. The area looked different by daylight, and at first she was uncertain. But wasn't that the house with the Tudor embellishments? And over there. She remembered thinking that place looked like an appropriate home for Hansel and Gretel.

It was a relief to discover that the Mediterranean palace looked humbler, more approachable, without the dramatic lighting against the backdrop of night. She parked outside the gate and, taking her note and courage in hand, approached the front door, half-expecting a guard to block her way. But no one detained her, and the door was answered by the same man who had greeted Peter and her the night of Ryan's party.

"Good afternoon. I'm Tara Nyborg. I have a note for Mr. Castle. I'm a friend of his brother, Peter."

He studied her. "The note is from Peter?"

"No, from me. I thought it would have a better chance of reaching Ryan if I dropped it off here." She suspected he was confusing her with a star-struck fan. "I have met Ryan," she said forcefully. "Peter and I attended a party here a week ago, and if you'll take the note—"

"That's where it was! I knew I'd seen you. Please step in."

"There's no need. Just give the note to Mr. Castle when it's convenient and—" He disappeared inside the house, and she stood there, feeling awkward.

"Tara?" Ryan was wearing cutoff shorts and a long-sleeved black pullover; his feet were bare, his chin was shadowed. Tara realized what an intrusion she was, but his smile helped.

"Where's Peter?"

"He's not with me. I'm alone." She thrust the note toward him. "I'm here about the job interview you arranged. Something went wrong. I thought if it wasn't too much trouble, you could call Mr. Adam again."

He beckoned her inside, but she didn't budge. "It was kind of you to make the contact for me, and I don't want to be a bother."

"Come on in!" He glanced at the note, then ran his hand over the stubble on his chin. "Your appointment with Brett was canceled because someone told him you'd gone to Seattle? I don't get it."

"I don't either. Do you have any idea how—"

"Hang on. We can get it straightened out, but first—I don't want to give the Castle brothers a bad name. Hank! Take Tara into the family room."

Before she could respond, Ryan double-stepped up a central stairway that ascended in a graceful arc. Pale yellow carpet seemed to flow down the white marble stairs, but everything else in the entry was white—and sensational.

Hank was the man who had answered the door, and after he led her to the family room—cozier than what she had expected—she declined refreshment. "No. I'll just wait."

A half hour passed. Tara was considering a quiet exit out the front door when Ryan reappeared. He had shaved, his hair was combed, and he wore slacks, a button-front shirt, and smart loafers. Tara was mortified. She had come to ask for a favor, and he'd felt obliged to dress. "Ryan, I never expected you to be here. I intended to leave you a message."

"I'm usually working this time of day, but tomorrow we're reshooting a couple of scenes from a feature we filmed up here. I drove up last night."

Tara had offered sufficient apologies. She was still here because he had kept her here, and he might be able to shed some light on what had happened. She let herself sink deeper into the soft leather sofa. "I can't imagine why my appointment was canceled. Do you have any idea?"

He dropped into a large armchair. "I may have it figured

out. You don't know Brett, but he's into perfection. I bet someone called *you,* maybe because the appointment had to be rescheduled and—"

She interrupted. "Mr. Adam *did* have a meeting this afternoon and I was told it would last several hours."

"That might have been the reason. Someone called your home to reschedule, was told you were in Seattle, and assumed you weren't coming back. In Brett's office, people aren't going to be quick to own up to mistakes. Easier to say you canceled the appointment and showed up anyway."

Tara leaned forward. "Of course! The receptionist all but told me they *never* make mistakes." She sighed. "Ryan, I was worried, I really was. So many strange things have happened. I mean, I have a good friend who kept warning me." She caught herself. "Forgive me. I'm not making much sense. But what happened at the studio was mystifying, and I'm grateful to you for explaining—" As she spoke, she picked up her purse.

"Hold on. Don't be in such a rush. Hungry? I am, but then I always am."

"It must run in the family. My uncle Matt claims Peter has the appetite of a lumberjack."

Ryan laughed. "Of course. He imitates me. When we were little kids, he'd try to eat as much as I did, but I was older and bigger, and poor little Pete never had a chance."

When he talked about Peter, Tara was again struck by— what could she call it? Maybe family camaraderie. But there was something—a warmth, a caring—and she wondered if she could ever experience that sort of a relationship with Walker.

Ryan's snack cart appeared, pushed by a tall, angular woman whose demeanor suggested she was the black equivalent of the receptionist in Brett Adam's office. "No pâté, today. It wasn't fresh, but I substituted the salmon log. And I added stuffed mushrooms. I thought you would approve."

Ryan was already lifting covers and examining everything. "Looks delicious, Ruby. As usual. Maybe one of these days I'll talk you into keeping house for me in Malibu."

Ruby was already retreating, and her soft "humph" translated as "not a chance."

At Ryan's insistence, Tara loaded a small plate with finger sandwiches, grapes, and a little of the salmon log.

"No, Ryan. I'm driving." He was pouring her a glass of wine. Then she remembered how proud he was of his wine collection. "All right. Just one glass. I'm sure it's very good."

The wine was slightly foxy and marvelous; the food tasted even better than it looked. She refilled her plate—cheese, and stuffed mushroom, a little more salmon. Earlier she'd hardly been able to down a bite of sandwich, but then she had been too uneasy to eat. She could admit that now. The strange call to cancel her appointment had unsettled her—but maybe the call hadn't happened. Not the way she thought it had. Ryan's explanation made her fears seem ridiculous.

Suddenly she put down her plate and headed for the door.

"Hey, where are you going?"

"To my car. I have an idea. Maybe, while we're eating, you'll glance at my portfolio. Then you can tell Mr. Adam you've actually seen my work."

"I'll send someone. Is the car locked?" Calling to Hank, he took her key, and a few minutes later she was arranging pictures on the center of a gleaming table. Ryan positioned himself behind her.

She showed him several groups of pictures, and his responses indicated he appreciated her side of the camera as well as his own. "And here are several portraits I did when I was working for a photographer in Seattle. He's well known, and I learned a great deal—"

She froze. Ryan's hand was under her skirt, stroking her thigh and gliding upward. His fingers were touching her, ready to explore between her legs. She gasped, not believing, but it was real.

"No!"

He stepped back, smiling as pleasantly as if she'd declined a second glass of wine. "Okay. I just thought it might be nice. You're lovely. Refreshing. But if you don't want to—" He shrugged. "Show me more pictures."

Her cheeks were burning, and she was unsure whether to be furious at him or herself. He was a famous actor and she had shown up on his doorstep, but he knew she hadn't expected him to be there. And she was his brother's girlfriend. Yes, for the moment, she thought of herself that way. Peter's girlfriend, and she wouldn't cause trouble between Peter and his brother.

She smiled and picked up her purse. "Sorry, Darnell, that's just not me."

He laughed. "Good! You're just right for Pete. Someone attractive, intelligent, sincere . . ."

He continued, but she wasn't listening. If he was trying to convince her it had just been a test, it wasn't going to work.

The front door had several inside bolts, and she struggled to undo them herself.

"Hey, don't get me wrong. And don't mention this because Pete is touchy and—"

"I won't say anything to Peter. And I understand—or at least I think I do. You're used to a different crowd, and it was my mistake coming here."

"Do you need . . ." He offered her something, but she couldn't hear. She was already in her car. Only after she had driven away did she realize she had forgotten her portfolio. She put her foot on the brake, but before the car stopped, she accelerated again. She was not up to another encounter with Tony Darnell.

CHAPTER 17

"Uncle Matt, did someone from Brett Adam's office phone me when I was in Seattle?"

"I didn't talk to anyone, but maybe your aunt—"

Tara was leaning over the banister and didn't wait for him to finish. "No, it had to have been a man. I'll ask Walker."

Uncle Matt was leaving for the station and paused, his hand on the doorknob. "No point in asking Walker. He pokes his head in here once in a while, but I doubt he's been around enough to answer the phone."

If neither Uncle Matt nor Walker had talked to anyone, then who had told Brett Adam's office that she was in Seattle? Tara shivered, but not from the morning chill.

"Tara!" Uncle Matt's voice boomed up the stairs. "I almost forgot. A letter came for you at the station. It's on the hall table, left-hand side." His tone mellowed. "And I don't know if your aunt told you, but we're having company for dinner tonight—Peter Castle."

She picked up her letter, noticing that her name was printed in professional-looking block letters. She started to open it, then called downstairs to answer Aunt Sylvia who'd asked if she wanted breakfast.

"Not yet, and please, don't go to any trouble. I can take care of myself." They fussed over her, and she was torn between

121

loving it and missing her independence.

She was dressed and brushing her hair before she remembered the letter. "Dear Miss Nyborg," it began, "I hope you will remember me and my son, Patrick."

She caught her breath. The letter was from Derek Bouchard! He reminded her that just before the police arrived to arrest him, she'd said she knew something—a reason why he couldn't have killed his wife if he had made the five o'clock flight to Phoenix.

I can't overlook anything that might assist my defense. My attorney said he would write to you, but I've met you and wanted to do it myself. I'll send this in care of your uncle.

He gave his phone number and address and asked that she please contact him. The entire letter was printed—uniform, concise letters—and she remembered that he was an engineer. Only the letters in "please" were jagged. It had been a difficult word for him, and that was more effective than an underscore.

She put the letter in her purse, trying to decide if she should get in touch with him. When the police arrived at his home, she had been about to tell him Pudget Vandermeer said she'd seen his wife after five o'clock, when he was already on a flight to Phoenix. But Uncle Matt and Peter both knew what Pudget Vandermeer had claimed. Neither was impressed.

She sat on the edge of the bed. Michelle had been convinced that Pudget was killed because she knew too much, and in her heart, Tara had never been convinced otherwise. She'd always suspected, wondered—

She jumped to her feet. She wouldn't allow herself to go over it one more time, but she would phone Derek—and hope Uncle Matt never found out.

She told Aunt Sylvia she was going shopping, because she couldn't bring herself to contact Derek Bouchard on Lieutenant

Matthew Nyborg's phone. She dialed Derek's number from a telephone booth and let it ring six or eight times. He wasn't going to answer. Good! She had made the attempt and could forget about it. Nothing she could tell him would be of help. Pudget's claims could never be proved, and if Derek didn't kill his wife, he was safe. Evidence couldn't exist to convict an innocent man.

"Hello."

After several heartbeats she said, "May I speak to Derek Bouchard please?"

"Miss Nyborg?" He'd recognized her voice, too, but another moment passed before she answered.

"Yes, I just got your letter, and—"

"Good! I wasn't sure it would reach you. And I didn't know if you'd respond—but I hoped."

"My uncle gave me the letter. But there's not much I can tell you. I don't know anything that can actually be proved, and—"

"Can I see you? When we were talking, something dawned on you. Something you thought was important. I could see it in your face."

"Mr. Bouchard, I don't think my uncle would approve of my seeing you and—"

"I'll meet you someplace—anyplace. And we'll talk."

Every law enforcement officer in Santa Barbara County would know Derek Bouchard was out on bail. He would be under surveillance, if not formally at least casually. Anywhere he went, he would be noticed. If he were with a woman, she would be noticed, too. Tara swallowed. She was Matthew Nyborg's niece. If she were seen with Derek, it might be an embarrassment to her uncle.

"I can't risk being seen with you."

"Come out to the ranch. You can drive your car right into the garage. I'm alone here, and no one will see you."

"Where's Patrick?"

His voice was muffled. "I don't know."

Closing her eyes, she tried to decide, but words were already forming. "I'll come. I'll be there within the hour."

Driving to Ballard, she puzzled over a strange mix of emotions. She felt guilty—in a way she was betraying Uncle Matt—and the apprehensiveness was back again, but something in her felt light. Despite everything, she wanted to see Derek Bouchard.

He was waiting at the gate and waved her into the garage. "Here," he said as she stepped out of the car, "we'll use the side door. No one will see you."

If she were going to be afraid, this was the time. She was all alone with a man charged with killing his wife, and he knew she would never have told anyone her destination. But she wasn't afraid. Looking at him, all she felt was concern.

"You look . . ." She stopped. *Pale?* No, he definitely wasn't pale. His skin had a healthy bronze tone, not quite a tan, but they were hardly into March. *Upset?* No, he seemed calm and in total possession of himself. He had to be worried, but he wasn't shattered. "You look," she repeated, "as if you've been through a lot."

"I'm okay. It's Patrick I'm worried about."

She followed him into the house. "You said you didn't know where he was."

"I don't. That was one of the conditions of my making bail. Patrick was to remain in protective custody and I wasn't to know his whereabouts." He gestured. "Do you mind sitting in the kitchen? No one's been in to dust or anything and—"

"The kitchen will be fine."

She perched on a tall stool at the counter and watched him pour two cups of coffee. She accepted her cup, then looked up at him. "Derek, I'm sorry about Patrick. It must be terrible for you."

"I'm not the one who matters. It's him. He can't understand what's happening. All he'll know is that he's lost both of us, his mother and me. I'm not even allowed to phone him. That's why I'm so desperate. I didn't kill my wife, but I can't get my son back until this craziness is cleared up . . ." He paced, and Tara shared his pain.

"I'll tell you everything I know, but first understand—I can't prove anything. And the police don't think very much of what I'm going to tell you."

He stood close to her, hanging onto every word. As undramatically as possible, she repeated Pudget's story about seeing his wife *after* he would have been on the way to Phoenix.

"Are you sure? Are you sure?" he repeated.

"Derek, I'm only sure of what she said. I don't know if it's true. And I told you—the police weren't impressed with her story."

"But I am!" He fisted one hand and slammed it into the other palm. "I want to talk to her. Where does she live?"

"Pudget Vandermeer? Didn't you hear? Didn't you read about it?"

"No. Since Jessie died, I've avoided the papers and the TV. I can't handle another word about the mission murder." He sighed. "That's what they call it. The mission murder. But what about Pudget?"

Tara stumbled over the words. "She . . . she's dead. When I was here before, I'd come straight from her house. We had talked—made friends. The next day . . . the next day I went back and found her. She'd been . . . she'd been . . ."

Derek's voice was soft. "Murdered?"

Tara nodded.

Derek stared beyond her into space. "Whoever killed her killed Jessie."

Tara nodded again.

Outdoors a bird called. A car roared down the road. The coffeepot gave up a lone gurgle. All else was quiet. In that quiet, a bond was formed. She would help him.

"Will you go see my son?"

"If I knew where he was . . ."

Derek touched the hand she rested on the counter. "Find out through your uncle. His office won't have any trouble getting that kind of information. You've met Patrick. It won't seem strange for you to decide to take him another gift. You won't be lying to anyone, and you can let me know——" His voice broke and his grip on her hand tightened. "Tara, I'm worried sick. Social services tell me he's fine, but what else can they say? That he's brokenhearted and terrified?"

She let her hand remain in his. "I could ask my uncle about Patrick. But he might think I was getting involved because I questioned his ability, and——"

"*Please.*"

She looked up, into his eyes. Brown they were, brown with a glint of green. Suddenly there was nothing to consider. "I'll do it," she said firmly. "I promise."

CHAPTER 18

It was late afternoon when Tara left the Bouchard ranch in Ballard and headed for the stores in Solvang. She had told Aunt Sylvia she had to shop, and now it was true. She needed a present for Patrick Bouchard to show Uncle Matt when she asked him to find out where the boy was, and the present had to be unusual enough for her to seem eager to deliver it herself.

The quick drive from Ballard to Solvang didn't give her time to come to terms with her encounter with Derek. Her reactions were strong, but impossible to define. She wasn't confused. To the contrary, she was clearheaded and certain Derek had not killed his wife. She was worried about Derek; her heart ached for his little boy, but those feelings didn't explain the awareness that something had happened to her. But something had happened. Even if she couldn't name it, it was there. She was different.

Answering Derek's barrage of questions, Tara had related everything she could remember about Pudget. Unfortunately, her recollections of that unique woman were forever linked with the shock of discovering her dead body. "When I think of anything else, I'll write it down," she had said. "I've been struggling to forget, but now I'll force myself to remember."

"Tara, let's go outside and walk around. You'll feel better— we both will—and we can talk about something else for a while." He touched a curl. "But I better get you a scarf so you can cover up this hair of yours. The color's magnificent, but it makes you too easy to identify."

They roamed the ranch. He showed her his horses. He had only three; he said he had intended to hire a trainer and buy more, but all his planning ended when . . . when . . .

Suddenly she blurted a question. "Derek, the evening that I came here—did you think the police—that my uncle—had anything to do with it? Did you think it was deliberate, so that I could keep an eye on Patrick until they arrived?"

They headed into a path that led beyond the stables to a small grove of cherry trees, and she waited for his answer. "Yes," he said slowly, "at first I did. Or at least I wondered. It was such a coincidence. But when I thought about how sweet you were with Patrick, it just didn't seem possible that you were anything but what you claimed to be—a friend bringing a gift for a little boy."

"That's the truth, Derek. I had no idea."

He took her arm. "I know that now. But it took more nerve than sense for me to write to you in care of the lieutenant in charge of the case against me."

Sending her letter to Uncle Matt had been an act of desperation. It was anything but funny, but unexpectedly they both laughed—the incongruity of it! Their laughter eased a strain. Their eyes met, and they stared at each other like children giggling over mischief.

They had walked on, and Derek talked again about the ranch, so exquisite now in the greens of new grass and leaf, the yellows and violets of early flowers, the pastel puffs of the blossoms dotting the fruit trees. The cool air carried the pungent smells of the earth, and it would have been so easy to forget everything. But they couldn't forget. Derek faced the prospect of a trial and agonized over the welfare of his son. When Tara finally left, his last words to her were, "Please, Tara, find out where

Patrick is and go to see him as soon as you can."

She had repeated her promise, and now she was in Solvang to buy Patrick a gift. The tourist mecca was awash in gift shops, and Tara parked near an interesting store that displayed the flag of Denmark—a slender white cross traversing a red field. She went in and was captivated by imports that included wood figurines, embroidered linens, and music boxes, but nothing that caught her eye seemed suitable for a young child.

She tried the next store and then the next. After nearly an hour of hunting, she found a delightful puppet, at least two feet long, and was about to buy it when it occurred to her that Patrick wouldn't be able to manipulate a puppet within a stone's throw of his own height. And his chubby little hands certainly couldn't manage those strings!

She remembered that Aunt Sylvia's store was nearby. Earlier Tara had considered it, but she intended to tell Uncle Matt she had just happened to see something for Patrick. Why run the risk of his finding out she actually searched for a gift? But if she just walked in and accidentally saw something . . .

It was dark and getting cold. She hurried the short distance, but stood in the doorway before entering. What was the name of the woman at the cash register? Inge, that was it. Too bad Walker wasn't there—but he was! She spotted him toward the back and opened the door. Her entrance was accompanied by a chiming of bells, and Walker looked up.

"Cuz, is that you?" He looked pleased, and she had an inspiration. Why not tell Walker the truth, at least about needing a present for Patrick? She wanted to feel close to him, to develop a feeling of camaraderie, and maybe a shared secret would be a good place to start.

She returned his smile. "It's me all right. And you have to treat me with respect because I'm here as a customer."

He performed a courtly bow. "Madam!"

Her laughter faded when she remembered her mission. "Walker, I need a present for a three-year-old boy. It's important, and well—perhaps I can talk to you about something."

"Of course, Cuz. Let's go in back. Inge! Holler if you need me."

She followed him to a room where a small Formica table and several chairs were surrounded by floor-to-ceiling boxes. The light was dim, just a low-watt bulb overhead.

"People usually don't look so serious when they come in here looking for a present," he said. "Something's weighing you down."

"You're right, but—" She broke off. She had already decided to tell him she wanted a present to take to Patrick Bouchard, but he was concerned about her. She wondered if she dared tell the whole story—carefully, so that he wouldn't think she had any doubts about his father's competence.

"What would you say," she began slowly, "if I told you I don't think Derek Bouchard murdered his wife?"

Time seemed to linger. When Walker finally spoke, his voice was a hoarse whisper. "Tell me everything you know."

She felt a rush of nervousness. "I don't know anything for sure. Well, that's not exactly right. I'm sure about Derek. He couldn't kill anyone. But what I'm going to tell you—*please* don't for a moment think I doubt Uncle Matt. He's good—wonderful—at his work and I'm sure Peter is competent, too."

"Peter the Great. Ah yes, he's very competent. Just ask Dad." Quickly, Tara pondered the sharp edge in his voice. It suggested a rivalry she'd been totally unaware of, but maybe, if she came down on Walker's side . . .

"Look, Walker, I know Peter is in charge of the investigation. And he's convinced he has a very strong case against Derek. But the evidence he has can't be what it seems to be."

"Such as?" Walker held a hand in front of his face. She couldn't read his expression. They were not close friends yet, and if she made a bad start, they never would be.

"I may be wrong. I shouldn't be telling you—"

Lunging forward, he grasped her arm. "Tell me everything. I want to hear it."

She eased back. "I will, but I'd hate to have Uncle Matt think—"

"I won't repeat a word."

"Good!" She plunged in. "Do you remember the day we all looked at photographs? Later I told you I was on my way to see Pudget Vandermeer."

"I remember." Walker's hand concealed the lower part of his face again, but she felt impaled by his blue-eyed stare.

"Pudget was killed that night—murdered. I'm sure you're aware . . ."

"Of course."

Tara pulled herself together. "I think that whoever killed Jessie Bouchard killed Pudget Vandermeer to keep her from giving Derek an alibi and sending the police searching elsewhere. And perhaps—at least it's possible—Pudget may have been able to identify the murderer."

Walker's voice was muted. "You may be right."

"I'm sure Derek didn't kill his wife. He's a nice man." She faltered. "It's hard to explain, but I'm positive—*I know*—he didn't do it."

Walker dropped his hand, but his face was expressionless. His arms hung limply at his sides. "Do you know who Vandermeer told about seeing Jessie?"

"Besides me? I have no idea. But she must have told *someone*. Someone who—" Tara shook her head. "This is all impossible. Everything that's happened—it doesn't seem real."

"I know exactly what you mean."

"Walker, I hope you won't tell this to your parents, but I saw Derek Bouchard at his ranch today. I promised him I'd try to see Patrick."

"So the present we need is for Patrick Bouchard." Walker said *we need*. He was identifying with her and ready to help.

"Yes, I've been looking but I haven't found anything. I don't know very much about children."

Walker grimaced. "I don't either—but believe me, I'm learning." Inge was calling, and Walker stood up. "We have something Patrick would like. It's recommended for five and older, but he's a bright kid. Come on, I'll show you."

Walker helped with a customer, then turned to Tara. "Look at this musical racetrack. The pedestals on the little horses fit into these parallel slots. It runs on batteries and the horses chase each other to several different tunes, including the Carousel Waltz and De Camptown Racetrack. The particular tune determines which slot will have the winning horse. Kids love it, especially when they realize the music tips them where to place their bets."

"Walker, it's perfect!"

"You can tell Dad you bought it because Patrick liked the other horse you took him."

"Good idea!" Tara took out her wallet. "I'll put it on my charge—"

"Nothing doing, Cuz. This is a present from me, to you, to little Patrick."

She tried to pay, but he insisted. It was his gift, and he carried the package back to her car. Suddenly he grabbed her arm. "Cuz, what we talked about tonight—you have to promise me, *promise me,* that you won't mention one single word of it to anyone. Not anyone. It's important. You have to promise."

His grasp was so tight, she felt pain and tried to pull away, but he wouldn't let her. "Promise. You've got to promise."

"Walker—my arm."

He let her go. "Sorry—but swear you'll never repeat a word—not a word—of what we talked about." His concern was startling, but it meant he cared about her.

"Walker, I won't tell anyone. I promise."

He sighed. "You want to help Derek Bouchard, and—if you come up with anything—let me know first. I'll know what to do." He held the door as she got in the car. "It's nice having a cuz, and I'm going to take good care of you."

Driving back to Santa Maria, she was absorbed in thoughts of Derek Bouchard when suddenly something struck her. *Walker had referred to Patrick as a bright kid.* Had he known Patrick? He certainly had never mentioned meeting the boy. *And Walker knew she had given Patrick a horse.* An odd feeling inched up her spine. She was baffled and would have to ask him—

A highway patrol was tagging her and flashing his beam at her rear window. Glancing at the speedometer, she hit the brake and pulled onto the shoulder. She hadn't been more than a few miles over the speed limit, but with her thoughts in such a quandary, who knows—

"Miss Nyborg?" The officer approaching the car knew her name.

"I'm Tara Nyborg. I hope I didn't do anything—"

He held up his hand. "I'm not stopping you for a violation. But a call came in a few minutes ago asking if there'd been an accident involving a green Camaro with Washington plates. I guess Detective Nyborg is worried about you. He's your uncle, isn't he?"

"Yes, but I can't imagine why he'd be—" She stopped. Of course he'd be worried! She had left in the morning, saying that she had to do a little shopping, and had never called to let them know she would be late. And Aunt Sylvia's last words to her had been a reminder that Peter Castle was coming for dinner! She looked at her watch. It was nearly eight and she still had a half hour's drive.

"Officer, there's nothing wrong. If it's all right with you, I'll just hurry—"

"Get a move on! I'll radio the station and have them relay the message that you're on your way." Rolling up her window, she heard him chuckle. "You get old Matt mad at you, and it'll be a hell of a lot worse than a speeding violation."

She ached to floor the accelerator, but forced herself to observe the speed limit—almost. The speedometer kept creeping up despite her efforts to remain light-footed. Living alone, she wasn't used to accounting for her time or having people worry about her if she wasn't home for a meal. She was too old and independent to need people looking after her— but, when she stopped to think about it, she wasn't too old to need affection. And that's what Uncle Matt and Aunt Sylvia were holding out to her—the affection and caring of a family. And Walker, too. He cared about her. They were wonderful, the three of them. How ridiculous that for a moment she had actually wondered if Walker might be hiding something.

Day after day, details of "the mission murder" case were splashed across the papers. Surely journalists eager to enhance their copy would describe Patrick as a bright, adorable kid, and she'd told the officers who arrested Derek about the horse from Pudget. Reporters would have latched onto that, too. *And she had thought about asking Walker how he knew . . .*

Forget the speed limit! She hit the accelerator. She'd be home in a few minutes. Home. And she would forget that such a disloyal thought had ever entered her mind.

CHAPTER 19

Walker Nyborg caught his reflection on the store window. He looked as worried as he felt, but he tried to convince himself he was chasing dragons. If there was enough evidence to convince a jury, Derek Bouchard would be convicted of his wife's murder. That was all there was to it—but Tara was convinced Bouchard was innocent.

She was bright and resourceful. She'd start digging, and where would it take her? Nowhere! He had checked back and come up with nothing. Or almost nothing—just a pair of earrings and a little boy who might recognize his mother's murderer. Not much. But what if Tara turned up other evidence? And what if she talked?

The sapling tree in front of the shop bent low in the wind. Passing tourists hunched their shoulders against the cold, but perspiration covered his forehead. He wiped his sleeve across his face.

What would happen if I tried to explain to Dad? For a blink he thought it might be possible. Then reality set in. Talk to Dad! He had to be losing his mind. He clenched his fists. Tara had promised not to tell her suspicions to anyone. She had better keep that promise. Her life might depend on it.

As he entered the shop, Inge held the telephone receiver out to him.

He wasn't up to one more thing, and even without hearing the deliberately provocative voice, he knew who it was going to be. He took the phone. She couldn't control him. He would just have to tell her—

"Walker?" A sweet voice, comforting, and he tightened his grip on the receiver.

"Nance! I thought it was— I mean you never call me here."

"I didn't want to call you at your folks'. Your mother answers, and when she knows it's me, she sounds so sad. I'm sad, too, Walker, and I want to talk to you."

He let the world vanish and basked in her warmth.

"I can drive down tomorrow, as soon as my shift ends, and spend the weekend. We can try to—"

He cut her off. "No, Nance, you can't come." He slumped against the counter. "Nothing can change things."

"Change what? Walker, something's wrong, and I'll help if you let me."

Again the urge to tell her, but he had made up his mind. *Leave her out of it.* "Nance."

"Yes?"

He cupped his hand around the receiver, enclosing the sound. "Nance, I love you." Gently, he hung up the phone.

Uncle Matt stood on the porch, hands on hips, as Tara pulled up in front of the house. "Uncle Matt, I should have phoned, but—"

He hugged her before she could finish. "We were worried and sure glad to hear you were okay." He looked a little sheepish. "I'm sorry you were flagged by the highway patrol. Hope it didn't bother you too much."

Aunt Sylvia met her at the door. "Forgive us for being anxious, Tara, but we couldn't imagine what had happened to you."

Tara swallowed. *They were apologizing to her.* "Please, it

was my fault. But I bought something. Uncle Matt, I'll show it to you later and explain—"

Peter put his arms around her and rested his cheek against hers. "Hmmm." It was a sigh of pleasure. "Tara, you are worth waiting for." He enunciated each word, highlighting the ambiguity of the statement: It was worth waiting for her to return for dinner? To come back from Seattle? Worth waiting for her, *period*.

Tara felt a rush of warmth. "Peter, it's nice to see you." She turned away. "Aunt Sylvia, I'm sorry I missed dinner, but I'm not very hungry."

"You didn't miss dinner. I've kept it warm in the oven, so let's eat now." She smiled. "But first, I think Peter has something for you."

"Just flowers, Tara. Sylvia put them in water." Peter handed her a vase containing several red roses nestled in a profusion of baby's breath. "Welcome to California."

"Peter, how sweet." Tara put her nose to the blossoms, but the fragrance was elusive.

Dinner was pleasant, but more than the food and the conversation, Tara enjoyed the wine. She sipped it slowly, welcoming the heady feeling. She even accepted a second glass, something she rarely did. As a rule, she drank very little, but now it was comforting to blur her thoughts.

The doorbell rang, and Uncle Matt jumped up. "No rest for the wicked." He waved Sylvia to stay in her place. "It's not Walker. He knocks."

He was gone for a few minutes and returned carrying a huge bouquet and Tara's portfolio. "More flowers for you, Tara, delivered in a limo. Any more and you'll be opening a florist shop. And I guess this belongs to you." He set the portfolio on the floor next to the buffet and handed her an array of exotic flowers in a silver container.

Tara couldn't identify all the flowers, but she recognized

cymbidium orchids. A card was attached to a silver card holder, and she knew whose the signature had to be. "I'll get something to put these in." The container held water, but she stood up, embarrassed and eager to leave the room.

"Did they keep your portfolio at the studio when you went for the interview yesterday?"

She paused in the doorway. "No, Aunt Sylvia. Not exactly. I left it—forgot it—someplace. It was nice . . . nice of him to return it."

"Who returned it?" It was Peter's question, but she couldn't look at him. And she couldn't lie, even though the truth was awkward.

"Your brother."

"*Ryan!*"

"Yes. I stopped to see him yesterday. No, not to see him— just to leave him a note, telling him there had been a mix-up in the interview he arranged. He was home. I showed him my portfolio. And . . . and I forgot it."

"You forgot it." Peter's tone was flat.

Tara sat down again, holding the silver container in her lap and looking at Peter through sprays of flowers and foliage. "That's right, Peter. I forgot it."

Struggling, she maneuvered the bouquet so that she could open the card:

Dear Miss Nyborg—A pleasure seeing you yesterday, and after you left, I looked at more of your work. It's terrific, and I've taken care of the confusion with Brett's office. They will call you. Please accept these flowers from the Castle brothers, and say hi to Peter for me. He's a lucky man.

Ryan Castle had chosen his words carefully, starting with the formal "Miss Nyborg." Tara felt a swell of gratitude. His sexual overtures had been offensive, but perhaps, in the values of the circles he spun in, he'd been doing what was expected. And he was certainly trying to make it right.

Tara was relieved to be able to read the message aloud, relieved to dispel any doubts about her visit. Her voice was calm, but she edited out the last sentence. It suggested a relationship between Peter and her that didn't exist—*and never would*. The thought was a surprise. Peter was handsome, intelligent, and interesting, and he certainly carried the endorsement of her aunt and uncle. What more could she want? It stunned her to realize that she knew.

CHAPTER 20

"Peter wasn't happy about his brother sending you flowers. He hardly said another word all evening."

Tara was helping Aunt Sylvia tidy the kitchen. She was aware that Peter's mood had changed after the flowers arrived, but wasn't sure what to make of it. "I hope he didn't think I was imposing on Ryan when I went to see him yesterday."

Aunt Sylvia stopped wiping the countertops. "Come now. You know better than that."

Tara shrugged. "Why else would Peter have been angry?"

"He wasn't angry. His feelings were, not hurt exactly, but maybe wounded a little. He brings you lovely flowers, but then his brother sends a bouquet that's just overwhelming. And Ryan's famous and can promote your career."

"But that was Peter's idea! He *asked* Ryan to help me." Tara stopped loading the dishwasher. "But it was hard for Peter to ask. In fact, Ryan said Peter had such a hard time getting the words out, he didn't make himself clear."

"That's your answer! Peter is very independent and responsible—like your uncle—and it's difficult for him to ask for a favor, even from Ryan. He asked because of you, and now he's afraid you'll get interested in the wrong brother."

"He can't think that I—"

Aunt Sylvia interrupted. "Would chase after Ryan? Of course

you wouldn't. I know that. But it's hard for Peter because women ask him about Ryan all the time." She giggled. "Did he ever tell you about the woman he arrested for helping her boyfriend hold up a bank? She was looking at a minimum sentence of ten years, but when she found out they were brothers, she asked Peter if he could get her a signed picture of Ryan. And do you know what? Peter got her one and told her to hang it in her cell."

Tara laughed, too. "No, he didn't tell me—and I see what you mean. It's too bad Peter has to put up with that all the time."

"He handles it well, but I don't think he wants to take chances with you." She put her arm around Tara. "It's no secret that he's very interested."

Tara pulled away. "It's certainly a secret to me! Aunt Sylvia, Peter and I hardly know each other." She and Derek Bouchard hardly knew each other, and yet . . .

"Tara, dear, I've made you blush. Well, enough said about Peter—at least for now." Aunt Sylvia finished wiping the counters and took the broom off a hook in the utility room. "When you were in Solvang, did you go into the shop?"

"That's where I bought the gift I want to talk to Uncle Matt about. Or at least I *would* have bought it if Walker had let me pay."

Aunt Sylvia brightened. "Did you and Walker have a chance to visit?"

"For a while. The store wasn't very busy."

"We keep open two evenings a week, but this time of year it's usually pretty slow. I miss the shop, but you mustn't tell that to anyone."

The kitchen was finished, but Aunt Sylvia seemed reluctant to leave. "Tell me," she said slowly, "how did Walker seem to you? I realize you don't know him that well, but did he act worried or distracted?"

Tara shook her head. "He seemed fine as far as I noticed."

Aunt Sylvia clasped her hands together. "I shouldn't tell this to anyone, but Tara, you're family now. I can confide in you." She paused. "When I have something on my mind, I usually talk to your uncle, but Matthew's been so hard on Walker since he moved back home." Suddenly she looked delicate, forlorn.

"What's wrong, Aunt Sylvia?"

Sylvia sat down and folded her hands in her lap like a little girl. "Six years ago Walker was engaged to marry a woman named Louise. She broke it off. In fact, she eloped with Walker's best friend." Sylvia hesitated and seemed to lose her train of thought. "Louise has a little girl. Kimberly, her name is. An exquisite child. I saw her in Solvang once with her grandmother. She'd be our granddaughter if—" She caught herself. "But that's not the point. Your uncle thinks Walker is seeing Louise again, and that they'll get married when their divorces are final. But Walker's so unhappy."

Tara struggled for something to say. "I didn't notice anything wrong tonight, Aunt Sylvia. We talked, he helped me pick out a gift, then he walked me to my car—"

"And you're sure he seemed all right?"

Aunt Sylvia was eager to be reassured, and Tara didn't know how to respond. Perhaps Walker *had* been in good spirits when she arrived at the shop, but when she left, he'd been worried about her! She could hardly mention that to her aunt.

"That day when we were looking at pictures—I remember one of a beautiful girl with dark hair. You didn't want me to look at it. Was she Louise?"

Aunt Sylvia sighed. "That was Louise. And if Walker actually is seeing her again, it means he's cared about her—" She choked on the words. "It means he's been in love with her all these years. So if they're together again, why is he so troubled? I don't understand."

Walker had heartaches of his own. Tara hadn't known. She was sorry she'd bothered him with her problem, but maybe he wouldn't give it much thought.

The blue light of the digital clock read 4:40 A.M., but Derek Bouchard couldn't fall back to sleep. He had slept almost three hours, more rest than he got most nights, and now there was nothing to do but wait for dawn—not that daylight would bring relief.

He shoved his feet into slippers, ice cold against the hardwood floor, and draped a blanket around his shoulders. He roamed the house, starting as he always did with Patrick's room. The bed had never been made since the child was awakened and carried into the night. The covers were tossed back, and a shaft of moonlight shone on the pillow that still showed the impression of his head.

The pain in Derek's chest tightened as he imagined how bewildered and frightened his son must be. Even his impending trial didn't make him as frustrated and angry as his concerns for his son.

An owl hooted. Derek took a deep breath. There was nothing he could do. Not right now, anyway. But hope glimmered in the distance. Tara would go to see Patrick. She was affectionate and would console him.

He went into their room. *Their room*—his and Jessie's. Since he returned from Phoenix, he had never slept in the bed they had shared. He wasn't avoiding tender memories of what he had lost. Far from it. He just didn't want to be reminded of her, and the deception she must have planned from the beginning of their so-called reconciliation.

The police had never searched the house, and something useful to his case might be concealed somewhere. He had tried to follow his attorney's instructions and search himself, but had never gotten far. Touching her belongings had angered him too much, but now he decided he could handle it. Tara's visit had had an effect.

He didn't know where to start. Jessie had adored clothes, and her closets and drawers were packed tight. Turning on the lights, he decided to do the closets first.

Could she really have worn all those dresses or needed so many shoes? Systematically he moved hangers and patted pockets. He didn't know what he was looking for, but gradually the search took on a value of its own. It was something to do, something definite, but more than that, his own power was growing. Jessie had haunted him even before she was dead, but now her aura, her presence, was fading.

She was an enigma, capable of warmth and also of glacial chills. From the earliest days of their marriage he had never known what to expect from one day to the next—from one hour to the next! She could blossom with charm and affection, but if her desires weren't catered to, her tantrums had no limits.

In the beginning, Derek *had* catered to her, but eventually he'd grown tired of her antics. He'd had enough and would have hung it up, but then they'd had a child. Jessie was fond of Patrick—Derek would never think otherwise—but she was negligent. Her needs came first. She complained about Patrick more than she tended him.

The closets yielded nothing, not even memories. Most of the clothes he sorted through had never been worn in his presence. He started rummaging through her dresser, knowing that this is where anything useful would probably be. He had postponed looking where looking was most apt to be fruitful until he had distanced himself from her. He threw aside garments that hinted of her fragrance, and ignored the soft fabrics and satiny textures that fell under his grasp.

Just as he was closing the last drawer, he realized that there was a bulge beneath the paper lining it. He patted the bulge, then slipped his hand under the paper and discovered several letters. There weren't many, only three or four, and the writing on the envelope was the rounded script of a European. But the address, not the handwriting, held his attention. The letters had been sent here to the ranch.

He sat on the edge of the bed, holding the letters at arm's length, knowing that once he read them, he would never be able to unread them. He would never be able to forget. Three were addressed to Jessie, and the fourth was an unaddressed envelope he thought was Jessie's own stationery.

Slowly he lowered the letters to his lap, sorting them again and again, top one to the bottom of the stack, as if he were shuffling cards. Maybe they were innocuous, nothing but personal letters from a friend, and he didn't have to read them. He could just turn them over to his attorney.

It was like watching someone else's hands take the first letter out of the envelope. He dreaded it, yet couldn't resist.

"*Meine Liebste . . .*" German! My dearest, my sweetheart, or something like that—

It is the middle of the night. Too late to phone to let you thrill me with promises of our next time together so I must write. But in my heart you are with me here in this room, lying beneath me and . . .

And . . . Still reading, Derek instinctively extended his arm and held the letter farther away. He had to squint to make out the small script, but distance helped him handle the repugnant descriptions of his wife's body in the arms of a lover who signed himself "Helmut."

It was hard to tell where the first letter ended and the second began, and by the third letter Derek was inured enough to focus properly. Instead of feeling grief or anger, he became aware of a totally different sensation. Each passionate sentence was a knife that severed the better, more tender memories that bound him to Jessie. By the time he folded the last letter and put it back in the envelope, he was a free man. *Free.* Her hold on him, the pain he'd felt for her, were gone forever.

In the unaddressed envelope was a neatly cut newspaper clipping:

> Andrew Mason, 32, has been reported missing by his aunt, Mildred Tatum. Mason, commonly called Handy, is a former rodeo rider who is known to suffer seizures as the result of a riding injury. Anyone with information about him is asked to contact the police . . .

The flip side of the clipping was part of an ad for a tire sale, so Derek turned back to the notice about the missing man. He read it a second time and wondered why Jessie had found it significant enough to save.

The hands on Jessie's porcelain clock pushed forward. Morning wasn't that long away. Derek still sat on the bed, a blanket around his shoulders, the letters in his lap. No one need ever know about them. He could take them downstairs and burn them in the fireplace, eliminating the risk that Patrick would ever find out about his mother.

Derek stood up. But Patrick needed him, and he didn't want to go to prison. He couldn't destroy anything that might help his case. The letters would have to be turned over to his attorney.

Someday this legal mess would be resolved. He'd get his son back. They'd spend time together; he'd build another stable, add more stock. The room faced east; a rosy dawn was breaking, and he envisioned a pretty, red-haired woman smiling at him.

CHAPTER 21

Uncle Matt took a dim view when Tara told him she wanted to visit Patrick Bouchard. "Tara, it's sweet of you to care about the poor kid—which is what I'd expect—but it's not a hotshot idea," he said, stirring sugar into his morning coffee. "People might think my department was trying to influence him through you, but that doesn't stick me as much as thinking you're setting yourself up to get hurt."

"Uncle Matt, I can handle myself. He's a darling boy, and the game is so unusual, I'd love to give it to him myself."

His grin was surrender, and he reached across the kitchen table and tousled her hair. "I guess I can't say no to you."

All it took was a few telephone calls. Patrick was in a foster home in the city of Santa Barbara. Tara had already met the child and could properly call herself a friend, so with Uncle Matt's endorsement, a visit was scheduled for Sunday afternoon.

On Sunday morning Tara left the house and phoned Derek from a filling station to let him know she would see his son later in the day.

"Tara, tell him I miss him, and that I'll see him as soon as they let me. See if he needs anything and find out if they're taking good care of him." He continued, giving her messages for Patrick and repeating his thanks.

"Afterward, I'll call you as soon as I can. And Derek, please try not to worry. I'll do my best."

His voice throbbed. "I know you will."

The morning dragged, but finally she was on her way to Santa Barbara. The inland drive was shorter, but she had time and stayed on the 101 until it reached the coast and dipped south. "Visiting hours are from two o'clock until four. If traffic stays light, we'll be early. I hope you won't mind waiting." Smiling, she glanced at her passenger.

"It's all right with me, Cuz, but if you'll loan me the car, I won't hang around when you visit the Bouchard boy. I have to see someone in Santa Barbara. I'll just scoot over and be back in time to pick you up."

Tara had been surprised when Walker wanted to go with her. *Insisted* he go with her, and Aunt Sylvia had encouraged it as a good idea. Tara had thought he intended to continue the conversation they'd had about Derek Bouchard, but he never mentioned it. His mind was elsewhere, but it was a peaceful day that didn't require conversation.

Pulling up at the address of the foster home, Tara felt encouraged. For starters, she would be able to tell Derek that the place looked pleasant and well kept. Carrying the toy racetrack, Walker accompanied her to the front door. Several children played in a large yard to the side of the house, but Patrick wasn't among them.

Tara's knock was answered by a short woman with a magnificent head of dark hair that crowned a cheerful face and plump body. "Mrs. Rose Ortega? I'm Tara Nyborg. I'm here to visit Patrick Bouchard."

Mrs. Ortega greeted them as she unlatched the screen door. "His worker phoned, but I didn't get him up from his nap because I wasn't sure when you were coming. You can wait in the living room while I wake him."

Walker thrust out his hand. "Mrs. Ortega, I'm Walker Nyborg, this red-haired lady's cousin. Lieutenant Matthew Nyborg is my father. It's a pleasure to meet you." When Mrs. Ortega extended her hand, he pumped it vigorously; then he turned to Tara. "Cuz, if you give me the car keys, I'll be on my way."

In the living room, Tara asked Mrs. Ortega how many children lived there. It wasn't an idle question. She had to find out as much as she could for her report to Derek.

Rose Ortega thought a moment. "Six. I have six now, but I can have up to eight. You never know. Maybe in five minutes Social Services will call and want to bring me two more."

Upholstered furniture, sagging and worn from use, and a scatter of toys gave the living room a homey, lived-in look, and Tara made herself comfortable in a large chair. Or tried to make herself comfortable. Suddenly she felt nervous. She had been so eager to see the boy that she hadn't thought much about what the visit would actually be like. She'd only met Patrick once, late in the evening, and chances were good, he wouldn't remember her. And if he did remember, he might also remember that she had arrived shortly before his father had been taken away. If he associated her with their separation—

"Patrick, this is your friend Tara. She's come to visit you."

He was rubbing the sleep out of his eyes with one hand, and with the other he carried the horse Pudget Vandermeer had made for him.

"Patrick." Dropping to her knees in front of him, Tara held out her arms.

He looked at her, his eyes widening and his sleepiness melting into a quizzical expression. Suddenly he thrust the little horse toward her. She reached for it, but he pulled it back. He held it tight, and she realized he had shown it to her to let her know he remembered.

"Yes, Patrick. It's me, Tara. And you're right. I gave you that horse. A wonderful lady named Pudget Vandermeer carved it for you."

"Where's my daddy?"

Mrs. Ortega stood in the doorway, certainly not a menacing figure. She had an obvious way with children, but Tara didn't feel easy with her overhearing their conversation. Tara had been strictly advised by Patrick's caseworker that she was not to question him about his mother or the charges against his father. She was totally committed to keeping her promise, but did that mean she couldn't answer Patrick's questions? And with Mrs. Ortega listening, did she want to reveal that she was in touch with Derek Bouchard?

"Timmy, you give that back to me! It's mine! Auntie Rose. *Auntie Rose!*" A girl was shouting, and Mrs. Ortega turned away.

"I have to see what's happening. Call if you need me."

Patrick had been perspiring, and a few strands of hair clung to his forehead. Gently, she pushed them back. "Patrick, your daddy is fine. He asked me to tell you he sends barrels and bushels of love. Just as soon as he can, he's going to see you."

"He's coming to see me?"

Tara put her arm around him. "Just as soon as he can," she repeated. She kissed his cheek. "That's a kiss from your daddy. And I have something for you, too." She reached for the package, and together, sitting side by side on the floor, they opened it. The track didn't interest him, but he was fascinated by the collection of miniature horses mounted by tiny jockeys in painted-on silks. One at a time, he picked up each horse and studied it.

"It's a game, Patrick. Do you want to play it?" She helped him pick a horse; then she selected one. "We put our horses in these slots. Let me show you how to do it, and we'll have a race. We'll see whose horse gets over there to the finish line first."

She showed him the power switch and turned it on. The first tune that played was "I Ride an Old Paint," hardly a racing song in Tara's estimation, but the two little horses bobbed up and down, rocking their way slowly down the track.

His expression had been solemn for a little child, but suddenly Patrick giggled and clapped his hands. "My horse is winning. He's a good horse and he's winning."

Tara kept her fingers crossed tighter than she ever had at a real racetrack. Patrick's horse *had* to win, and it did. They played again, and when her horse won, Patrick didn't lose his smile. "Your horse is good, too."

"Do you have a nice friend here that you can play this with?"

"Timmy. He's here. But he said maybe he's going away soon. He's awarded the cat. He says I'm awarded the cat, too, but I don't know."

"Awarded the cat? Patrick, I don't—" But then she did understand. *A ward of the court.* Tears flooded her eyes and she looked away.

Tara stayed as long as she could, talking to him, playing with him, and promising to visit again. "Next Sunday. That's a whole week, but I'll be here. And I'll find another nice game for you or something else that you'll like."

"My daddy *never* comes to see me." Patrick had been having a good time, but suddenly he looked desolate. Tara caught him in a hug and felt his little body tremble. "I'm waiting and waiting, but Daddy never comes. And Mommy never comes."

"Oh, Patrick, I'm sorry. I'm so sorry." Tara's voice was choked. Kissing him, she left a trail of tears on his cheek. "You'll see your daddy soon. I know you will. He loves you bushels and baskets full, and you'll see him soon."

CHAPTER 22

After Tara said good-bye to Patrick, she went outside and looked for her car. She didn't see it and it took her a moment to remember—*Walker*. Hands on hips, she wondered what to do.

"Over here, Cuz." Walker called to her from the far end of the block. He was leaning against the car, and when she reached it, he held the passenger door open for her. "I'll drive."

She was still fastening her seat belt when he lunged behind the wheel, turned the key, and roared away from the curb. The car lurched as he rounded the corner.

"Walker!" He didn't respond, and she pulled back in her seat, watching him. The muscles in his arms and neck were taut; his jaw was tense. He was driving too fast through residential streets, and it was a relief when they reached the freeway. But he accelerated on the ramp and immediately cut across to the fast lane. From where she was sitting, the speedometer appeared to be in the eighties. The angle was deceptive. They couldn't be going that fast, but surely they would hear a siren at any moment.

Abruptly he took his foot off the accelerator. The car slowed. He sighed. No, it was more like a gasp, and the tautness seemed

155

to drain. He glanced her way. "Sorry, Cuz. Guess I was heavy on the gas."

"What's wrong?"

He shook his head. "Nothing. The whole world is absolutely great. Haven't you noticed? But don't let me spoil *your* day. Tell me about your visit with Patrick."

Tara decided to practice her report before she delivered it to Derek. "Patrick is well cared for. The home is pleasant, and the foster mother is intelligent and caring."

"And he's fine?"

"Yes, I think so. He looks good—adorable, actually—and healthy. We had a nice visit. And, Walker, you were right about the racetrack. He loved it."

Walker spoke very slowly. "Tell me, Cuz. Did Patrick Bouchard remember that he had seen you before?"

"Oh, yes! I was surprised because I'd only met him one time. But he recognized me right away."

"Did he remember your name?"

"Yes—no. I'm not sure. Mrs. Ortega told him my name. But he was carrying the horse that Pudget Vandermeer made for him, and he knew I'd given it to him." Blinking away tears, Tara stared out the window. "It's such an odd toy for him to be attached to, but he received it right before he was separated from his father and maybe it has special significance."

"But he remembered you and knew you had given it to him? You're sure of that?"

"Yes, I am, but Walker—how did *you* know?"

"About the horse?" He pondered. "I think Mom told me. You told her all about going to the Bouchards, didn't you?"

"That's right!" Tara was startled at the memory. "Aunt Sylvia made me go shopping the next day, and she bought me a lovely dress. My mind wasn't on shopping though. I kept talking about Pudget and . . . and everything that had happened since

I arrived in California." She trembled. "I saw two women who were dead, murdered."

His eyes weren't on the road. He was staring at her. "That's right, Cuz. You certainly have a knack for putting yourself in harm's way."

Walker took the inland route, and when they reached the turn that led to Ballard, Tara was sorry she didn't have the car to herself. She envisioned Derek pacing near the phone, waiting for her call. It would have been so nice to arrive in person and give him the news he was so desperate to hear.

She and Walker talked very little on the remainder of the drive, but as they were getting out of the car, he reminded her of her promise. "Watch your step. Don't go telling your suspicions to anyone—*anyone*. You've got to trust me."

The urgency in his voice touched her. "I promise, Cuz," she said, using his nickname for her. "I want to help Derek. I have no idea where to start—but no matter what happens, I won't mention a word to anyone until I've talked to you. I promise."

At the door, he raised her hand to his lips. "Good girl. Keep that promise, and I'll do my best to take care of you."

Tara ached to get in touch with Derek, but she didn't have a phone extension in her bedroom, and anyway she still had qualms about calling him from Matthew Nyborg's home. She would respect his principles and point of view, at least when she was literally under his roof.

But while she was under his roof, she might be able to get additional information about the case. Or the cases. She was sure of it now. Pudget Vandermeer had died at the hands of the person who had crushed the breath out of Jessie Bouchard.

Walker was home only long enough to change his clothes, and then Tara was alone with her aunt and uncle. She waited until Aunt Sylvia was busy in the kitchen and the news broadcast Uncle Matt was watching broke for a commercial.

"Uncle Matt, I haven't seen much about it in the papers, and I'm wondering what's new with the investigation of Pudget's murder."

He looked troubled. "I wish I had something encouraging to tell you—and the D.A. Truth is, we haven't turned up any significant leads. It's been two weeks and with random crimes— Well, Tara, I'm afraid the longer it goes, the less chance we have of bringing him in."

She kept her voice easy. "Are you sure it was a random crime?"

"Tara, we're sure as hell not overlooking anything. We checked into her past, people she knew—everything—but what we're dealing with is a murder committed for robbery. The lab crew couldn't lift any usable prints, except hers, and—"

"Uncle Matt, *my* prints should have been there! I was in the house twice, and the first time she showed me around. I know I touched things. She had a creation—*Meditation,* it was called—that I touched. I even turned the handle. Why didn't my prints turn up?"

"You've got a good mind, Tara, and you're on the right track. The fact that we didn't find your prints, plus several other things, indicates that the killer took the time to obliterate his traces."

"So it wasn't a random crime!"

"We think it was, but the killer knows he's on file somewhere and could be traced. But that's the best clue we've got. I've assigned as many man-hours to it as I can. We've checked out burglary and assault ex-cons in the area. That didn't lead to anything, but the networking is statewide, and—"

"But, Uncle Matt, if my prints weren't on the handle of the *Meditation* sculpture, then the killer must have touched it. Otherwise, he wouldn't have cleaned it off. That means he was a guest, someone she let into the house. She told me she showed it to everyone."

His program was back on, but ignoring the remote control at his fingertips, Uncle Matt vaulted across the room to switch off the set. He didn't sit down again, but walked the room, his energy surging until he looked like a great cat bounded by the bars of a cage. "When we didn't find your prints on objects you said you'd touched, we did tests to see how easily the surface on that handle retained prints—and I'll tell you something. The lab man was able to lift excellent samples of *his* prints from that handle. But that doesn't mean Margaret Vandermeer let the killer in. Everything points to a break-in, and the asshole—pardon me—the killer wiped the handle clean because he touched it, probably planning to take it, but then decided it was too risky to rip off anything so unusual."

Tara took a deep breath. "Could someone have deliberately made Pudget's death look like a robbery so that you wouldn't be suspicious?"

"Of what?"

"Of the fact that Pudget knew Jessie Bouchard was still alive after her husband left for Phoenix. Pudget was sure she had seen Jessie. Absolutely positive, and she knew what she was talking about."

"Tara, this is what I was afraid of."

"What do you mean?"

"You were hell-bent on seeing the Bouchard boy, but I should have refused. It's my fault, but now your feelings are involved. You want to come up with a solution that will give the kid back to his father. Well, take it from me. Tough as it probably is for him now, that boy is better off. He doesn't belong with a man who would do—well, I don't have to go into it. You *saw* what he did to her."

"He didn't do it! Not Derek." She blurted the words. "Whoever killed Jessie Bouchard killed Pudget, too. I don't have evidence, not the kind of evidence that means anything

to you, but I know it. And, Uncle Matt, Derek couldn't have
killed Pudget. You know I left her alive and went directly
to see him. I was with him until *your* office arrested him."
Without meaning to, she stressed the "your," making the word
sound like an accusation.

His usual animation vanished. He looked deadly solemn.
"Promise me you won't get involved in the Bouchard case."
His voice mellowed. "Your aunt and I know it's been terrible
for you—being on the scene when her body was found and then
meeting her little boy—but have more confidence in Peter. He
deserves it, and Bouchard is his case. So promise—"

She loved him and Aunt Sylvia as dearly as if she'd known
them all her life. It was hard to look at his determined face
and refuse, but she couldn't turn back. "I can't promise. I'm
already involved, and I guess I was from the moment I saw
Jessie Bouchard in that *ropa*. Or at least from the first time
I talked to Pudget."

Uncle Matt put a hand on her shoulder. "Well, you wouldn't
be Johnny's girl if you weren't willing to stick your neck out.
I just don't want you to be disappointed and hurt."

"I'll try not to be, Uncle Matt. And I'll promise never to do
anything that would reflect badly. I mean, you're the lieutenant
in charge and—"

"And I will be for longer than I thought. I never handed in
my resignation." He glanced toward the kitchen and lowered
his voice. "Never was too keen on it, and I'm certainly not
going out now with two unsolved murders on the books."

A silent protest rose in her throat. *Three, Uncle Matt. Add
Jessie Bouchard's murder. I don't care what you think—I
don't care how good a detective Peter is—you're both making
a terrible mistake. Derek and I will prove he didn't kill his
wife.*

"This sort of situation is new to you, Tara, but it's Pete's
job, so don't worry. Bouchard won't get anything worse than

he has coming to him, and with the courts the way they are, he may not even get that. Put it all out of your head, and I won't mention a word to Peter."

Won't mention a word. Those were the exact words she had said to his son, and with a rush of guilt, Tara realized she had broken her promise to Walker. She was chagrined. If Uncle Matt knew how worthless her promises were, he wouldn't have asked her to promise *him* anything. Her only consolation was that Walker would probably have made an exception of his father.

CHAPTER 23

Tara went to bed early, but when she closed her eyes, she envisioned Derek pacing near the phone, still hoping to hear from her. She intended to contact him first thing in the morning, but morning seemed a long time away, and it was less than forty miles to Ballard. She could be there within an hour. Derek would be awake—she was sure of it—and she would return home before anyone realized she was gone.

She pulled on slacks and a sweater, and ran a brush through her hair. No makeup; there wasn't time. Clutching the handrail, she crept downstairs and out the front door.

She drove without lights until she was several yards from the house, then she hit the light switch and floored the accelerator. Her cousin drove fast and she could, too.

The rural darkness was relentless, and occasionally her headlights caught a mist that seemed to rise from the earth. She encountered few other cars, but her anxiety wasn't the result of being all alone in the dark. For once she couldn't repress the thought that Jessie's murderer had killed a second time to protect himself, and Tara was the only person who knew—who could swear—that Pudget Vandermeer had seen Jessie alive after her body was allegedly already lifeless. Perhaps the killer thought Tara was a threat, too.

The car veered and hit the shoulder, but she straightened the wheel. She couldn't lose control of herself.

She was driving through rolling hills, a beautiful terrain by day, sinister by night, but taking a deep breath, she loosened her death grip on the wheel. The darkness was getting to her. What she was thinking was impossible. She'd been in California only a few weeks. She hadn't met many people and couldn't know the murderer; he could not know her.

Lights were still burning at the Bouchard ranch, and Derek opened the door at her first knock. "Tara! I'd given up hope."

When she went inside, he grasped her shoulder. "Did you see Patrick?"

"I was with him for nearly two hours." The reassuring report, the carefully chosen words, fell out of her head. With a burst of emotion she described the home and Mrs. Ortega. "She takes good care of him. He likes her, but Derek, he misses you terribly."

Derek looked at the floor, and the hand on her shoulder trembled. "Thank you. Needed . . . so badly . . . to know." The words were broken and she shared his pain. No wonder she hadn't found a way to phone him. She'd wanted to be with him when he heard about his son, even if it meant sneaking out at night after her aunt and uncle had gone to bed.

He asked about Patrick again, sometimes repeating the same question several times. "And he was all right? Did he seem all right? Clean and well fed?"

They sat together on the couch, and Tara stroked his arm. "Derek, they're taking excellent care of him. Mrs. Ort—" She caught herself, not wanting to reveal the name. "His foster mother has a real way with children."

"I wish there was something I could do to thank—"

She held a finger to his lips. "He's a wonderful little boy, and I was happy to see him again."

Derek looked pensive. "Tara, maybe I shouldn't do this, but

here are some letters I want you to read." He dashed upstairs, but when he returned, he hesitated. "I wouldn't do this—I swear I wouldn't—but I want you to know how it was with Jessie and me. And this will explain it better than anything I could ever say." He thrust several letters at her that were addressed to Jessie Bouchard.

Derek tapped the address with his finger. "Notice where they were sent."

Tara slipped the top letter out of the envelope, and Derek switched on a table lamp, giving her more light. She began to read, but after a few paragraphs, she recoiled. "Derek, I can't . . . I don't want to read this."

"Read!"

Her cheeks burned at descriptions of lovemaking between Jessie and—who had signed the letters? Someone named Helmut. Tara read the second letter, then held out the third. "Do I have to read this last one?"

He shrugged. "They're all the same."

"I'm sorry . . . about this, but I'm glad you wanted me to know."

He propped his elbows on his knees and rested his head in his hands. "It's crazy. The position I'm in. I have no right to think about—"

She handed the letters back to him. "And this small envelope, is it the same as the others?"

"She was saving this newspaper clipping. Something about a missing man. I have no idea why she kept it, but take a look."

Tara read the article, and had started to put the neatly cut clipping back in the envelope when suddenly the blood drained out of her hands and feet. Her fingers and toes tingled. Moving slowly, she took a second look at the name.

"Tara, what is it? What's wrong?"

Tara's first attempt to speak ended in a gasp, but then she

forced herself to form words. "The missing man—Andrew Mason—his body was found in a dry bed at Lake Cachuma. He was buried there . . . murdered."

"Tara, are you sure?"

The temperature in the room must have plunged, and Tara shivered. Derek put his arm around her. Their faces were almost touching; they stared into each other's eyes. A slight nod. Yes, she was sure.

She felt his body tense. "My wife must have known him. He must have meant something to her, or she wouldn't have saved the clipping." Eagerness edged his voice. "Whoever killed Jessie may have known Mason, too. And maybe . . . at least it's possible—" He broke off, but she nodded, grasping his thought. "Do they know who murdered Mason? Do they have any suspects?"

She turned her face away. "I don't think so. Not from the way my uncle talked this evening. He said he had two unsolved murders on the books. Pudget Vandermeer is one of them and I think Mason is the other."

"Your uncle doesn't know it, but he has *three* unsolved murders." Derek sounded angry. "I didn't kill Jessie, but if the cops ever find out who did, they'll have Pudget's murderer, too."

"And Andrew Mason's."

"It's possible, Tara. Now tell me what you know about Mason. How he died, when his body was found—everything." Derek's voice was low, and Tara whispered in response. It was a grim conversation, and though no one could overhear, it seemed out of place to let their voices carry.

After she told him the little she remembered from newspaper accounts of Mason's death, Derek rested his head against the back of the couch. "None of this makes sense, Tara. None of it. But what baffles me most is how Jessie was put in that chest or *ropa,* whatever they call it, after the mission was locked up r the night. And that's what had to have happened."

He hit his hands together. "But unless the murderer is
ompletely insane, he wouldn't have killed Pudget just because
e claimed to have seen Jessie. Are you sure she didn't tell
ou anything else?"

"Pudget saw a man getting out of a car just inside the entrance
f the Ballard cemetery, right after she passed Jessie. She didn't
e Jessie and the man together, but they were the only people
round. Pudget didn't describe the man. All she said was that
e looked familiar."

"And this happened after the mission is supposed to have
een locked up." It was a statement, not a question.

"Do you think there might be some way to get into the
ission at night? A way that wouldn't be obvious?"

Derek shrugged. "There has to be. Jessie was at the airport
ith me less than an hour before the mission closed. So
hoever killed her hid her body later. Jessie was slender,
ut still he couldn't have fit through a transom with her. But
aybe a window—"

"Maybe the door was left unlocked."

"Maybe."

They were quiet, and Tara realized they shared the same
ought.

"I couldn't let you risk it."

"I wouldn't be risking anything." She stood up and headed
oward the door.

"Wait, I'll get my jacket and an afghan for you. It'll be cold
ut there."

What they were contemplating took a touch of madness,
ut either they did it now, when the idea was fresh, or they
ould never do it at all. She drove, and silently he pointed out
e turns.

The cloud cover had drifted away from the moon, and lunar
ght silhouetted the mission. Tara drove to the remote corner

of the parking lot, the gravel crunching under her wheels impos-
sibly loud. She turned off the ignition. They sat in darkness an
found each other's hand.

"C'mon." A single word and she followed him out of th
car. He helped her drape the afghan around her shoulder:
then they crept slowly toward the shadow of the long, lov
building.

"The chapel is at the far end, toward the road," he whispere(
"but I don't know where—"

"I know where the *ropa* is." Tara had never told him she'
been on the grounds when his wife's body was discovered. H
had no idea that she had seen Jessie. Now wasn't the time t
tell him, but she led him toward the door near the *ropa*.

The door was old, a massive piece of carved wood, an
possibly part of the original structure. Tara couldn't remembe
it from the first time she'd stood here, but then she'd been to
jolted to be attentive to anything. Now she was calm, detache(
almost as if she were viewing herself in a dream. "The *ropa* i
through here, just a few feet away."

Derek touched the door, then fingered the heavy chain tha
was slipped through the iron handles on the door and the frame
The chain was secured by a large padlock. He tugged the loc
and it held firm.

Derek slapped the door with his open palm. "It's not eve
a regular lock. I thought that if it was something standard,
person with an assortment of keys might have gotten luck
and hit on a key that worked. But this—" He touched th
padlock again. "There's no way anyone could have gotter
past this."

Gravel crunched. A highway patrol was headed towar
Tara's car. "Derek, they mustn't find you here! That bench—
get down behind it."

"I can't leave you to face—"

"Hide! I can handle this." Tara stepped out of the shadow

and into the moonlight. She waved to the deputy who was getting out of the patrol, flashlight in hand.

"That's my car, Officer. I hope it's all right for me to park here for a little while."

He turned the flashlight on her. "What are you doing here?"

"I'm a photographer. I'm doing a study of the mission for a calendar assignment, and I was hoping to get a few shots of the mission by moonlight." The beam never left her face, and squinting, she shielded her eyes with her hand.

"You're out here in the dark taking pictures? Where's your camera?"

"In the trunk of my car."

With the light in her face, she couldn't see anything, but she heard a second voice. "What's under the blanket?"

"Just me. It's cold out here."

"Let the blanket drop and put your hands on your head."

Tara obeyed, pushing the afghan off her shoulders and slowly raising her hands. She was terrified, but not for herself. She hadn't done anything, except possibly trespass after the area was closed to the public, and she couldn't be in serious trouble. But if they discovered Derek, it would look suspicious. His bail might be revoked, and some journalist would wax creative and write about a killer returning to the scene of the crime.

She was afraid Derek would show himself and explain what they were doing. She had to keep him in hiding. Taking a sharp breath, she spoke as loudly as possible. "I'm Tara Nyborg. Lieutenant Matthew Nyborg is my uncle, but please don't tell him I was out here all alone." All alone, that was her command to Derek. *Stay where you are.*

"Nyborg's niece?" The flashlight beam was turned away from her face. She blinked, blinded by the sudden plunge into darkness.

"Let's see some ID."

"It's in my purse, on the front seat of the car."

She blinked again and shapes became visible—the two deputies and the cars. She went for her purse, showed them her identification, then opened the trunk so they could see her camera equipment. The deputies held a low-toned conversation; then one of them told her to leave. "If you're going to try to get pictures here at night, get permission from one of the padres and bring someone with you. You shouldn't be out here by yourself."

"You're right, Officer. It was just that the moon seemed so bright tonight . . ." As she spoke, she slid behind the wheel of the car. The sooner she left, the sooner they would leave and allow Derek to get away.

She drove out of the parking lot, hoping to see the lights of the patrol car behind her, but she didn't. The two officers were still on the grounds. Looking back, she saw a part of the building illumined by a flashlight beam. *They were searching.*

She didn't dare return. Derek was on his own. Fighting tears of fear and frustration, she headed toward the Bouchard ranch. She drove about a mile, then parked on the shoulder of a lonely stretch of road. She would have to wait . . . and hope.

It was too dark to see her watch. Surely in her anxiety, time would pass slowly, but still, it seemed too long. The police must have found him, and he wouldn't have been able to explain. She should have stayed with him, told the truth and backed up his story. A noise—someone was approaching on foot. She jumped out of the car. "Derek?"

"Tara, where—" He gathered her in his arms, and they clung to each other. The cold was biting, but she felt his warmth, the brush of his lips against her cheek.

"I was so afraid they had found you."

"They came close!"

He drove the remaining few miles to his house, and now she knew the time—*almost three in the morning.* He tried to convince her it was too late for her to drive home, but her aunt and uncle would get up in a few hours. She had to be there.

Their good-bye was wordless. He caressed her hand, then taking it firmly in his, raised it to his lips. She felt his firm grip, the moisture of his kiss. A lingering, shared squeeze and then she left.

Was it only a few hours ago that Walker had kissed her hand? She and Derek had been through so much since then that it was almost impossible to believe so little time had gone by. She floored the accelerator, trying to blot out the awareness that what they had gone through was nothing compared to what lay ahead.

CHAPTER 24

"Tara, I don't understand. You're going out *now* to take pictures of the mission by moonlight?" Dawn streamed through the window, and Aunt Sylvia was reading the note Tara had placed on the kitchen table when she crept back into the house.

"No, Aunt Sylvia. I wrote that note last night, after you and Uncle Matt went to bed. I couldn't sleep. Guess it was the moonlight, and I decided it would be the perfect time to get a few moonlit shots of the mission."

"You went out last night, Tara?" Uncle Matt was always light on his feet, and she hadn't heard him come downstairs.

It had been agony for Tara to get out of bed so soon after getting into it, but chances were good that he would hear she had been at the mission. She wanted to seem as rested and unconcerned as possible, but she had to stare into her coffee mug when she answered. "I wanted night shots of the Santa Inez Mission to complete my calender layout. I . . . I'm not sure they'll come out . . . wasn't as bright as I thought." Her words were garbled. Telling lies didn't come easily to her.

"Tara, let me get this straight. Last night after we went to bed, you drove down to the Santa Inez Mission?" His tone was brisk—Lieutenant Nyborg, not Uncle Matt.

"That's right," she said, swallowing. "I wrote you a note, then I drove down in hopes of taking pictures in the moonlight."

"Pictures in the moonlight." He didn't believe her, and she felt like an insect impaled on a pin. She'd been afraid to tell him the truth, but too late she realized a lifetime in police work had made him impervious to lies. He wouldn't have believed her even if she'd managed a more plausible story.

"The mission is well patrolled at night, isn't it?"

She'd had an encounter with the police. Her claim to have been taking pictures was an excuse in case he heard about it. Her real purpose was her interest in the Bouchard case. He understood it all. There was nothing left for her to explain, and she was too mortified to try to justify herself.

He put his hand on her shoulder. He was Uncle Matt again and affectionate. "Tara, I know you mean well. You're concerned about the Bouchard boy, but there's nothing you can do to help him. Going down there late at night—at anytime—is foolish. What could you hope to accomplish?"

"I don't know. I just thought . . . maybe the mission wasn't always locked after closing hours. If Pudget saw Jessie Bouchard when she said she did, then—"

"That again! I should have realized. Now, little girl, you listen to me. My department has done a thorough investigation—thanks to your friend Peter. He's painstaking and very proud of his ability." He rubbed his hand between her shoulders, a soothing sensation. "You have to learn to have more faith in him!"

"I do have faith in him, Uncle Matt. But I met Derek Bouchard, and he's just not a murderer."

"They never are—until they kill someone. Let go of it, Tara. For your own good."

"Matthew, she meant well and you know it." Aunt Sylvia sounded just as she had when Tara heard her defending Walker.

Uncle Matt must have recognized the tone, too, because he bristled.

"Now, Sylvia, I don't want to make an issue of this, but Tara isn't using the best judgment, and I want to protect her."

"Uncle Matt, I don't agree with the charges against Derek Bouchard, but that doesn't mean I'm not using my head. I've thought about this very seriously and—"

"Tara, I'm not concerned because you think Bouchard is innocent. That's your privilege—it's anybody's privilege! But as for second-guessing a police investigation, you have no experience evaluating—"

"Matthew, don't raise your voice."

He put his hands on his hips. "Now listen, Sylvia, I don't need to be told—"

Tara jumped up. "This is my fault. I shouldn't have lied about last night. You're both so good to me, and I'm sorry." She ran up the stairs, almost bumping into Walker.

"Walker . . . I didn't know you were here."

He didn't answer, but his stare held a message. *He had overheard and knew she had broken her promise.*

She backed into her bedroom and fell across the bed, exhausted and despairing. Uncle Matt and Walker—her new family. They were both disappointed in her and for good reason. And Aunt Sylvia and Uncle Matt were arguing. But she was too tired to think about them. She was too tired to think about anything. Closing her eyes, she took a deep breath. A lingering gasp and she found herself in space, whirling toward a comforting blackness. She had to sleep, and when she woke up . . . when she woke up . . . she would help Derek.

Walker felt as if a blast furnace had suddenly roared in front of him. *He'd been so sure he had taken care of Tara.* Using his handkerchief, he mopped the perspiration from his forehead. *If only she had listened to him!* But she hadn't, and now he had to decide what to do.

He paused outside the kitchen. Mom and the old man were still going at it, and he heard his name. No matter what started an argument, eventually he was the bone of contention.

The aroma of fresh perked coffee was tantalizing, but he wasn't up to a confrontation. He had to be alone until he'd had time to think. He eased out the front door—and bumped into Peter Castle.

"Walker, you look strange. What's wrong?"

"Nothing . . . nothing's wrong." Try as he might, he couldn't stop staring.

Peter had on a sports coat and tie, and his easy smile suggested he was at peace with himself and the world. "Well, maybe it's just too much love life."

"How's *your* love life?"

"We're putting in round-the-clock hours, and I'm afraid there's not much time for anything else. But speaking of love life—do you know if your cousin is up?"

Walker felt another wave of heat. *Tara had told Dad her suspicions. She would tell Peter, too. And Peter would listen.* If Walker were going to do anything, he would have to be fast. He forced out the words. "There's something I want to talk to you about."

"Pete, is that you out there?"

"Yeah, Matt, I'll be right in." Peter's eyes narrowed. "What's up?"

Let's talk about the Bouchard case. It would be a risk, but Walker knew he had to get to him before Tara did. But he wasn't ready, not yet.

"Pete! What's holding you up?"

For a quick beat Pete's stare locked with Walker's. "I'll stop in at the shop, maybe tomorrow."

Walker watched Pete go inside; then he looked up at the window to Tara's room. "Tomorrow."

After sleeping until noon, Tara went downstairs, wondering if she had forfeited her loving welcome in the Nyborg home. The house was quiet, but through the dining room window, she saw Aunt Sylvia on the porch, tending her dainty jungle of potted plants. Tara waved, and Aunt Sylvia rushed in, still carrying her watering can. She squeezed Tara in a one-armed embrace. "Let me put this down."

She didn't pause to let Tara respond. "You had a call from Brett Adam's office, but when I peeked in, you were so sound asleep, I didn't want to wake you. Perhaps you can return the call now, while I fix you something to eat. You must be famished."

"I'll get myself something. But I want to apologize. I—"

"No! Don't apologize. You only did what you thought best, and your uncle had no business scolding you. But we're family now, and all families have their little rows." She patted Tara's arm. "Only now you know—that uncle of yours has a quick temper. And, I might add, your father did, too. The two of them would argue until I thought they'd tear each other limb from limb, but when it was over, they were as devoted as ever."

Tara loved to hear about her father—even that he had fought with his brother—and it was comforting to know she was still dear to her relatives. *Family ties.* She had done without them most of her life, and it would take more than a disagreement to shake her loose. She would find a way to make things right with Walker, and she already had an idea for mending the rift with Uncle Matt.

She called Brett Adam's office and talked to Mike Clark. "Yes," she told him. "I'll be happy to meet with Mr. Adam tomorrow. That's Tuesday at one o'clock." She repeated the day and time twice to eliminate the possibility of confusion.

"And *please,* Mr. Clark, don't accept a cancellation from anyone but me."

The soup Aunt Sylvia ladled out for her smelled delicious, but Tara was too preoccupied to feel hungry. "Aunt Sylvia, do you know where Uncle Matt put the carton of pictures and awards that I took down when I was helping in his office?"

"I think it's in the hall closet." She joined Tara at the table, bobbing a tea bag in her cup. "You know that was all a hoax, don't you?"

"A hoax? What are you talking about?"

"Your uncle! He wanted me to think he was serious about retiring. Oh, perhaps he was for a while. He even talked about making sure Peter was named to replace him. But in his heart— well, I just don't believe he ever came to terms with the idea of walking out of that station for the last time."

"Was that the hoax? His talk of retiring, I mean."

"Of course! Having you gather up his mementos was supposed to appease me. It did, too, but then he admitted that no retirement date was set, that he hadn't even turned in his resignation. Humph!"

Her aunt was exasperated, but Tara laughed. "I think you're right! Yesterday Uncle Matt said he'd changed his mind about retiring, at least for now. And that gave me an idea. Do you think I could hang his pictures and awards back where they were? Would *you* be disappointed?"

Sylvia shook her head. "Not really. He's not ready to retire, and he can't fool me anymore with talk of cleaning out his office." She smiled. "I don't really mind. Life could be a lot worse than having a husband who loves his job. And that's something for *you* to remember, Tara."

Tara wondered if now was the time to tell her aunt that fascinating as Peter was, he hadn't set the flame burning. For a breathtaking moment it had seemed that he would, but it just hadn't happened—at least not with Peter Castle. Her aunt and uncle were both building their hopes on seeing the two of them together, but they were building for disappointment.

Tara caught herself. She didn't dare say anything. It was incredible—bizarre—but she *was* falling in love. If she gave herself away, better to have them think it was Peter. The truth was impossible to explain, even to herself.

She put her dishes in the dishwasher. "Do you think it would be all right for me to take his pictures back to the station? Sort of a peace offering to tell him I'm sorry."

Her aunt looked amused. "A peace offering's not necessary—but it would be nice. And tell him I said it was a good idea. Then he won't have to figure out a way to tell me his retirement is on hold."

CHAPTER 25

In less than an hour Tara was en route to the station, the bulky carton of Uncle Matt's mementos and personal belongings in the backseat. The drive took her through blocks of condos surrounded by neat patches of grass and spindly trees. Tara had been told Peter's condo was halfway between the Nyborg house and the station, and she assumed that this was where it was. He was almost a neighbor.

Almost. It was a painfully appropriate word. She'd been concerned that her aunt and uncle would be disappointed because the romance they'd promoted wasn't going to happen, but she hadn't considered Peter. He was very attentive, but she hoped that in his estimation, she was an *almost,* too.

Lugging the carton in front of her, she entered the station. "I'm Tara Nyborg. Is Lieutenant Nyborg in his office?"

An officer near the reception desk looked familiar. Ream, that was his name. She'd met him a couple of times, and he recognized her, too. "Tara, the lieutenant went out a little while ago, but he could be back anytime. Do you want me to put that carton in his office?"

It was a relief to let him take the carton out of her hands. "Maybe I can get this stuff back up before he returns. I took everything down so I should be able to figure out where things go." She followed Ream to Uncle Matt's office.

Ream set the carton on the floor, and when he pulled the door shut behind him, Tara got to work. Uncle Matt had more than a dozen framed awards and commendations, and through the years, he'd had his picture taken with an assortment of VIPs. One eight-by-ten colored enlargement was in a silver frame. The photographic study wasn't very good. The scene should have been shot from a higher angle, but Tara understood why the picture merited the expensive attention. The photo showed a dignified Uncle Matt shaking hands with a man in cowboy attire who smiled directly into the camera. *Ronald Reagan.* He owned a ranch in the Santa Inez Valley, and law enforcement officials were alerted whenever he was there.

She would hang that picture first, but darn—she hadn't thought to bring a hammer, and she'd taken down every hook she'd been able to pull out. But maybe Uncle Matt had something she could use. She checked the top of his desk, then pulled open the top drawer, hoping to find a heavy Scotch tape dispenser or paperweight.

She rummaged a moment, but saw nothing but several folders and a memo pad. She started to slide the drawer shut, then jerked it open again. Clipped to the top of one of the folders were mug shots of Derek. There were two views, front and sideways, and the date and county identification were mounted on a small board hung from a chain around his neck. He looked agonized even in the side view, and she winced. How demoralizing it must have been.

Telling herself she couldn't—wouldn't—look at private papers in her uncle's desk, she watched her hands open the folder. She couldn't stop herself. Derek had not killed his wife, but as she started to read, horror crept over her. The notations were in her uncle's own handwriting and more of a list than anything else, but the impact was paralyzing. *Poor Derek.* How could he stand up against all this?

A name caught her attention—Helmut Lauer. A notation identifying him as a former love interest of the deceased said he had participated in a contest in the Hollywood area at the approximate time Jessie Bouchard was murdered. Another blow. After Derek had shown her Helmut's letters, they had speculated that perhaps Lauer was the man the police should be investigating. She moaned, knowing now she had to tell Derek that Lauer had to be eliminated as a suspect.

She had started to turn a page when suddenly the enormity of what she was doing caught up with her. Overcome by shame, she closed the folder and was about to slam the drawer shut when she felt a tight grip on her arm. "I would never have dreamed it. Not you. Not Johnny's girl." Her uncle's voice trembled. "You got in here to search through my files."

"No! You don't understand. I was looking for something to use . . . hang pictures. Saw Derek's photos . . . Uncle Matt, I'm sorry."

He released her arm. "You'd better leave—now."

"I lied to you this morning. I shouldn't have, but now I'm telling the truth." Snatching up the picture of Ronald Reagan, she held it toward him to give credence to her words. "I needed something . . . hang it back up. I'm going to put everything back exactly the way it was before." She talked faster and faster. "Aunt Sylvia said to tell you she thought it was a good idea. She knows you're not ready to retire, and—"

He stood next to her, his fierce energy radiating in waves. "Tara, I meant what I said. I want you to leave."

"Uncle Matt, please I . . . I—" She caught his expression. He was angry, but she saw something even worse. He looked disappointed—grieved. She closed her eyes tight. When she opened them, she grabbed her purse and ran out.

Walker approached the preschool-kindergarten, and when he was as near as he dared go, he inspected the children playing in the yard. At first he thought she wasn't among them, but then he caught sight of her on the steps that mounted the slide. Her dark hair was almost hidden under a pink knit hat that exactly matched her jacket and pants, and even without seeing them, he knew her shoes were pink, too. She might get short shrift when it came to care and attention, but her outfits were always the best juvenile fashion had to offer.

When it was her turn, she seated herself, but clung to the side bars. She looked frightened, but she usually did, a little girl lost in a threatening world. Suddenly she jerked hard. Her arms swung forward as if she'd been put in motion by a shove, and the boy sliding down behind her looked gleeful.

She landed hard, but picked herself up and wandered off alone. The children would go inside soon, and Walker headed toward his car. His chest felt weighted, and by more than just the forty-odd pounds of a five-year-old. Now there was Tara, too.

He glanced at his watch and decided it was late enough to go see another child. Mrs. Ortega would remember him—he had made sure of that. He was the son of a police lieutenant and the red-haired lady's cousin.

She answered the door, and he donned a sun-bright smile. "Mrs. Ortega, how's it going?"

Her expression showed dawning recognition. "You're the man who was here last Sunday with—"

"My cousin, Tara. We came to visit Patrick, but I was picking someone up at the airport and couldn't stay. D'you think I could see him now?"

She looked doubtful. "His worker didn't call me, and I'm not supposed to—"

"Just for a minute. I have more horses for his game, and . . . well, I'd like to say hello to the little guy." He heaved a sigh.

She unlatched the screen. "Well, you've been here before. It will probably be okay, but I think I should call—"

He bounded inside. "I can only stay a few minutes, then I have to make a dash for the airport. I have another friend to pick up."

Mrs. Ortega smiled. "The children just love that game. I never saw anything like it." She started through the house, and he stayed at her heels.

Patrick was in the backyard with several other children, and before she could call to him, Walker said, "Let me just run this out to him. Then I'll be on my way." He was out the back door before she could answer. Waving, he called out, "Patrick! Come see what I have for you."

The child stopped riding his tricycle and looked at him, but didn't approach. Walker's smile was gone, but his voice was soft and coaxing. "Patrick, come here. Don't you want to see this? It's for your racing game."

Patrick didn't budge, and Walker knelt alongside the trike. With the little boy watching, he unwrapped the gift. "See, more horses for your game. And here's a stable to keep them in. You know what a stable is, don't you, Patrick?"

The boy nodded. "My daddy's horses sleep in the stable."

"Sure. You remember what a stable is. And you remember me, too, don't you, Patrick?"

The child nodded again, a gentle smile on his face.

"And do you remember where you saw me?"

"Sure. I remember good."

Walker glanced back at the house. Mrs. Ortega wasn't in sight, and he slipped his arm around the boy. He had to find out exactly what other memories lingered behind those trusting eyes. He had only a few minutes, but it was time enough.

Patrick knew, *he knew.*

Stumbling to his feet, Walker shook his head to clear it. "Here, Patrick." He shoved the package at the little boy and left through the side gate.

He drove for miles before he could trust himself to think, not that thinking got him anywhere. There were no answers, no solutions. Not anymore.

In Solvang, he recognized the dark sports car parked in front of the shop, and the knot in his stomach tightened. Pete Castle had spotted him, too, and was on his way over. Walker stayed in his car, staring straight ahead, and Pete assumed a stance like a patrol cop writing a ticket. For an insane moment, Walker expected him to ask for a driver's license.

"Hey, you wanted to talk to me. What's up?"

Walker had to find out if Tara had talked to Peter. Despite her promises she'd blurted everything out once, and he could almost hear her telling Peter his investigation had taken him in the wrong direction. But Walker couldn't take Pete on now. If he broached the subject, he stood a good chance of revealing a hell of a lot more than he learned.

Lowering his window, Walker hoped his smile didn't look like a grimace. "Nothing that important. I was just wondering. One day I hear the old man is retiring. The next day he's still glued to the job—"

"Get out of the car." He sounded like a patrol cop, and Walker climbed out. They stood face-to-face. Pete was taller, and Walker had to look up a couple of inches.

Pete stood hands on hips. "Walker, you're not concerned about whether Matt is retiring. What's really on your mind?"

"Nothing important."

Pete shrugged. "Maybe not. But I have a hunch it has to do with the Bouchard case."

The knot in Walker's stomach turned to lead. "What gave you that idea?"

"I saw Matt about an hour ago. He was raving and everyone at the station was lying lower than the down side of a snake. All I could get out of him was that Tara had been in his office snooping and that she had it in her pretty red head that

Bouchard was innocent. I thought maybe you knew what had set her off."

Walker laughed and convinced himself it sounded genuine. "Tara! Come on, Pete. She's no snoop. Don't have to worry about her putting her nose where it doesn't belong." He laughed again, but this time he knew it sounded hollow.

Pete shook his head. "You don't understand. I'm concerned about her. Bouchard's dangerous, but he's out on bail because a half-witted judge decided he wasn't going to run for it. It's risky for Tara to get mixed up with him."

Walker turned up the collar of his jacket. "You're reading it all wrong. She met the Bouchard kid—Patrick, I think his name is. He's her only interest. She feels sorry for him, but if she had a run-in with Dad today, that should cure her. Don't worry about her." Walker hesitated, then said it again. "I mean it, Pete. There's nothing to worry about with Tara."

Pete didn't follow him into the shop, and Walker jerked up the phone and punched in a long distance number. "Nance Nyborg in ICU. This is her husband and tell her it's important."

He held his breath. *Please, Nance, please—be there for me one more time.*

CHAPTER 26

Tara almost floored the accelerator getting out of the parking lot, but a block from the station she pulled to the curb. *Uncle Matt.* He was a cherished replacement for his brother, the father she'd never known, and without meaning to, she'd done her best to wreck their relationship.

Pulling herself together, she tried to decide what to do. Uncle Matt had told her to get out, but did that mean out of his home as well as his office? She sighed. His exact meaning didn't matter. She had to leave his house to spare him the pain of ordering her away.

She had returned to California riding high hopes. A loving family had been waiting for her, and she'd had the prospect of an exciting new job. Nothing had worked out. The job had been smoke, and she'd alienated her relatives. And despite herself she felt as if Walker was right: she had stumbled into harm's way. She wasn't frightened, just apprehensive. Something was wrong, something close to her, and now she had no one to turn to. A name formed on her lips, but she rejected it. He had troubles enough of his own.

At home, she let herself in and tiptoed up the stairs. First she would pack; then she would say good-bye to Aunt Sylvia—quickly and tearlessly if she possibly could. She couldn't take everything with her, but would pack enough to get by for several days. Perhaps then she would know where she wanted her things sent.

She loaded two suitcases and assembled her photographic equipment. Then she sat down atop the quilt decorated with gaily colored spring flowers. It was time to go, but how could she tell that dear woman—

The door opened. "Tara, I *did* hear you up— My goodness, what are you doing?"

Tara stood up. "Aunt Sylvia, I hate to tell you this, but Uncle Matt thinks I deliberately went through his desk. I opened a drawer looking for a hammer. I saw the Bouchard folder. I'm terribly sorry. I shouldn't have looked at it, but I did. Uncle Matt caught me. He was furious and told me— Well, I want to leave now, before he comes home."

Aunt Sylvia pressed her hand to her mouth. Her eyes widened, then filled with tears. "Oh, Tara, how dreadful! But it's my fault. I encouraged you. I wanted you to go. I'll explain it to him. He'll understand."

Tara stood up. "Aunt Sylvia, I've caused enough trouble, and I have to leave, but I'll keep in touch if you let me. I love both of you very much."

It took Tara several trips to put everything in the car, and Aunt Sylvia watched, looking forlorn and disbelieving. Finally there was nothing left to do but say good-bye. The words Tara wanted to say wouldn't come. She would have to write and explain everything—how much her aunt and uncle meant to her, her strange feeling of involvement with the Bouchard case, maybe even her feelings for Derek. But now all she could do was get away.

She drove for several miles in no particular direction and considered stopping at a motel. But she couldn't face being alone and finally she U-turned at an intersection and headed south. It was almost dark when she pulled up at the Bouchard ranch. "Derek! It's me, Tara."

He didn't answer, and she pounded on the side door. Still no answer. She glanced back at her car. Even in the fading light, the Washington license plate looked glaring. If a patrol car passed by, it would be noticed, and she had distressed her uncle enough.

The garage door was heavy, but not locked, and after a couple of hard tugs, Tara got it up. But after driving her car inside, she didn't know what to do. Derek's car was gone. He might return in a minute or he might not return at all. She waited awhile, then decided to try the doors, starting with the one in the garage. She didn't have to go farther. The door opened. She hesitated, wondering if she wanted—or dared—to go inside. Derek wouldn't mind. She knew that, and yet it would seem strange to be in that house all alone.

Her grip tightened on the knob. She felt hollow, deserted, and Derek loomed as her only comfort. She would wait, at least for an hour. If he didn't come, she would leave a note telling him she was checking into the motel in Buellton where she'd stayed before.

Inside the house, she felt awkward, but at least she could make herself useful. Dirty dishes soaked in the sink, and dropping her jacket and purse on the kitchen table, she drained the water and started over, washing the dishes, then scrubbing down the countertops and wiping out the microwave. Housecleaning didn't usually get her best effort, but now it was a relief to have something physical to do. She even swept the floor—and still Derek wasn't home.

Waiting for water to boil for tea, she went into the living room. With Derek at her side, the room had seemed pleasant or at least normal. Now she couldn't shake the thought that this was Jessie's house. Crossing her arms, she hugged herself to ward off a chill.

A clutch of framed pictures was on top of a spinet piano, and the first one Tara looked at was a professional study of a woman whose hauteur and dark-haired beauty blended into a striking presence. So this was Jessie Bouchard in life. Tara set the picture down, wishing she could forget the other Jessie Bouchard—the twisted body, those eyes, bright and confident in the photo, staring blankly in death.

From the moment she'd seen Jessie in the *ropa,* Tara had been pulled into the case. It was eerie, but after she had had that terrible nightmare, she had sensed she was involved, that she wouldn't be able to just walk away and forget.

She poured the boiling water into a mug, splashing the table because her hands were shaking. She slammed the pan down. Why was she so afraid? And where was Derek?

Eight o'clock. Nine. *Ten.* She couldn't stay any longer. She'd go to the motel in Buellton, but now, just for a moment, she'd rest here on the couch.

"Tara! Tara, wake up."

"Derek . . ." His living room belonged to a dream, but he was real. "I . . . I didn't think you'd mind if I waited for you." She squinted at her watch. It was past eleven.

"I'll turn the thermostat up and start a fire. You must be freezing."

"I have something to tell you, but I'm afraid you won't like—"

"I had no idea you were here or I'd have been back long ago." He was piling wood in the fireplace and hadn't heard what she said. "I went to Hollywood, but it was a waste of time. I'm no detective and didn't come up with anything."

"What were you trying to—"

"Helmut Lauer." He spat the name. "I got to thinking. Maybe Jessie tried to break it off with him. If he was as crazy about her as his letters indicate, then maybe—"

"Derek!"

He stopped stoking the fire and looked at her.

"I started to tell you. I found something out today—about

Lauer. He was in a bodybuilding contest on the night Jessie was murdered. And he won. According to the notes, the contest started in the afternoon and lasted into the evening. He couldn't have gotten up here, then back down to Hollywood—"

She had expected him to be disappointed, but instead he raised his eyebrows. He was thinking and looked intrigued. "Tara, that doesn't make sense. Jessie died on a Monday night. Don't you think that sort of contest would be held over the weekend? Maybe I'm grasping at straws, but a Monday seems phony."

Tara sat on the floor and reached her hands toward the feeble blaze. Derek eased down alongside of her. The only sound was the first crackling of the fire. "If you're right," she murmured, "if he *wasn't* in a contest that night, it won't be hard to prove."

He nodded, and they stared at each other. "Tara, how did you find out about the contest? I don't think Lauer's name was mentioned in any of the reports and—"

"I'm ashamed of what I did. I want you to know that, but if what I did will help you, well . . ." She touched his hand.

"Okay, Red, so tell me."

She smiled, responding to the tenderness in his voice, not the flip words. Briefly, she told him what had happened. "So you might say, I wore out my welcome at my uncle's home. I have a job interview in Hollywood tomorrow, but I'm not sure I'll keep it. I may just head back to Seattle."

He took her hand. "I'm sorry your uncle blew up at you, especially because it was on my account. But he'll forgive you."

His breath warmed her cheek. "Tara, you did the right thing coming here, and you have to go for that interview tomorrow. You have to get the job. I'm in no position to say this, but I'll be damned if I'll let you go back to Seattle."

Nestling her head on his shoulder, she closed her eyes. After the long, agonizing day, it was comforting to be close to him,

sharing the glow of the fire. She would leave in a few minutes,
but right now—

"Derek! I have an idea. I'll go for that interview tomorrow.
And I'll go see Helmut Lauer, too. I'll tell him I'm a reporter
working on a feature. If I can get him to open up to me, maybe
I can learn something, starting with the dates of any contests
he's won. If he lies, we can check."

He caught her excitement. "He has a gym on La Brea. I have
the address. But promise me you'll be careful. You can't risk
letting him realize you suspect—"

She pressed a finger to his lips. "I've interviewed people
before for photo layouts, and he'll never suspect anything.
Don't worry."

He winked at her. "I'll worry. You can bank on it."

They were silent. He seemed lost in thought and she waited.
"What can you remember about the last time you saw Jessie?"

"When she took me to the airport that afternoon, the road
was blocked because of a chemical spill. It was going to be
hours before traffic was flowing again. Meantime, only one
car at a time would be let through in either direction."

His arms were around her, and Tara felt his body tense. "I
think whoever killed her had her body in his car and was
driving someplace where he could hide it. But when he saw
the traffic snarl and all the police, he got frightened. He had
to do something quick. He turned onto the mission grounds,
just to avoid the police. And then somehow—" Derek sighed.
"Last night we couldn't do it, but he did. He got inside the
mission and put her in the *ropa*. He probably could have just
left her, but hiding her ensured he would have more time to
get away."

She realized he had gone over it a thousand times. "Derek,
if you're right—if the murderer was on his way to hide her
body, maybe he was headed for Lake Cachuma. The man whose
body was discovered—they say he could have remained buried

for years, forever if the lake ever filled up again. But children were digging and found him."

His voice was hollow. "Jessie could have been buried out there, and I would never have known what had happened to her. I'd have spent the rest of my life searching for Patrick's sake."

Tara wanted to hold him, stroke him, comfort him, but she held herself in check. *Not now, but maybe someday.* Pulling away, she stood up. "I have to leave. The motel in Buellton is only a few miles—"

"No, Tara! Stay here—in Patrick's room. We don't know who's behind all this, and it's too risky for you to be alone."

She didn't want to resist. She would stay the night, and tomorrow she would have two interviews—one with Brett Adam and one with Helmut Lauer.

CHAPTER 27

Matt Nyborg sat on the edge of the bed and bent to tie his shoes. "Are you sure she didn't say where she was going?"

Sylvia sat up and folded her hands atop the bedspread. "Matthew, I answered that question last night—every time you asked."

Matt felt as if he were tethered to the bedpost. He needed to move around, exercise until his head cleared, and then he had to figure out what to do about Tara. That damn temper of his. It shamed him to remember, but when he saw her going through his desk, the lid had blown off. He hadn't listened when she tried to explain, but later he'd heard plenty of explanations from Sylvia. Now she was giving him a review, but he couldn't get worse than he deserved.

"I still can't imagine what you were thinking of. Poor Tara had no idea you'd be out of your office. She was just going to put your pictures back, and she expected you to be right there while she did it." She shook her head. "All that talk about sorting through everything in your office, getting ready to retire. Why, Matthew, you never did one thing except have Tara take those pictures down and sort through personal belongings and that was just to placate me."

He tried to pace, but their king-size bed and fancy bedroom

set didn't leave much room. "Doggone it, Sylvia, we've gone over that. Tara was eager to be of help, and it was just something to keep her busy so she wouldn't get bored. As for retiring, it's still on the back burner."

"Yes, and I know just how far back it is."

He held up his hand. "Okay, okay—but now I have to find out where she went. And you stay in bed. It's early and I'll fix my own—" Too late. Sylvia was already slipping into her robe.

He cherished their mornings together, but not *this* morning. He didn't mind her being hard on him. Her censure was nothing to the riot act he was reading to himself, but he couldn't stand that wounded look in her eyes. And her questions sure didn't help.

"Matthew, I still don't understand why you thought she hoped to find something. Nothing about the Bouchard case is secret, is it?"

"No, of course not. Everything we have is available to his attorney."

"Then why—"

"Sylvia, I told you. I had just heard that her car had been spotted at the Bouchard ranch. What she was up to there beats all hell, but when I saw her going through my files, I blew up. Thing now is to find her."

"I thought she was interested in the Bouchard case because of the little boy. She's tenderhearted." She poked him in the ribs. "All you Nyborgs are, even the ones who hide it under a thick skin—but now I'm wondering. Do you think she could actually be interested in Bouchard—personally, I mean? I can't imagine that she'd pass up Peter for—" Her voice broke. "No, it's not possible. She just couldn't care about Bouchard."

"If she does, then we have two of them—Tara falling for a wife murderer and our son panting to take a turn in his ex-sweetheart's stable of lovers." Matt could have bitten his tongue. Things were bad enough without starting in on Walk-

—but of course any mention of him and his mother was up
n arms. When would he learn!

She tugged his arm. "There's not more about Walker? Not
nore than you've told me?"

"No, Sylvia, nothing that concerns Walker directly. But I
nderstand Brian Holmes is naming his wife's lovers in his
ivorce action, and we shouldn't be too surprised if Walker's
ame makes the list."

Sylvia's eyelashes lowered and her nose tilted skyward, the
oyal gesture that always bewitched him. "Humph. Brian can't
ossibly have nerve enough to accuse our Walker of anything.
t's his fault Walker and Louise weren't married in the first
lace, not that I'm sorry about that now. And what reason
ould he have for exposing his wife's filthy linen?"

"As I hear it, an aunt of Louise's died and left her estate to
he little girl. We're talking seven digits, and Brian and Louise
re fighting for custody—of the money if not the kid."

Matt made a quiet beeline for the bedroom door. A quick cup
f coffee and he'd be on his way. He'd put out word that he was
ooking for a green car with Washington plates. If Tara was in
anta Barbara County, he'd find her. He hustled downstairs. If
e didn't find her, he'd have one hell of a time making peace
vith Sylvia—and himself.

Tara wasn't as excited as she'd been the first time she parked
n the visitors' lot near Building E of the sprawling studio. The
ocus of her life had shifted, and the job that had once seemed
o important was now little more than a distraction. But getting
ut of the car, she put everything else out of mind. It was time
o make a good impression.

When she stepped off the elevator, she was greeted by Mike
lark. "No mistakes this time, Miss Nyborg. Brett is waiting
or you."

Brett Adam's office was a dazzling white space pierced with

sharp black. Walking across the carpet was like sinking into a cumulus cloud. The walls and window coverings were unblemished white, and so was a centered desk, several chairs, and a long leather couch. A small white piano shone like a mirror, the black keys remarkably vivid, and a clock in a long ebony case hung on the wall. When Brett Adam rose and extended his hand, Tara saw that his chair was black. She blinked. It took effort to pull her attention away from his surroundings and concentrate on the man.

"Mr. Adam, I appreciate this interview. If you look at my portfolio, you'll see that I've done a variety of assignments—"

Brett Adam was still clinging to her hand. His office was impressive, but the man wasn't. He needed several more inches to be average height and many pounds fewer to be average weight. "Tara, what a pleasure." His smile was possessive. She tugged in an attempt to reclaim her hand.

"Ryan asked me to do something for you, and I'm sure we won't have any problem finding a spot. But now he tells me you're not an actress. At first he said you were, but if that's your preference, we could try you out and see—"

"I'm a photographer! A professional." Jolted, she realized she wasn't being interviewed for an existing job. She was "a favor" Brett Adam was doing personally for one of his network's reigning stars. "I think there's been a mistake. If you don't need a photographer, then—"

Brett Adam studied her, then released her hand. "Sit down. We'll talk while I take a look at that portfolio."

He put the portfolio on a low table as white and gleaming as the piano, and as he examined her work, he asked astute questions. "Tara, you have talent, and I think we will be able to assign you occasionally—as a professional—to some of our publicity layouts. But it would be on assignment."

She settled back in her chair. "That's fine, Brett. That's the way I usually work."

When she left his white cocoon, he promised to line up a challenging job for her. "Perhaps not for several weeks, but Mike will keep in touch, and I'll have him notify our publicity department to expect creative work from you!"

Tara couldn't care one way or the other, because the interview that mattered was still ahead of her. It was time to call on Helmut Lauer.

His gymnasium wasn't far away, a couple of miles at most, but in the few minutes it took to reach it, she completely shifted gears. Her portfolio was in the trunk out of sight, and she bounced out of the car with her camera bag and equipment slung over her arm. She *felt* like a news photographer chasing a feature and whatever evidence she could uncover.

Staying at Derek's, she hadn't been able to make an appointment with Lauer, because the Bouchard phone number was probably familiar to him. If he had asked for a number in case he had to call her back, she'd have been stuck and perhaps stirred his suspicions. But this was better anyway—take him completely off-guard, just a reporter eager to do a story about a bodybuilding champion. And Helmut Lauer certainly looked like a champion.

"Hey, Helmut, a reporter's here to see you!"

The man who answered the summons to the reception desk had a full mane of platinum hair, chiseled features, and the body of a classical statue—but not a marble statue. Only bronze could depict a man whose time on earth had to be divided between the workout bench and the tanning booth.

"My name is Tara Nyborg and I'm a free-lance photojournalist. I tried to reach you by phone, but perhaps I had the wrong number. I've heard about you—that you've won a notable bodybuilding contest. I hope—"

He flung a blue towel over a bare shoulder, a studied gesture. "*Which* contest do you mean? I've won . . ." He calculated.

"*Sieben, acht*—I'm not sure. But you want to write a story about me?"

"Yes, possibly part of a larger feature, but if I get enough information on you, I'll do an exclusive—*if* you're interested." *And he would be interested.* Vanity exuded from him like flame from a torch. He would be easy to flatter, easy to catch off-guard. She had seen the steamy letters he wrote to another man's wife and suspected he might be a murderer, but she could have disliked him under any circumstances.

The office he took her to was as nondescript as Brett Adam's was dramatic, but this time it was the man who held her attention. He showed her his trophy case, quickly spieling off the details of each win. She threw in personal questions and scribbled notes as quickly as she could, wishing she'd thought to carry a recorder. He wasn't going to be the subject of a feature, but she had no way of knowing which bit of information might give him away.

"And your most recent win, Mr. Lauer—when would that have been?"

He paused. "*Vor drei oder vier Wochen*—three or four weeks ago." Although strongly accented, his English was easy to understand—and he could write it well enough to describe his passions—but he still counted in his native tongue. He stroked the base of a trophy as if it were a pet. "This is my latest. It had to be corrected because the engraver did not have my name right. I just got it back."

Tara sucked in her breath. "But the date on the trophy is correct, isn't it? February 23, a Sunday?"

He nodded. "The date is correct."

She tried to keep the eagerness out of her voice. "And it was a Sunday?"

He glanced at her. "*Ja,* it was a Sunday."

Sunday, not Monday. The contest he had used for an alibi had been the day before Jessie was murdered. And he knew it.

He had deliberately lied to the police, and they hadn't checked his story. The hand holding the pen shook, but she kept writing, sensing she was close to something.

Her pen stopped. He had lied to the police—*Uncle Matt and Peter Castle.* Together they were in charge of the Bouchard investigation, and she was discovering evidence that would discredit their work. The knowledge stabbed. She adored her uncle and hoped to keep Peter Castle as a friend. But she couldn't feel disloyal. No matter the consequences, her loyalty belonged to Patrick Bouchard and his father.

She forged ahead. "Mr. Lauer, I'm sure my readers—my female readers—will be interested in romantic revelations. Is there a Mrs. Lauer? If not, what can you tell us about your romantic interests?" Her voice wavered, but surely his preoccupation with himself would keep him from noticing.

"There is no Mrs. Lauer."

"Maybe you can describe the type of woman that appeals to you."

Staring at her, he shook his head, but she wasn't ready to quit. "You're so blond—maybe brunette ladies are your type. Do you have—or have there been—any special brunettes in your life?" She was going too far—babbling—but if she could just get him talking . . .

"Why do you ask about brunette ladies?"

"As I said, you're so blond—"

"Perhaps I like red-haired ladies."

She smiled. "Perhaps, but—"

"Perhaps," he echoed. "But I am curious about your questions. I have been interviewed before. The information you want—it is different."

"I intend to do an original piece, and—"

"For what newspaper?"

"I told you, I'm free-lance." She rattled off several publications for which she had actually done work. "And I do calendar work, too. Currently I'm completing a layout of the California missions, but after that, maybe a calendar featuring something handsomer—"

His cultivated bronze complexion didn't disguise that he had gone pale. "The California missions?" he repeated. "You have something to do with the missions?"

Too late she realized she had said something that had to conjure Jessie. Her corpse had been discovered at a California mission, and perhaps Tara was face-to-face with the man who had put it there. She stuttered. "No, I . . . I don't have anything to do with the missions. Just taking pictures. That's all."

"You haven't asked to take any pictures of me."

"But I'm going to, right now. Perhaps we should start out in the gym, with you on the equipment."

The azure eyes piercing her looked cold. Jolted, she realized vanity did not preclude intelligence.

"Your name again, please."

"Tara Nyborg. I'm a free-lance—"

"I don't think so." He muttered something in the language in which he did his best thinking, and she couldn't understand. "You are here for another reason. What is it?"

The question was so blunt, it was a struggle to stick to the lie. "I'm doing a feature about bodybuilders. If you don't want to be included—"

Again he muttered in German. "What you are saying—*nein!* It is not true. You want information, but your questions—you are not writing about me. I think"—he paused and nodded to himself—"I think you want information about Jessie."

She gasped. "Why I . . . No, what makes you think—"

"I told the detective everything, all about Jessie and me. But you're not with the police. It is something else." He slammed the door and stood with his back to it. "Now tell me why are you here, *Fraulein.*"

The walls of the tiny room seemed to move toward her,

narrowing her space and safety. An anvil pounded in her chest. If he had killed once, twice, maybe three times before, he might kill again if he thought she was a threat.

"Why are you here?"

"Because I . . . It really doesn't matter and I want to leave. If you don't let me out of here, I'll scream."

Moving slowly, he opened the door. "Scream, *Fraulein*. Scream loud if you want. It won't bring Jessie back."

She didn't stop running until she reached her car, but then she was disgusted with herself. *He had mentioned Jessie.* She should have kept her composure, questioned him. He couldn't have done anything to her with a half dozen people only a few yards away in the gym, and he might have let something slip.

But now she knew he had lied to give himself an alibi— and how quickly he had connected her with Jessie. The dead woman was obviously forever on his mind.

Suddenly Helmut Lauer's parting words echoed. *Scream loud if you want. It won't bring Jessie back.* The tone, the words, had sounded like grief not guilt, but maybe he had loved her. His letters had boasted of love, and perhaps he had killed her because she wanted to break it off.

His motives didn't matter if they could prove he had killed her. And they would prove it. Suddenly she felt light, as if she were floating. She should have been terrified. Helmut Lauer knew she suspected him. He might inscribe her name on his list of victims, but instead of fear, she felt relief. A burden had been lifted, and now that it was gone, she could admit it. Until she suspected Lauer, she'd had the eerie sensation that the murderer was close to her, watching her. It was crazy, but she'd had the feeling he was someone she knew.

CHAPTER 28

Driving north on the 101, Tara whizzed past other cars. She felt daring. Her detective work had been clumsy, but she'd discovered something worth knowing. She couldn't wait to tell Derek, but suddenly she had an idea. It was risky, but she was up to it.

In Santa Barbara she left the freeway and drove to the foster home. "Hi!" she said when Rose Ortega answered her knock. "I guess I'm early, but I don't mind waiting if he's not ready."

Mrs. Ortega stood, hands on hips, at the open door. "Miss Nyborg, no one told me you were coming. Did you talk to Patrick's worker about visiting him today?"

"Visiting him? I have permission to take him out for the rest of the afternoon and for dinner. Didn't you get the call?"

"No, I didn't and—"

"It must be my uncle's fault. He promised to arrange it. I suppose I could try to get Uncle Matt on the phone, but—" She paused, shaking her head. "Of course he may not be at the police station, but he talked to Patrick's worker. Everything was approved except the actual day, because I wasn't sure just when I'd be free." Tara fretted. "I've driven all this way and I promised Patrick that soon . . ." She let her voice fade, knowing she had given it her best effort and just had to wait.

Mrs. Ortega waved her inside. "It'll be all right. Your cousin brought Patrick a present yesterday, and—"

"What? Walker was here yesterday?"

"Yes, and when I told Patrick's worker, she said it was fine. If she's already told your uncle you could take him out, I know it will be all right. Wait here—it'll take me a few minutes to get him cleaned up."

Tara was surprised to hear that Walker had visited Patrick. It was sweet of him to be kind to a little boy he didn't know, and she took it as evidence that he wasn't angry with her. Mentally she crossed her fingers. Perhaps she could salvage one relationship with a Nyborg relative.

When Patrick saw her, a shy smile crept over his face. "It's my Tara friend."

His Tara friend. She knelt to hug him, and all sense of guilt vanished. What she was doing couldn't be wrong. Her uncle was furious at her, erasing almost all chance of her being allowed an approved visit, and this time she had something else in mind.

Tara remembered hearing that California law required a child under forty pounds to ride in a car seat. She didn't have one, but she secured Patrick with the shoulder holster and seat belt. "There now, Patrick. We'll be on our way, and I think I have a surprise for you."

"Am I going to see my daddy?"

She smiled at him.

Traffic was slow, and the ride to Ballard seemed incredibly long even though she and Patrick kept up a conversation. "Oh, yes, Patrick, Auntie Rose told me you had a visitor yesterday and that he brought you a present."

"A stable and more horses for my good game that you gave me."

"That's wonderful! And the man who gave you the present, he's my cousin. You don't know him, but—"

"I knowed him. I knowed him right away when I saw him. I remembered. And he asked me if I remembered."

"You knew him—the man who gave you the new horses?"

"Uh-huh." Patrick's attention was diverted. They were getting close enough to Ballard for him to recognize the terrain. He strained to see out the window. "We're going home!"

"Yes, Patrick, yes we are—but the man you saw yesterday. Where did you know him from?"

"Mommy took me by the water to play, and he was there."

"He *knew* your mommy?" Her grip on the wheel tightened, and she felt an odd sensation.

Patrick struggled unsuccessfully against the seat belt, trying to get up on his knees. "I want to see! We're getting to my house!"

Tara took her foot off the accelerator. "We'll be there in a few minutes, Patrick. But now listen to me. I want you to tell me about the other time you saw the man who brought you the present yesterday."

Patrick squirmed. "It was by the water. I was playing. Mommy had new earrings. In the car, she looked at them in the little mirror like that." He pointed to the rearview mirror. "She said she was going to buy me an ice cream bar, but she didn't."

"Where did she get the earrings?"

"Her friend."

Braking, Tara eased onto the shoulder. She felt numb, and the late afternoon sunlight was slipping into a burgeoning darkness. But she couldn't let herself faint. She had to take care of Patrick—and she had to find out . . .

"Why are we stopping? Why aren't we going home? Where's Daddy?"

Patrick's eager voice jarred her, but it would be a while before she could drive. "Patrick," she whispered, "was the man who came to see you yesterday the friend who gave your mommy the earrings?"

"I don't know. Where's Daddy?"

"Did you see the man other times?"

"Maybe. I don't know. Why can't we go home? Is my daddy there?"

Tara started driving. "When he talked to you yesterday, did the man want to know if you remembered him?"

"Yes, he asked and asked."

Every breath she took stabbed. The wheel was wet in her hands. *Walker had known Jessie Bouchard. He had given her earrings. He'd wanted to find out if Patrick remembered him.* A scenario was forming in her mind, a scenario too hideous to look at, too frightening to ignore.

At the Bouchard ranch, she tapped the horn and signaled to Derek to open the garage door. She drove in quickly, wanting to get her car out of view from the road.

"Tara, I've been worried about you. Did everything go— Patrick!"

Patrick was frantic with delight, and as soon as he was free of his seat belt, he scrambled into his father's arms. There was a flurry of arms and little legs, and Tara turned away. They deserved privacy.

Derek carried Patrick into the house, and they both seemed determined not to let go of each other. When Derek finally turned to Tara, his voice was ragged. "How . . . how did you get permission . . . and how long . . ."

"Just until tonight. I have to take him back, but he needed to see you."

Derek gathered his son in a bear hug. "And I needed to see this little guy. Daddy misses you, Patrick, a thousand muches."

While the two of them basked in their reunion, Tara checked the refrigerator and dug through the cupboards, looking for fixings for dinner. Grocery shopping obviously wasn't one of Derek's priorities, but she found pasta, sauce, and frozen zucchini, and set to work on a one-dish menu.

When her little dinner was ready, they ate, but no one had much appetite. Derek and Patrick were busy being thrilled with each other, and Tara . . . Tara was busy trying not to think . . .

The reunion was exhausting for a three-year-old, and after dinner, Patrick fell sound asleep in his father's arms. Derek wouldn't lay his son down, but sat on the couch, holding him close.

Tara had been impatient to tell Derek that he'd been right— the contest Helmut Lauer had used for an alibi had been on Sunday, not on the day Jessie died—but a crawling feeling told her that might not be important. Derek noticed her silence.

"Tara, you've hardly said a word. Did everything go okay with the job interview—and with Lauer?"

"The job interview wasn't what I expected, and Lauer . . . well, I told him I was working on a feature, and we talked."

Derek stopped caressing his son's hair and looked at her. "Did you find out anything about that contest?"

Tara ran her hand across her forehead. "Derek, you were right. The contest was the day *before*. He told me—"

"Wait! He gave you the actual date or he told you it was on a Sunday?"

"Both. He'd won a trophy. It was dated, and I asked him if it had been a Sunday. He said yes, or more likely *ja*. He has a strong German accent and—"

"Tara, I have to understand this. Helmut Lauer told you the contest was on a Sunday? You're sure he said Sunday?"

"Yes, he did, but—"

"Then I guess we were chasing shadows. If he had deliberately lied to the police to give himself an alibi, he certainly would have lied to you, too. There has to be some other way to explain the mix-up on the day."

"Maybe he thought if I wrote an article, the date would be mentioned . . ." Her voice faded. What Derek said made sense. She'd been complimenting herself for being such a clever sleuth, but she had missed the obvious. Lauer hadn't tried to disguise the date, and what had made him suspicious of her were all the ridiculous questions about brunettes. The man might have a flawed character, but his intellect was intact—which at the moment was more than she could say for her own.

She felt drained, defeated, and it wasn't merely because her precious evidence didn't really exist. Devastating was the realization that if Lauer were innocent, she might still know the name of the . . . No! She wouldn't let herself consider it. She had totally misinterpreted the situation with Lauer, and she was still misinterpreting. Uncle Matt was right—she had no experience with murder. All she was doing was jumping from one ridiculous conclusion to another.

Derek was staring at her. "There's more, Tara. I can see it in your face."

She squirmed. "No, there's nothing. Nothing. I had an idea— a terrible idea. It can't possibly be true."

"Tell me about it."

"No!"

"My God, Tara, you're not beginning to think that I . . . that I actually did—" His voice throbbed.

She knelt on the floor in front of his chair. "Not for one minute. I know you didn't. You couldn't have."

He cupped her cheek with his free hand. "Then tell me."

She closed her eyes, savoring his touch. If only the moment could linger, Derek holding Patrick and her in his arms, the three of them safe and together. But she had to open her eyes, and Derek stared into them, waiting. She glanced away. "Derek, after I talked to Lauer, I convinced myself he was guilty. Now I realize how ridiculous I was. And I'm doing it again. I don't have any evidence—nothing at all—but I'm trying to persuade myself that someone I know is . . . is responsible . . ."

Patrick stirred. "Daddy."

"I'm here, Patrick."

Yawning, the boy came to life. "I want to pet the horses. Can we go to the stable? And can I give Sundelion a carrot?"

"Sure thing, Patrick." Derek stood up. "Let's go in the bathroom, then visit the horses." He gave Tara a pleading look.

"How long do you think we have?"

She shook her head. "I have to take him back soon, but maybe another hour."

He tightened his grip on his son. "I don't know how you managed this, but I won't do anything to jeopardize you. I'll show him the horses, then you can take him." He cleared his throat. "When you return, we'll talk."

CHAPTER 29

Tara persuaded Derek not to accompany them when she took Patrick back to his foster home. The child was drowsy when she put him in the car and comforted with promises that he would see his daddy again soon, but mist filmed over Tara's eyes when she glanced back and saw Derek walking down the driveway, still waving good-bye.

Evening traffic was light, and after she had kissed a sleeping Patrick and put him into Rose Ortega's arms, she returned to Ballard via the inland route that passed Lake Cachuma. Of course there wasn't much of a lake, at least not visible from the road. She'd been told that years ago, before the long drought, Lake Cachuma had been a mystic blue jewel set in drifting fogs and pastel vapors, visible for miles from the highway circling through the mountains. It was dark now, but even by daylight, the lake had receded far out of sight. A large portion of it was nothing but dry bed.

Dry bed—that's where the body of Andrew Mason had been found. The area was a sinister reminder, and she had to sort her thoughts before she got back to Ballard. Derek would be waiting, and what would she tell him?

This afternoon she'd been convinced Helmut Lauer had murdered Jessie Bouchard. Now she suspected Walker Nyborg.

It was as simple as that, as ridiculous—and as terrifying. In her mind, she had fabricated a case against Lauer. Could she allow herself to put together a case against her cousin?

Why not? He wasn't guilty. He couldn't be guilty, but she wouldn't be convinced until . . .

She steeled herself. *Okay, start from the beginning . . .*

Walker knew Jessie Bouchard and had given her a pair of earrings. He had been curious about whether Patrick remembered him. She swallowed. Not too damning. Hadn't Walker mentioned the boy to her and described him as a bright kid? Of course he had. She remembered it distinctly. She had shopped for a gift for Patrick and eventually found the racing game in Aunt Sylvia's store. No, she hadn't found it. Walker had called it to her attention. *We have something Patrick would like. It's recommended for five and older, but he's a bright kid.*

He hadn't tried to hide that he knew the boy. Nothing suspicious there—but still, driving home that night she'd felt uneasy. She'd sensed something in Walker's manner and had wondered . . . And he had made her promise never to tell anyone about her suspicions.

She recalled their first meeting. What a day! She'd been at the mission when a body was discovered; she had met Peter, and that evening he'd introduced her to her aunt and uncle. While they were at dinner, Walker had arrived. He'd acted stunned, but Aunt Sylvia had attributed his daze to meeting his cousin. But thinking back, it occurred to her that Walker's strong reaction followed Peter's comment that he was in charge of the Bouchard investigation.

It couldn't be true. The whole idea was incredible—but what had Aunt Sylvia told her about Walker and his former fiancée? They had been seen together, boating on what was left of Lake Cachuma. But what if . . . what if the woman with Walker wasn't the old girlfriend? Perhaps he'd been seeing Jessie. Tara tried to visualize the picture she'd seen of Walker's fiancée the day she and Aunt Sylvia had sorted through family photos. Dark hair, that's all she remembered, but Jessie Bouchard's hair was dark, too. Maybe from a distance . . .

Tara shook her head. She was letting her imagination run wild again, just as she had with Lauer. But she hadn't imagined that Patrick had told her Walker had given his mother earrings.

Earrings. The word stirred a memory.

Pudget Vandermeer had said that in the Ballard cemetery Jessie Bouchard was wearing a pair of earrings that Pudget herself had made. *Jessie was wearing my earrings—bright blue abalone-shell seahorses in a gold-and-magenta setting. And I saw a man near the entrance of the cemetery. I bet he saw her, too. He looked familiar, so he must live around there. I said good evening and he sort of waved.*

Tara had repeated every word to the police, but had anyone paid attention? A vital clue from a woman who wore a possum? And would Peter—would anyone—waste a moment suspecting Matthew Nyborg's son, especially when poor Derek was available as just another spouse killer?

And how could she have forgotten! Pudget had shown her a collection of earrings on a velvet display board. She'd said she had rushed to finish them because they were going to be picked up that night. Picked up. By whom?

If Uncle Matt had investigated and found out Walker picked up an order of earrings, would he have thought anything of it? *Or* . . . Tara could hardly breathe, and one at a time, she dried her hands on her skirt. If he *had* thought it was significant, what would he have done? He was critical of Walker, but still, his only son . . . and Uncle Matt adored Aunt Sylvia—

She blinked, trying to make the scene go away. *Walker arriving at Pudget's sky house. Pudget telling him she'd seen him the other night in the cemetery . . .*

Pieces tumbled into place to form a grotesque picture. That afternoon at Aunt Sylvia's she had told Walker that Pudget had seen Jessie after the mission was closed. If the unthinkable were true, Tara's own name might be the signature on Pudget's death warrant.

Tara wanted to scream until she couldn't hear herself think, but there was still more. Someone who knew her schedule and whereabouts had called Brett Adam's office to cancel her job interview. Someone—*Walker!* He'd been home, sitting at the kitchen table just a few feet away from her when she made the appointment. He knew she believed Pudget. Surely it would be safer for him if he could get rid of his precious Cuz.

Tara felt dizzy. She adored Patrick and wasn't brave enough to give a name to her feelings for Derek. She would do anything to help them, protect them, but what if helping them meant her exposing Walker? What would happen to Uncle Matt and Aunt Sylvia if they knew their son was a murderer?

Derek was waiting for her, and suddenly she knew what she would tell him—*nothing*. No matter what she felt for Derek, Walker Nyborg was her cousin. She couldn't reveal her suspicions about him to anyone, not even Derek Bouchard.

"Tara, about five minutes after you left, your uncle came. He was looking for you." Tara was hardly out of the car when Derek broke the news.

"Uncle Matt! How did he know—I mean, really, I can't believe . . ." She fumbled for words.

"He knew you had been here. But how was Patrick? Did he cry when—"

"He was sound asleep, and in the morning he'll wake up in a familiar bed. And I'm sure that seeing you did him a world of good—but my uncle. I can't get over it. Exactly what did he say?"

"He was very courteous and identified himself as your uncle, not as a police lieutenant. He said he knew you were here and he wanted to talk to you." He put his arm around her. "Tara, I'm in no position to play it cagey, so I told him you were gone, but were coming back. He left you this note."

It read, "Tara, I apologize for the misunderstanding. Please, phone home immediately, love, Uncle Matt."

The word *love* was squeezed in, an afterthought, but he had told her to call home—she still belonged. She slumped against Derek and trembled with silent sobs. "Derek," she gasped, "Derek. I love you, and I don't know what to do."

CHAPTER 30

Tara's dreams were fragmented, kaleidoscopic images, and she stirred long before dawn. Half-awake, she tried to get comfortable in Patrick's narrow bed, and suddenly a memory surfaced—those photos, the film she'd shot at the mission! She waited until the little hand brushed seven; then she hurried downstairs and picked up the kitchen phone.

"Michelle, it's me, Tara. I know it's too early to call, but I need a favor immediately. It's urgent."

"Tara!" The drowsiness disappeared from Michelle's voice. "I've been trying to reach you. A man called yesterday and left a message for you on the machine."

"Who was he?"

"He . . . he didn't say. He just left the message."

Tara waited, but the line was silent. "Michelle?"

"I'm still here. It's just that—well, it's so scary. He said—he said you should leave California and come back up to Seattle. Tara, he said your life was in danger and that you should keep your guard up at all times."

Tara swayed and had to brace herself against the wall. "He said *what*?"

"Your life is in danger and you should stay on your guard. Listen, I'm worried sick, and I think you should do what he says. Come back to Seattle."

Tara caught her breath. "Describe his voice—what did he sound like?"

"I couldn't tell. The message was muffled. He could have been holding something in front of his mouth."

"And that's all he said?"

"Good grief, Tara, that's enough! You throw your clothes and equipment in the car and get back up here."

"I can't, not yet." It took effort to steady herself, but she had to focus on why she had called. "Please, do something for me right away."

"I'll do anything, but what's going on? You're in danger, and I want to know—"

Tara swallowed. "In the darkroom are negs of my shots of the missions. Go through them and find the ones of the dead woman in the *ropa*. Print the negs. Do a couple of blowups of the head and be sure to catch the ears." She repeated it. "I need blowups of the ears. It's urgent."

"Blowups of the ears!"

"Please, Michelle. There's no time to explain. I need you to get going on this now."

"Okay, okay, I will. But Tara, please be careful."

"Do you have a pen? Here's the address where you're to send the prints and use Federal Express. Get them to me as quickly as you can."

"I'm on it as soon as I hang up the phone."

"Good, then I'll say good-bye."

"Wait!"

"Yes?"

"Ryan Castle—have you seen him again?"

Tara gasped. "Yes, I saw Ryan. I was in his home and I left when he got fresh and put his hand up my dress." She slammed down the receiver.

She thought Derek was tending the horses, but he was in the doorway. "Tara, what in the world—" He grimaced. "Pictures of a dead woman in a *ropa!* Jessie?"

Tara sat down and folded her hands on the table. "I never saw any reason to tell you. It didn't seem important, but—" She caught her breath. "I was at the mission when Jessie's body was discovered. A woman was screaming. I ran to her—everyone did—and she was standing over the open *ropa*. My camera was in my hand. I snapped pictures. Automatic—I didn't even think."

Derek went white. "You saw her. You saw Jessie."

"It's horrible to talk about, but I wasn't trying to keep it from you."

"Why do you want the pictures? You said you needed a blowup of the ears. What possible reason . . ."

"There's just something I want to see—find out for sure."

He sat down across from her and put his hands over hers. Last night they had talked, not about the case or the criminal charges against him, but about each other—about the two of them together when all the ugliness was over. And now he was waiting for an explanation.

"Derek, please, you have to be patient. There's something— but I have to be sure before I talk to anyone, even you."

He shook his head. "That sounds dangerous and I don't like it. If you're on to anything, I want to know about it. Or if you won't tell me, go to your uncle. I don't think much of the investigation his office did, but he'll protect you."

She closed her eyes. *Uncle Matt, I found out who really killed Jessie Bouchard. It was your son, Walker. I don't know why he killed Jessie, but he killed Pudget to keep her from talking. And the man buried at Lake Cachuma—check into that one, too. One more thing—now I think he's trying to scare me out of California.*

Derek squeezed her hand. "Tara, don't take any risks. I dragged you into this, and I couldn't stand it if anything happened to you."

That erased all doubt. She didn't dare tell him about the threatening phone message. "Derek, believe me, I'll keep my guard up at all times, and I promise—as soon as I can, I'll tell you everything."

When the morning traffic thinned, she headed toward Santa Maria, hoping that Uncle Matt would be at the station. Just seeing Aunt Sylvia would be painful enough.

They had welcomed her as their own, yet she was trying to do something that might destroy their lives. But she had no choice. If Walker had already murdered several times, he might murder again. And if he wasn't exposed, Derek might go to prison in his stead.

When she pulled into the driveway, her aunt rushed to greet her. "Tara! I'm so glad to see you. Your uncle and I have been so worried. And Walker, too. He's very concerned about you."

Yes, Walker was concerned enough to phone Seattle and threaten me. Pricks of fear jabbed through her, but she kept her voice calm. "Aunt Sylvia, I'm fine and you mustn't worry. I can take care of myself."

Aunt Sylvia fussed, offering her coffee or breakfast, and assuring her that her uncle was sorry he'd lost his temper. "That temper is a Nyborg trait, and I wouldn't be surprised if you had your share of it. But Walker doesn't. He's calm and easygoing, and I think his father wishes he were more aggressive."

Tara turned away. She had read about people like that—murderers whose acquaintances were incredulous when their gentle friend or cordial neighbor was exposed as a vicious killer. But the woman fussing over her would be more than incredulous. Aunt Sylvia would die. She couldn't survive the agony of seeing her adored son—her only child—sent to prison for the rest of his life.

Murderers can kill again! Tara had to focus on that. She had to remember Patrick crying for his daddy, Derek following the car down the driveway, waving a pathetic farewell.

"Tara dear, you're so distracted. I know something's bothering you, and if you let me, I'll try to help."

"No, Aunt Sylvia, it's just that I want to look at those photos of the family. I'll take a few if you let me. I'll duplicate them and return the originals."

"They're still in the bottom drawer of the dresser in *your* room." She stressed *your*, conveying a message.

Tara had never looked at the photos since the afternoon she pored over them with Walker and Aunt Sylvia, but she'd intended to spend a relaxed day studying them until she could identify every face. But now was no time to reminisce. Putting several boxes on the floor, she sorted through the photos quickly, pausing only once to stare at the face of her father. *Johnny Nyborg*. His vitality, his zest, were apparent even in black and white. Wincing, she thrust the photo aside.

She found what she was looking for—one photo of the woman all alone, the other of her with Walker. Tara slipped the photos into her pocket. She'd had a few minutes of privacy while her aunt made a phone call, but now Sylvia appeared in the doorway.

Tara held out several photos of her father and one of her parents together. "After I have duplicates made, I'll send these back to you."

"*Send* them back! Don't make it sound as if we won't be seeing you!"

Tara's voice caught between sobs. "Aunt Sylvia, I love you. And I love Uncle Matt. You're the two best people I've ever met."

"Tara—"

"Please. I have to go." A final, clinging embrace, then Tara broke free and ran down the stairs. At the door she collided with her uncle.

"Tara, where are you going? Your aunt phoned and told me you were here. I got here as fast as I—"

"Uncle Matt, I'm sorry for all the trouble I've caused you. Forgive me. And know that I care about you—no matter what happens." She plunged toward her car. He shouted apologies, but she couldn't trust herself to look back.

She trembled so badly that keeping the steering wheel steady took concentration. *Check the speedometer. Let up on the gas.* She had over thirty miles to go, and the long drive would give her a chance to calm down and plot her next move.

The photos of Walker's ex-fiancée were in her pocket. *Louise*—Aunt Sylvia had once referred to her by name. Tara would show the photos to Derek. If he saw a resemblance to his wife, it would confirm her suspicion that it was Jessie Bouchard, not Louise, who had been seen with Walker. Perhaps, between her encounters with Lauer, Jessie had let Walker think she was interested. When he found out she was only teasing, all the anger and frustration he'd felt when his fiancée jilted him poured out and then . . .

Tara clicked on the radio, loud. She wasn't a psychiatrist any more than she was a detective.

Solvang. She hoped Walker wouldn't be in the store, but when she saw his car, she wasn't unnerved. It was strange, but she felt calmer, more in command, than she had at her meeting with his mother.

Chimes accompanied her entrance, but Inge was waiting on a customer and Walker wasn't around. The costume jewelry display was toward the back of the store, and almost holding her breath, Tara approached it. Several pairs of earrings matched the ones Pudget had shown her—shell flowers, fish, seahorses. Pudget had sold earrings to Aunt Sylvia's shop. When Tara met her, she'd been in a hurry to catch the bus back to Ballard—she didn't drive—so who but Walker would have picked up the orders?

"Walker, I'm not willing to cave in. And you shouldn't either, not unless there's proof."

Tara froze.

"Nance, I wanted to spare you. But if you think there's a chance—" His voice broke. "I can't think straight anymore. I must be going crazy."

His companion sounded gentle. "Didn't you know you could tell me—that no matter what, I'd help you? And you're not going crazy. The predicament you're in—the whole thing . . . it's hard to believe—but let me think . . ."

The woman's voice was muffled. Tara strained, and the next words she heard sounded decisive. "Walker, make arrangements for us to go to Santa Barbara this afternoon. When we get there, I'll be able—"

"Nance, you can't just—"

"Shhh, Walker. I'm a nurse. When I do it, she won't even know. But the second thing is—you have to tell your father everything, just the way you told it to me."

Walker's laughter sounded wild. "If I do that, I really am crazy. And Dad will make sure I spend the rest of my life assigned to a padded room at Atascadero."

Atascadero, the state mental hospital for the criminally insane. Tara felt eerie. Part of her wanted to run; part of her couldn't stop listening. The woman had to be his ex-wife or almost ex-wife, but she sounded devoted.

"Walker, I know how you feel, but you can't keep this to yourself. You *have* to talk to someone, and I think you're wrong about your father."

"Tara, I was busy with a customer and didn't see you. Walker is in back. Let me call—"

Tara held up her hand. "No, Inge. I had a couple of minutes and thought I'd look—" Her feet were moving now, quickly and toward the door. It was too late. Walker glanced out from the back room.

"Cuz?"

Tara's lips formed a greeting, but sound didn't come and she raised her hand in a floppy wave.

A woman stepped out from behind him. "Walker, is this . . . ?"

"Yes, my cousin Tara."

"I'm Nance Nyborg. Walker told me about you." She extended her hand. She looked older than Walker. Her face was more agreeable than plain, and Tara couldn't tell if the rings around her eyes were sleeplessness or tears.

"Nance, yes of course, how nice."

"Just stopping in, Cuz, or did you want—"

"Earrings. I was interested in a pair of earrings." This was probably their last encounter. She had to rally her courage. "Pudget Vandermeer made the shell pairs, didn't she?"

Nance shot Walker a look. Their exchange was quick, the span of a heartbeat, but it was real. Tara saw it.

Walker took earrings from the case. Was it her imagination, or did his hand shake? "Here. She made this pair and those down in front."

So much of that darling woman's heart went into all her creations that when Tara touched the earrings Walker laid on the counter, she felt Pudget's presence. She wondered if he felt it, too, if he cared. It was an effort, but she kept her voice brisk. "Walker, that day at the house when I told you I was going to see Pudget, you didn't mention that you knew her."

"I didn't know her—not by that name. I think she signed herself Margaret, or something."

Nance made a funny sound, then cleared her throat. "Why are you interested in those earrings?"

Tara felt dizzy. Nance Nyborg knew she had an ulterior motive. Minutes ago Nance had assured Walker that he could tell her anything, but surely what Tara was imagining wasn't possible. He couldn't have told her about Pudget and Jessie.

t the woman facing her was frightened.

The silence was ominous. Tara had to respond. "I thought
d get a pair of her earrings as a sort of remembrance. That's
. Inge can ring them up."

"Cuz, they're yours. Take them."

She backed out of the shop. "Thank you. I appreciate— And
ance, it was nice to meet you."

They must have answered, but all she could hear was her
wn thoughts. She had crossed the line. She no longer suspected
m. She was convinced. Her cousin, John Walker Nyborg, had
lled at least twice.

CHAPTER 31

he front door slammed, and Tara glanced out the window of
atrick's bedroom. A uniformed man was walking away from
e house. She tensed, thinking he was a policeman. Then she
w the van. *Federal Express.*

Pulling on her robe, she ran downstairs barefoot. Derek was
the hallway, an open package in his hand. He was staring
a photo, and his eyes looked glazed.

"Derek, you shouldn't have opened this. It's awful for you
see . . ." She jerked the photos away, and several scattered on
e floor amid a flutter of negatives. Dropping to her knees, she
athered the prints and negs and stuffed them into the envelope.
he would look at them after she took care of Derek.

He stood immobile, his hands positioned as if he were still
olding the photos. She shook his arm. "Derek. *Derek!*"

He slumped against her. She thought he was going down,
nd she pressed her body against his, pinning him against the
all. "Derek, hold onto me."

She clung to him, and gradually his eyes seemed to focus.
linking, he looked at Tara. "I knew—I'd been told. But we
ept her casket closed. I never saw . . . never imagined what
was like . . . how she looked . . ."

"Derek, how horrible for you."

"I'll be okay. Just give me . . . minute."

He pulled himself upright, and Tara tucked the package under her arm, concealing it as much as she could with the sleeve of her robe. "I'll get dressed. I won't be long, and then maybe we can go into Solvang for breakfast. No one will notice us early in the morning, and you need to get out."

Derek shook his head. "You shouldn't be seen with me. And I want to look at those pictures. I'll hold myself together and whatever's going on—whatever you know—you have to tell me."

"But—"

"No buts. Let's go in the kitchen. I'll get us some coffee and you'll tell me everything."

Tara placed the photo packet on the table. She composed herself, then picked up a print. All it would take was a moment, one quick look, because she knew what she was looking for—but it wasn't there. Jessie Bouchard's right ear was clearly visible, and there was no earring. Tara stared, reluctant to believe it. She'd been so sure.

Derek put his hand on her shoulder. "Okay, Tara. Tell me what you're looking for."

Tara's voice was flat, drained. "An earring. I was positive she would be wearing earrings. Pudget said that in the cemetery, Jessie was wearing a pair of shell earrings shaped like seahorses. But she doesn't have earrings on."

Derek took another photo out of the package. "What do you mean? She has an earring." He held a blowup toward her.

Tara gasped. The blowup showed the left side of Jessie's head, and an earring was visible—an earring shaped like a bright blue seahorse in a gold-and-magenta setting. Apparently when Tara snapped the pictures, she had automatically gone through all the right motions, moving and angling, and had taken different views.

"She would never have removed just one earring, so she must have lost one," Tara said, comparing the two photos. "But one earring proves Pudget was right!"

"Okay, Tara, now you have to tell me—"

Tara withered. The photos might save Derek, but they condemned Walker. She couldn't feel compassion for her cousin, but his parents would suffer. Pushing the photos away, she started to cry.

Derek comforted her, but when her sobs subsided, he was adamant. She had to tell him what was going on.

It was hard to get the words out. "I . . . I know who killed Jessie and Pudget. And we'll be able to prove it."

Derek slammed his fist on the table. "Who? Who killed her?"

She closed her eyes. Dead silence, and then from far away she heard a voice. "My cousin, Walker Nyborg, gave Jessie those earrings. And he killed her. And Pudget, too. I'm sure of it."

"Your cousin! You mean your uncle's son?"

She heard the voice again, distant and singsong. "Yes, Walker Nyborg."

Derek sputtered. "That . . . that's not possible."

Tara opened her eyes and the voice she heard was her own. "It's possible, Derek. And it's true. My cousin killed them."

He sat facing her while she explained all of it. At first he was quiet, but then he started taking notes and asking questions.

When her voice finally faded away, they stared at each other. *Walker*. It was almost impossible to believe, and yet—analyzed and laid out on paper, the evidence against him was stunning.

Derek looked at her. "No wonder you couldn't go to your uncle."

Tara jumped up. "There's one more thing." She ran upstairs and got the pictures of Louise. She thrust them at Derek. "Does this woman resemble Jessie?"

He studied them for several minutes, then shook his head. "Not really. Her hair is dark and in the picture it's long, the way Jessie usually kept hers, but there's no facial resemblance. Is your cousin tall? If he is, then this woman is tall, too, maybe close to Jessie's height."

"Hmmm. That might be enough. The same height, similar hair—from a distance one could possibly have been mistaken for the other. I wonder—"

Tara hadn't heard a car pull up, but there was a sharp knock on the door. She was still in her robe and stayed out of view when Derek answered. Men were talking, but the only words she caught were "remanded to custody."

"My bail's revoked without a hearing? Why? What's going on?"

Tara rushed to the door. Two police officers stood to either side of Derek. "Derek, what do they want? What's happening?"

"They're taking me back to jail."

"*Why?*"

"I don't know."

One of the officers cleared his throat. "Miss Nyborg, I think his bail is revoked because he had a forbidden contact with his son."

She screamed. "That was my fault! Derek didn't have anything to do with it. I picked Patrick up and brought him here. You can't take him back to jail for that."

"Maybe his attorney can get it straightened out. But meantime . . ."

With the officers' permission, Derek checked his horses and told Tara what instructions to give to the stable helper who came daily.

"Derek, this is terrible! I never dreamed anyone would find out. Patrick talks about you all the time, so even if he mentioned the visit, I didn't think anyone would pay any attention. I'm so sorry."

Derek looked angry, but held out his fists to be cuffed. "Tara, don't blame yourself. I'm glad I saw Patrick, and my attorney will straighten it out. Just promise me you'll be careful." He was being led to the police car. "Wait! I know what you should do. The detective who met me at the plane and told me about Jessie—his name is Castle—talk to him. He may be your best shot. Tell him everything, just the way you told it to me."

Tara was dazed and lingered at the porch railing even after the patrol car was out of sight. Only when her feet stung with cold from the concrete did it occur to her that she was barefooted and still in a robe. One of the officers had called her by name. Her presence would get back to her uncle—to everyone—and be misinterpreted. But perhaps that wouldn't matter. *Once Derek was cleared and Walker's guilt was established* . . . She moaned. She wanted the one so badly, yet dreaded the other.

After she dressed, she wrote a note and tacked it on the stable door for Derek's helper. Then she did up the coffee cups and a few dishes that were in the sink. She would leave the place tidy. Derek had wanted her to stay, but she couldn't. By day the house would be endurable, but by night the loneliness would be overwhelming. By night she wouldn't be able to forget the eyes staring at her from the *ropa*. The pictures had renewed the horror. If she were alone in Jessie's house, Tara would see those eyes—feel those eyes—watching her.

But the real threat came from the living, not the dead. Walker knew she was tracking Jessie's murderer, so he had called Seattle and left the warning for her on the answering machine. He hadn't succeeded in scaring her away, so now he would come after her. For her sanity and her safety, she had to get away.

She packed her suitcases and camera equipment into the car, then locked the front door. The horses were temporarily provided for, and if Derek were in jail longer than a day or two, she would locate a stable where they could be boarded.

After she checked back into the motel in Buellton, she considered Derek's advice. At first it seemed impossible. After all, Peter's investigation had led to Derek's indictment. But Peter Castle was her friend. She could trust him, and he would take her story seriously.

CHAPTER 32

Detective Peter Castle sat at his desk, reviewing the file on the Andrew Mason murder. He wasn't assigned to the case, but he stayed close to the investigation, not that there were any new developments. Mason had relished beer and arguments, and had indulged both tastes as much as possible. That much they were sure of. But even though his muscular frame had towered over six feet, he hadn't been a scrapper. A talker, *yes,* and a braggart, mostly about his days on the rodeo circuit. He'd been picked up and questioned a couple of times for hanging out near the high school, but if he was selling marijuana out of his boots or Stetson, they had never nailed him for it. His claim was that he just liked being around kids.

The medical records engrossed Peter. A bronco had thrown Mason, and he'd suffered a severe concussion. He hadn't regained consciousness for three weeks, and his recovery had been only partial. Following the accident, he wobbled when he walked—one person had described it as a port side list— and his doctors had warned him that even a slight head trauma could be fatal.

Light bruising on his cheeks indicated he had been struck, but according to the autopsy report, the blows would hardly have stunned a normal person. But they had done more than stun Mason. Within seconds he had lost consciousness, and death had followed quickly.

Peter nodded, remembering. He had read the entire report before, and nothing new had been added. The case was stagnating. No new clues and no witnesses.

The surmise was that person or persons unknown had hit Mason and panicked when the guy literally dropped dead. Instead of notifying the authorities, whoever landed the punch had planted Mason's body in Lake Cachuma, undoubtedly hoping it was a permanent arrangement. Peter closed the folder. They weren't getting anywhere, but he couldn't fault their conclusions.

The phone rang. "Detective Castle."

"Peter, it's me, Tara. I have to talk to you."

"Good to hear from you. What's up?"

"It concerns the Bouchard case."

Peter gripped the receiver. "The Bouchard case," he echoed. "Sure, but we've got our man."

"You've got the wrong man. But I *know* who killed Jessie Bouchard—and Pudget Vandermeer, too."

Peter hesitated. "Tara, what are you talking about?"

She was crying. "It's so terrible. I hate to tell you—but Peter, it was Walker. My cousin Walker. He killed both of them, and maybe that man in Lake Cachuma, too."

Peter couldn't believe what he had heard. The insanity of it left him dazed. "Tara, stop crying and listen to me. I think we should talk about this in person. Where are you?"

"I'm at the motel in Buellton where I stayed before. You picked me up here and took me to meet my uncle. Remember?"

"Of course, I—"

"And Peter, there's no mistake." Her words were coming in a gush, and Peter didn't quiet her. "When she died, Jessie Bouchard was wearing the earrings that Pudget said she'd had on. Pudget made those earrings and Walker gave them to her."

Walker gave them to Jessie. Peter was stunned, but he answered in the noncommittal voice he'd developed interrogating suspects. "Tara, when Jessie's body was found, she wasn't wearing earrings. I have the pictures our crime photographer—"

"Your photographer shot her from only one side. The same thing happened to me. At first I thought she wasn't wearing earrings, and then I saw the blowup of her left side and—"

"*What* blowup?"

"A blowup of one of the shots I took."

"*You* took pictures of Jessie Bouchard?"

"Yes—before you arrived at the mission. I had my camera in my hand. It was automatic, but I took different angles—"

"Before we go any further, I need to see those pictures. Sit tight, and I'll get there as soon as I can."

After they hung up, Peter Castle stared at the phone, drumming his fingers in steady cadence on the desk. His case against Derek Bouchard was solid. He had gone over every detail, but he figured he'd better take a look at those pictures.

The phone rang again.

"Pete, the judge signed the bail violation, and we picked up Bouchard. I think you were right to move on it. Now that he knows where the boy is, he could pull something. And anyway—I'm worried about my niece." Matt grunted. "I sure as hell didn't expect her to become pals with Bouchard, though I imagine you already know what I had in mind."

Peter cleared his throat. "Tara feels sorry for the little boy, and Bouchard must have filled her head with a lot of nonsense. But she's one terrific woman, and I expect to have another turn at bat." He considered telling Matt he was on his way to see Tara, but decided against it.

On the way out of the office, he dropped Mason's folder back in the file. He was stymied. What could Tara possibly have come up with to make her suspect Mason's death was linked to Jessie Bouchard's?

The bell jingled. Several people entered the shop, and Walker went out front to wait on the trade. He didn't care whether he made a sale, but going through the motions made the time go faster. "May I help you?" Donning his proprietor's smile, he helped several women select items at the linen counter.

"Oh look, isn't this the cutest—and it'll make a perfect gift for my daughter-in-law."

"This is something that might interest you. We have only one left, and it's marked— Excuse me while I get the phone."

He picked up the receiver and heard Nance's voice. He listened to what she had to say, but one recital was not enough. She had to repeat everything a second time. "Walker, there are more refined tests, but they actually aren't necessary. The initial tests indicate that it's just not possible—"

For a stabbing moment, there was a sense of loss; then he was free-falling through space.

"Walker, why did she lie to you?"

"It has to be because of the inheritance."

"Can you tell me the price of the one on the wall?"

"Nance, Nance." He repeated her name, wishing he could take her in his arms. "I'll come up to San Francisco—"

"Wait! I have to know how you feel. I mean—"

"I love you—no one else. I just didn't know how much I loved you until after we separated." The words gushed out and he didn't care if anyone overheard.

"Walker, I want you to come—but you can't forget Tara."

She was right. He had to take care of Tara.

"Please, I don't have all day. Can you help me over here?"

Walker hung up and finished waiting on the customers. Inge was still at lunch, but as soon as the store cleared, he locked the front door and headed for his car.

Last night, after he'd taken Nance to the Santa Maria airport for her flight back to San Francisco, he had stopped at the house. His mother had been in a frenzy of concern. "Tara's staying at the Bouchard ranch. It seems impossible, but your father is positive. Can you believe it?"

Walker believed it, and he knew Bouchard's bail had been revoked. Tara would be all alone. He turned off the main road. That had to be Bouchard's place over there.

He knocked on the front door. "Tara! Tara, are you here?"

No answer, and he walked around to the back. The screen on the back door wouldn't budge when he tugged it, but near the side porch was an old-fashioned window. He whacked the frame of the lower pane, and it moved. A second blow loosened the pane enough for him to raise it. The window was small. It would be a tight squeeze, but definitely possible.

"Hey, no one's home. What are you doing?" A young man in overalls shouted from the door of the stable.

"Know when they'll be back?"

"The note they left me said they'd be gone for a few days. I help take care of the horses."

"Are you here at night?"

The man stepped closer and stood with his hands on his hips. "Nope. Just a couple of hours in the afternoon."

Walker waved again, then headed back to the car. He had to do it. He dreaded it—but what choice did he have?

CHAPTER 33

"It's me. Open up."

It was daylight, but Tara didn't unbolt the door until she recognized Peter's voice. Without a word, he crushed her in his arms. His mouth was vibrant against hers, and she was gasping when he let her go.

He grinned. "Sorry. That's no way to greet a friend, but I still have hopes. Meanwhile, just what were you trying to tell me on the phone?"

Tara felt slightly off balance. "I guess . . . well, I should begin by showing you the pictures."

He gave her shoulder an affectionate squeeze. "Sure, let's take a look." There was only one chair, and he sat down on the bed. "You sit there, pretty girl detective, and show me all your important evidence."

Despite his warmth, she caught a certain amusement in his attitude. He was very conscientious and proud of his work—Uncle Matt had assured her of that—and she was telling him that she, not he, had solved the Bouchard case. He wasn't ready to take her seriously. *But he was going to take her seriously.*

Sitting stiff and upright, she opened the packet of photos, then handed him the blowup of Jessie Bouchard's left ear. "See the earring? It's shaped like a seahorse—exactly what Pudget described." Tara hated touching the photos, but she remained crisp and businesslike. She tapped a spot with the tip of her finger. "There, Peter, right there."

"I see. That does look like an earring and—"

"Of course it's an earring!"

"Yes, I think so." He returned the photo. "But I doubt that it has any significance."

"It will have—when I explain all of it to you." She steadied herself. "I know what I'm doing is incredible. You're in charge of the Bouchard investigation, and here I am, asking you to believe that you're wrong and I'm right. But there's no one else I can go to, and I know you. You don't want the wrong man to be convicted or the real murderer to go free—even if establishing his guilt would . . . shatter people we both care about."

"Of course I want the D.A. to prosecute the right man. And I'll listen to everything you want to tell me. But I have to say— on the phone you weren't making a lot of sense."

"Just listen to me. What I'm going to tell you makes all the sense in the world."

It was hard to know where to start, but she had reviewed everything with Derek and had his notes. "To begin with, Walker was seen several times with a woman who matched the description of Jessie Bouchard. His parents thought she was an old girlfriend named Louise, but—"

"How do you know the woman wasn't Louise?"

"I don't—not positively. But wait, you'll see. It all fits."

She proceeded, detailing everything she knew in an attempt to convince him, but the information that had seemed so conclusive to Derek and her hardly raised Peter's eyebrows. He listened intently, but was clearly skeptical. She paused, exasperated, but his nod prodded her on.

"The most important thing is that Pudget definitely saw Jessie after Derek was already on a plane for Phoenix. The earring proves Pudget knew what she was talking about, and that means Derek couldn't have killed his wife."

Peter frowned. "Vandermeer may have seen Jessie Bouchard *sometime* when she was wearing those earrings. But for all we know, Jessie wore them frequently. They may have been her favorites. Tara, don't you see—Pudget couldn't have seen Jessie on the night she was killed. Jessie's body was found at the mission the next morning. I don't have to tell *you* about that. And the mission is locked up tight every evening at five."

Tara faltered. "That's the one thing I don't understand. There has to be a way—probably something very simple— that everyone has overlooked. But whoever killed Jessie got into the mission that night."

"Don't you think our department investigated? Your uncle and I went over everything, all the possibilities."

Tara couldn't let herself be defeated. "I'm sorry. What I'm saying suggests you didn't do your job right, but—"

"It sure does." He sounded wounded. "And it's not just me. You must think your uncle is a numbskull, too."

She wasn't getting anywhere, so she tackled something new. "Jessie Bouchard had this newspaper clipping carefully hidden with some letters. It's about a missing man, but I'm sure you'll recognize his name. *Andrew Mason*. He's the man who—"

"Sure, I know the name, but what's the connection? For all you know"—he flipped over the bit of newspaper—"she might have been interested in a tire sale."

Tara sighed. "I'm not convincing you, but I know Derek didn't kill his wife. And even though it's torture for me to know it—I'm just as positive that Walker did. And he killed Pudget, too. She had recognized him and—"

"Recognized him! You never said that."

"I did! In the note I left for Uncle Matt—Pudget said the man she saw in the cemetery looked familiar."

"And she said he was Walker?"

"No! Of course not. But Walker *would* have looked familiar to her. She sold earrings to my aunt's shop—"

Peter raised his hands, cutting her short. "Tara, you know Bouchard, and apparently he cuts a whole lot deeper with you than I do. I'm sorry about that, but you're letting your feelings boss your brain."

"I know it seems that way, but if you would only listen."

"I've been listening." He stood up. "As a friend, let me tell you—put this behind you. You'll hurt yourself and a couple of very fine people if you persist."

Tara's composure shattered. "I *can't* put it behind me. If you won't help me, I'll find someone who will. There has to be someone—" She burst into tears.

He stroked her hair. "Hey, you really are serious about this, aren't you?"

She looked up at him. "I'm dead serious."

He continued to soothe her. "Okay, you win. Never could stand to see a pretty woman cry. You're wrong, but I promise to do everything I can to prove you're right."

Overcome, she grasped his arm, trying to convey her gratitude.

"You'll hear from me soon, but meantime, you'd better not talk to anyone. It wouldn't take much for word to get back to Matt."

"I understand."

He picked up the photos. "I'll take these and see what other information we can dig up on those earrings."

When he left, Tara kissed him on the cheek, almost regretting that her admiration for him hadn't developed into a real attachment. He had character; he was bright, considerate, responsible—all the qualities a woman could want in an enduring romance, and he was even better to look at than his screen-hero brother. But something in her had held back, and then she had discovered his flaw. He wasn't Derek Bouchard.

Derek. He was in the Santa Barbara jail, but they hadn't put her call through, and she needed the name of his lawyer. She hadn't thought to look for it before leaving the ranch, so now she would have to go back. The lawyer had to know that she alone was responsible for Derek's visit with his son.

A dark cloud cover was rolling across the sky, certain rain where she came from. This wasn't Seattle, but from force of habit, she took her raincoat. She drove straight to the ranch and parked in the driveway, no longer concerned with hiding her car. Her precautions hadn't worked.

Just as her key touched the lock, she heard someone creeping up behind her. She froze, too frightened to scream. Thoughts flickered. Could she get inside and bolt the door, or should she try to make it to her car?

Run! Turning, she charged right into the arms of the man who helped Derek around the stables.

"What's wrong? Did I scare you?"

As she jerked around, her ankle twisted. Pain inched through her foot. "No . . . I . . . it's all right. I'm glad you're here."

"I'm about done for the day. Be back tomorrow though, and I'll see that everything's taken care of."

She started to thank him, but he interrupted. "Someone was snooping around a little while ago. Pried one of the back windows open, but I shut it. Didn't know whether I should call the police or what, but he acted nice and friendly."

Tara went rigid. "Describe him."

"A tall guy, slender, with blond hair. Neat-looking. I told him my note said Mr. Bouchard would be gone at least a few days and—"

He was still talking, but a roaring through Tara's head deadened all other sound. *Walker.*

"Hey, are you okay?"

"Yes, but will you wait right here while I look for something? I won't be long." She hobbled inside. "Don't leave! I'll hurry."

A manila envelope full of legal papers was in the top drawer of his desk. *Waldon*. The attorney's name was Francis Waldon. She copied his phone number, then rushed outside.

It was dark by the time she got back to the motel and could pack ice from the vending machine around her throbbing ankle.

The first time she had stayed at this motel, a bag of sweet rolls had appeared at her door, and the birds that pecked at them had died. She'd never discovered where the rolls came from, but then it had seemed impossible that anyone could have tried to poison her. It didn't seem so impossible now.

Could Walker have . . . ? She shivered and not from the ice. Her motel had been mentioned at dinner, and Walker would have realized that the pink bag—anything that might be traced back to him—would be tossed out by maid service long before poisoning was diagnosed. But why would he have wanted to harm her then? She hadn't heard Pudget's story and didn't know Derek. She'd seen Jessie in the *ropa*, but so had lots of people.

Tara tried putting weight on her foot. It still throbbed, but she could walk. No, she told herself, Walker would have had no reason to harm her then—unless . . . unless . . . The thought when it struck was staggering. Could Walker have found out she'd taken pictures of Jessie? It was possible, but how could he know that her shots were a different view from the ones taken by the crime lab?

Oh God! He was the son of the lieutenant in charge of the case. Somehow he'd used his father's position as an excuse to see the crime photos. Panicking, he'd had to know if anything at the scene might incriminate him, and he'd stolen or destroyed the shots that revealed the earring he had given Jessie.

So she and her photos had been a threat to him then—and she was certainly a threat to him now. Hopping to the door on one foot, she checked again to be sure it was locked.

• • •

Damn! When everything was said and done, Matt Nyborg loved his son, no matter what. That made it hard, and telling Sylvia . . . He'd never dreaded anything so much in his life. He paced back and forth in his office, then sat down to keep himself from attacking the walls.

The story he'd just listened to—hell, it just wasn't possible. He knew it wasn't possible, but he had to behave like a cop instead of a father.

He pulled the files on the Bouchard and Vandermeer cases. He'd review everything. In case—just in case—he found anything that looked different from another angle, he'd take action.

CHAPTER 34

The cloud cover was gone and the long, low silhouette of the Santa Inez Mission was distinct in the moonlight.

Tara saw a man retreat into the shadows and heard the crunch of gravel under her tires. When she slowed, the man came forward and waved her to the far corner of the grounds. She parked under low-hanging trees and stepped out of her car.

Her ankle throbbed when she put her weight on it, but she ran toward him. "Peter, on the phone you said you had discovered the way Walker got into the mission—"

"That's right. Grab your camera. You can get some night shots, and it'll provide a good excuse if we're interrupted."

She was surprised, but went back for the camera. "Tell me! How did Walker get inside after the mission was closed?"

"Simple." Peter beckoned and, limping, Tara followed him. "Sometimes the toughest things are easy."

"What do you mean?"

He stopped in front of the heavy door. "Look," he said, wiggling the padlock. "This is supposed to be locked. But what if it wasn't? What if that night the old caretaker forgot?"

"But how would Walker have known?"

"Maybe he didn't. Maybe he just got lucky." He pointed at the mission bell tower, stark against a shaft of moonlight. "There's a good shot for you."

251

Tara adjusted her camera and took the shot he indicated. "But I don't understand. Why did Walker bring the body to the mission?"

Peter shrugged. "He was driving Jessie's car. He had her body stowed in the trunk and was headed to Lake Cachuma to bury it."

"Lake Cachuma? That's where Mason was buried! So you must think Walker killed him, too. Peter, you're amazing. In a few short hours, you've turned your whole case around."

Peter went on as if he hadn't heard her. "There was a chemical spill on the road. A road block was set up not far beyond the mission. He drove in here to avoid it."

Tara nodded. "That makes sense. Lieutenant Nyborg's son would be recognized—"

"He found a way in and dumped his cargo in the *ropa*."

He was pointing toward the sky where a flurry of clouds obscured the silvery moonlight. Tara shot the scene in the split second before the clouds scudded away.

They were walking toward the graveyard. The earth was soft, and her ankle smarted with every step. "Poor Aunt Sylvia and Uncle Matt. They'll be devastated."

"You're right. It's going to be a hell of a loss."

"I thought of something else. Patrick Bouchard remembers his mother's boyfriend."

"He does?" He grasped her arm. "Can he identify him?"

"I think so. He's little, but he has a very good memory. He even remembers that his mother's friend gave her earrings."

"You're positive?"

"Yes. And my interview that got canceled. I should have suspected Walker, because no one else knew about it."

"I knew."

"Of course, but that's not what I mean."

"Maybe Walker figured you'd outlived your usefulness and wanted you back in Seattle where you couldn't bend old Matt's ear about Vandermeer—how you were so sure that crackpot knew what she was talking about."

"She wasn't a crackpot. She was an artist and—"

"You call that art? A crazy wheel with flashing lights. What did she call it? *Meditation?*"

"You saw *Meditation?*" It was a question, but she already knew the answer. He had to have seen it, because the lights only flashed when it was operated . . .

Peter sounded distant. "She showed it to me when I went there to take her report."

Tara was baffled. *Uncle Matt said his men had never talked to Pudget—had never taken a statement.*

"Here," Peter said, still holding her arm. "You'll want some shots from the top of the grotto."

The grotto was high, and climbing it in the dark seemed insane. Peter wasn't making sense. Something was wrong, and terror iced up her spine.

Suddenly Tara remembered her nightmare. She'd been trapped in a dark cemetery. A figure had taken her hand to guide her, but the figure hadn't been a friend. It had been death.

She tried to jerk away from him, but his grip on her arm tightened. "What's the matter, Tara?" His voice was in her ear. "Is it beginning to add up? But you don't care *who* killed Jessie as long as it wasn't Derek."

Tara struggled, but couldn't get away. Her camera clattered to the stones.

"Don't . . . don't scream. If you scream, I'll have to hurt you."

Tara heard a roaring in her ears. A scream died in her throat.

"You wanted to know, little girl detective. So now you'll hear it, all of it." He pulled her to the ground and thrust a hand over her mouth.

"I took Jessie to a little club off the highway, and all she talked about was my brother. Ryan this, Ryan that—how she wanted a chance to be on his show. After the place closed, we were out in the parking lot. Mason showed up. He looked drunk and I threatened to run him in. He mouthed off, and I decided to show Jessie a real cop in action, not some cardboard actor—"

Tara was rigid, listening, waiting for a chance.

"I whacked him, and he went down. He was dead, and Jessie played it for everything it was worth. Promised me a circus when the media found out Ryan Castle's brother had killed a man. *Ryan Castle's little brother . . .*"

She felt his whole body shudder. Maybe this was her moment. Tensing every muscle, she jerked hard. She pushed his hand away from her mouth, but he grabbed her hair. The pain was unbearable when she tried to pull away. He was breathing hard, but still talking. He wanted her to know. "I asked Ryan to get Jessie an acting role. But that wouldn't have satisfied her. She knew I'd buried Mason and would have screwed me forever."

Peter seemed to catch his breath. "First class police work. I built a case against Bouchard for a murder I committed."

Tara pleaded, but Peter was caught in his narrative. "I got her in the *ropa* just the way I told you. I drove her car to the airport and hitched a ride back here—hung around until the call came in after Jessie's body was found . . ."

"Why . . . why are you telling me all this?"

"Why not? You'll never repeat it." He hissed. "Tara, you were a blessing and a curse. Matt's a good cop—the best. And just when I needed to distract him, you came along. I didn't want you to get away. But the rolls I left you didn't make you sick. God, they should have! There was enough insecticide in them to send you to the hospital—"

Tara couldn't struggle anymore, but she had to struggle. She had to try, but he was straddling her and holding tight to her hair.

"Matt believed in me. That was the hardest part—deceiving the one man I respect . . ."

Tara strained against him. "He . . . he respects you, too. Likes you. Won't turn you in . . ."

"Tara, Tara, you know better than that."

"Pudget, why did you—"

"She called the station to say she realized who the man in the cemetery looked like. I took the call."

The man in the cemetery had looked familiar to Pudget, because he was a ringer for his actor-brother . . .

Peter released Tara's hair and ran his fingers down her cheek. "When I checked Jessie's corpse in the *ropa,* she had on only one earring. I removed it in case the other earring turned up in the wrong place." He snarled. "This is your own fault, Tara. Your photos are damning evidence. I'm the only person who was alone with the body—the only person who could have taken the earring. And I can't have anyone wondering why."

Tara could hardly breathe. *He's going to kill me. He really is going to kill me. And Patrick will be next.*

"Poor Tara." His face was so close she could feel his breath. "She was so lovely. And so foolish—taking photos of the mission at night. What a horrible accident. She must have climbed up to the top of the grotto. She slipped, smashed her head on the stones . . ."

His fingers slid down her neck. She felt his thumb against her throat, gagging her, choking her. She was losing consciousness.

"Tara!"

From far away, she heard her name. *Uncle Matt! Oh, God, Uncle Matt . . .*

EPILOGUE

The TV faced her hospital bed, and Tara watched a familiar face. It was Ryan Castle, but the movie star facade was gone. His movements were weary and his eyes were dark hollows. He struggled past reporters at the entrance to the county jail and talked over his shoulder. "The charges against Pete are devastating, but I'm standing by him. He's my brother."

Shaking his head, Uncle Matt snapped off the set and came toward her. "Enough of that. Tara, how do you feel?"

She smiled. "Pretty good, thanks to you."

He took her hand. "Thanks to Walker. I was damned near ready to have him locked up in the loony bin when he came to me with his suspicions about Pete."

"A loony bin! Matthew!"

"Mother, he means Atascadero," Walker said, grinning.

Uncle Matt stood still long enough to gaze at his son. "I was wrong, and I'm ashamed of it. But I'm proud of you. And, Walker, I think you'd make one hell of a cop."

Walker shook his head. "I'm on my way back to San Francisco. Nance is waiting for me."

Tara felt a flood of tenderness, but there was something she had to know. "Uncle Matt, how did you know where I was?"

He paced by her bed. "After I talked to Walker, I had you watched. I was alerted when you drove onto the mission grounds with your lights off, and I hightailed it down there."

Tara sank back against the pillow. It was so incredible Walker had been suspicious of Peter from the beginning. That was why he'd acted so strange the first time she'd met him. He'd been stunned, not by the appearance of a cousin, but by Peter Castle's nonchalance toward Jessie Bouchard's murder. "I made so many mistakes about you, Walker. When Patrick told me you had been with him and his mother on the day that she was given those earrings—"

"I know. You thought your Nyborg relatives had the bad habit of being killers." He laughed. "I'll get even, Cuz, but I'll wait until your leg is healed."

Tara's face had to be one big grin. *Walker!* They were going to be pals after all.

"But why did Peter leave a message in Seattle warning me?"

"Cuz, that was me. I didn't expect to scare a fiery redhead out of California, but I wanted you to know you were in danger and put you on guard. I was worried sick about you."

Aunt Sylvia broke in. "Don't talk, Tara. You need rest."

"No, Mother." Walker's voice was firm. "She won't rest until she understands." He came closer to the bed. "I was happy with Nance. I wouldn't have come down here when Louise called, but she told me—she said that Kimberly was my daughter. I couldn't ignore that."

Tara reached out to him. *The ties that bind.* Of course he couldn't ignore his child.

Walker grasped her hand. "I got to know Kimberly, and she seemed starved for love. That still bothers me, but she's not my daughter. Blood tests proved it. But that's how I met Patrick. I took Kimberly to a playground, and he was there alone. I looked after him until his mother showed up—wearing earrings I'd sold to Pete Castle. Later I spotted Pete and Jessie together. I knew they were seeing each other."

"Why did you go to see Patrick in the foster home?"

"I wanted to find out what he knew, and when I asked him the name of his mommy's friend, he didn't hesitate. He said 'Peter.'"

Tara shook her head. "Walker, why didn't you tell me?"

He gestured. "I *wanted* to tell you I suspected Pete, but I was afraid. If you decided I was crazy, you might tell him everything and put yourself in danger."

Tara closed her eyes. "You were right on target. I did go to him."

Walker was still holding her hand. "When Bouchard was rearrested, I went out to the ranch to see you. I realized how easy it would be for Pete to get to you there, so I knew I had to alert Dad." Her eyes were still closed, but she heard the grin in his voice. "I knew he'd think I was nuts, but I took my chances. I had to."

"Rub it in. I've got it coming." Uncle Matt slapped at his side. "But I'm a cop, and when I reviewed the files again with Walker's allegations in mind, I came up with a couple of dandy questions, like how in hell *had* Castle come up with so many answers so fast, and why hadn't he gotten a warrant to search the Bouchard ranch."

"Maybe he was afraid that searching the ranch might turn up something that tied him to Jessie."

"Right. Walker, you're thinking like a cop, and there's a place for you at the academy."

"I don't think so, Dad. At least not right now. But thanks for the vote of confidence."

Tears shone in Aunt Sylvia's eyes, and Tara smiled at her, letting her know she understood. Father and son had made contact at last at a time when it counted most, and Matt's pain over Peter Castle was canceled by pride in his son.

"Tara?" Derek was in the doorway, and he had Patrick in his arms. The tension lines across his brow were gone. He looked younger, more appealing—oh, God, he looked wonderful. She leaned forward, unmindful of a stab of pain, into a three-person embrace.

Patrick pulled back and reached into his pocket. "Tara, this will make you feel better." He handed her Pudget's little carved horse, and she felt her eyes fill.

"Patrick, Derek, I want you to meet my family—my uncle Matt, my aunt Sylvia, and my wonderful cousin, Walker."

A murmur of greetings, and then Uncle Matt extended his hand to Derek. Her uncle and the man she loved grasped hands. If they had met before, it was in the past. This was a new beginning.

417